Mother
Love

Mother Love

ELIZABETH BROWN

Matador
9 Priory Business Park,
Wistow Road, Kibworth Beauchamp,
Leicestershire. LE8 0RX
Tel: 0116 279 2299
Email: books@troubador.co.uk
Web: www.troubador.co.uk/matador
Twitter: @matadorbooks

ISBN 978 1838591 878

British Library Cataloguing in Publication Data.
A catalogue record for this book is available from the British Library.

Printed and bound by CPI Group (UK) Ltd, Croydon, CR0 4YY
Typeset in 11pt Sabon MT by Troubador Publishing Ltd, Leicester, UK

Matador is an imprint of Troubador Publishing Ltd

To Chloe & Ted

"They fuck you up, your mum and dad.
They may not mean to, but they do.
They fill you with the faults they had
And add some extra, just for you."

Philip Larkin

Prologue

MRS ROSE WESLEY HAS PLEASURE IN INVITING

....

on the occasion of the marriage of her daughter Margaret to Mr Clive Johnson to be held at Knight Road Congregational Church, Bedford at 3pm on 2nd March, followed by refreshments in the adjoining Church Hall.

* * *

The White Lodge
Chearsley
Aylesbury
Bucks
19th February

Dear Margaret

You could have knocked us down with a feather when Mother and I heard your news. We didn't even know you were courting again! You certainly got over that other chap pretty quickly! We will be delighted to attend your wedding on Saturday week, and we look forward to meeting your intended.

With our warmest congratulations,
Harriet and Aunt Ruby

Dear Aunt Ruby and Harriet

Thank you for the napkin set you gave us for our wedding gift. Did you work the embroidery yourself Harriet? You were always handy with your needle. What an unusual colour combination you picked out! I'm sure we will use your gift regularly.

Clive and I had a very enjoyable honeymoon in the Cotswolds. It's such a pretty area of the country, we only wished we had more time to explore the scenery. Sadly, Clive had to return to work on the Thursday, they really cannot manage without him.

We are settling nicely into our new home, which is small but very cosy. Oh Harriet, I can't tell you how gratifying it is to have a place of my own. I'm learning to be a housewife and enjoying myself very much indeed. Let's hope you are lucky enough to find yourself a husband before too much longer! I assure you it's a very pleasant accomplishment!

Love always
Margaret

The White Lodge
Chearsley
Aylesbury
Bucks

Dear Margaret

It sounds like you're revelling in your new married state! Mother and I visited the Cotswolds last Spring and couldn't stop remarking on the beautiful countryside. We were lucky enough to have a full fortnight allotted to our little holiday and as you may imagine, we didn't waste a moment of our time. We stayed in a very comfortable boarding house in Broadway, so we had ample opportunity to get out and about. We felt we had become quite intimate with the area by the time we left and our landlady, Mrs Hayle, was very pressing in her invitation to return soon. Our duties at home have prevented us from doing so to date, but we hope to go back as soon as the opportunity arises.

I thank you for your kind wishes regarding a future husband, but my life is so full at the moment that I find it difficult to imagine how I should fit one in! He would have to be an unusually obliging and adaptable man if he is to meet my requirements! I suppose I always feel that no one can be quite the man my Father was, and I would be fortunate indeed to meet someone who matches his standards. You will know what I mean, of course, you were so fond of my Father, an affection I thoroughly understood when compared with your own Pa. He was certainly one of a kind!

Mother sends her best wishes. We are pleased that you liked the napkin set. It gives us pleasure to think of you in the evenings sitting to your supper and using the gift we worked at so assiduously. I hope Clive is appreciating your devoted care as he should!

Affectionate wishes,
Harriet and Aunt Ruby

Dear Harriet

What extraordinary news I have to tell you! I haven't been feeling very well lately and it turns out that I'm expecting a happy event! A honeymoon baby! I can't tell you how excited we are. I'm feeling a bit rough unfortunately, but the doctor says it's nothing to be concerned about. I just need to have plenty of rest and everything will be fine. Clive is so good to me, quite happy to turn his hand to all manner of domestic chore and fussing over me as though I'm a piece of precious porcelain. Do you know, Harriet, I really think I struck gold when I met him! Perhaps one day, you will be lucky too.

It is possible you will be surprised when I tell you that Clive has no idea about the things that Pa used to do. I really didn't want to tell him and I would prefer it if he never knows. So please don't mention anything in future. I'm sure you understand my feelings and I need not say anything more on the subject. I'm just looking forward to creating a new family of my own which will grow up without any shadow looming over it. It's like having a fresh page, snow white and crystal clear. I'm going to be so careful to watch over my children and treasure them so nothing bad can ever happen to them.

Listen to me! It's the hormones!

Love always
Margaret

The White Lodge
Chearsley
Aylesbury
Bucks

Dear Margaret

Well done to the proud parents! We were desperately worried when we heard you had given birth so prematurely, but when your Mother told us the baby was almost eight pounds in weight, we felt a huge relief. In fact, I should think you were pleased you didn't go to full term, or goodness knows how heavy baby Caroline would have been!

I hope you like the little matinee jacket that Mother knitted, it will be very useful now the weather is getting chilly. I thoroughly enjoyed quilting the tiny bonnet and like to think of it snuggling your darling baby's little head.

I'm sure you are relishing motherhood very much, Margaret, and doubtless Aunt Rose must be thrilled to be a Granny again. You're lucky that she is so fit and well, I expect she will be an eager babysitter for you as Caroline grows. Mother says I must tell you to enjoy these infant days as they are so fleeting. We do hope to be able to see your new little family one day.

Affectionate wishes
Harriet and Aunt Ruby

Flat 3
Ivy House
Ivy Terrace
Bedford

Dear Harriet

Thank you for the sweet gifts you sent for Caroline. I don't know why Mother told you she was almost eight pounds, she barely tipped the scale at seven pounds six ounces, but she is thriving now. Though I must tell you, babies cry a lot, which is rather wearing after a day of it. Still, the midwife says she will grow out of it so I must be patient with her. She's such a little thing, but it's one long round of endless demands. Change nappy, feed her, bath her, wash nappies, and just when you sit down with a cup of tea, she wakes up and we start all over again. You should see the bags under my eyes!

As for Mother babysitting, over my dead body is all I can say. You of all people know she wouldn't protect me as a child, so why would I trust her with my own children? Who knows what harm might come to them if I left them in her care?

It would be nice to see you and Aunt Ruby but I can't see my way clear just yet. I hardly find time to brush my hair so we'll have to wait until I establish a routine and can at least manage a civilised visit. I'm so dreadfully tired I can barely string a sentence together when Clive gets home in the evening. Anyway, thank you for your kind wishes, and please accept my apologies for the lack of promptness in my correspondence.

Fond love
Margaret

The White Lodge
Chearsley
Aylesbury
Bucks

Dear Margaret

Oh my dear! We were quite concerned at your letter. You seem to be having a hard time of it. Mother thinks perhaps you have a case of the "Baby blues". She says it's not unusual, and you mustn't worry because it's quite natural and you will recover in due course. She says she felt rather overwhelmed when she was a new Mother. But she had plenty of help from her family and she was soon back to normal.

Would you like us to come and stay for a little while? Of course I understand your reluctance to trust your Mother, but we feel that it might help you to get back on your feet if we can take care of the household chores for you and help you with your little baby. You needn't worry about respectable appearances, we won't take notice of all that unimportant nonsense. We'll take lodgings nearby so we won't intrude or be a nuisance to you. Just let us know when we can come and we will be on the train in an instant.

Affectionate wishes
Harriet and Aunt Ruby

Flat 3
Ivy House
Ivy Terrace
Bedford

Dear Harriet

I don't know what you're trying to insinuate, but I assure you I am perfectly capable of looking after my own child. As it happens, Mother has turned over a new leaf, and has become very involved with Caroline. She comes every day and is very caring and attentive to her every need. I can't remember now exactly what I wrote in my letter to you but I think you must have misunderstood quite wilfully.

Just so you are absolutely clear in your minds: Clive and I and baby Caroline are well and extremely happy. There is no question that I need to get "back to normal" as you rudely suggest. I am as normal as ever and there is no reason for you to fill your empty lives by worrying about me.

Please do not bother visiting. I do not wish to feel like some medical exhibit to be pawed over by nosy relatives who have nothing better to do. On consideration, I think I would prefer not to hear from you again.

Margaret

One

MARGARET

It's thanks to me that my children have grown up balanced and normal. They've been lucky. I didn't share their good fortune.

I could easily have been someone else, someone different: carefree, happy-go-lucky, maybe even a little reckless sometimes. But I didn't get to choose. Circumstances made me the keeper of the secrets. Every family has them, it's just that some secrets are deep and dark, too dark to be allowed to surface because they pollute everything they touch. I wouldn't allow my family to be afflicted with the burden of the secrets so I have had to bear that burden alone. That has been the sole purpose of my life and I have never relaxed my grip on the destructive forces rattling in my mind. My job has been to protect my family from the secrets and I did what I had to do. That's Mother Love.

Not that they thanked me for it of course, especially the older two. It seemed like the whole point of their existence was to make my life as difficult as possible – like the time my son caused an argument with the neighbour so bad that I couldn't bear to live there any more. Mind you, Addy was a right snob, looked down on us because my husband Clive worked for her husband at weekends. The families all around used to get on OK,

1

we had some great bonfire night get-togethers with the Dads all taking turns setting off the rockets in the milk bottles and nailing the Catherine wheels to the shed door....but Addy.....I always felt the undercurrent when she was laughing and joking with me; just passing the time of day, I could sense the unspoken contempt she felt for me. Two faced bitch quite frankly.

Anyway, young Matthew told her straight one day what I really thought about her and she burst into my kitchen like a madwoman, tears smearing her perfect make up, and gave me an earbashing like you wouldn't believe. Poor Caroline witnessed the whole thing; she was standing in the middle of the kitchen doing the ironing. You shouldn't subject a child to a hysterical scene like that, should you? She started snivelling but she clammed up later when Clive asked her about it. The last thing she would do was come to my defence, just whimpered that Aunty Addy was crying. I'll never forgive Addy for what she put Caroline through that day. Don't worry, I gave as good as I got, but I would never speak to her again, and I told my children they were never to speak to her either or play with her children. To be honest, it made it a bit awkward with our husbands, but they refused to take part and carried on as though nothing had happened. That's men for you.

No more Catherine wheels though.

CAROLINE

There was a big upset between Mum and Aunty Addy. Mum said it was the last straw, because she didn't get on with the neighbours the other side either, always complaining how difficult they were. In those days we didn't get the luxury of a phone line for each household, so we shared a party line with next door. Mum was convinced they listened in to her phone calls and there was a bit of a doorstep ruckus one day when she wanted to use her telephone at the same time they were using theirs.

So I suppose it was no surprise to come in from school one afternoon to find that Mum had hammered a home-made sign in the front garden. "For sale. Apply within". She didn't agree with paying good money to a smarmy estate agent to do what she could do better herself. And she searched out a new house that was miles away from our old neighbourhood. We moved there when I was 10.

Dad refused to uproot us from the primary school we had always attended, so he took the bus to work and left the car at home for Mum to use. The school-run was a chore she did not enjoy. Chloe was still in the Infants, which let out earlier than the Juniors where Matthew and I lingered for an extra half hour. Mum got so impatient hanging around outside school that quite often she couldn't stand it and went off with Chloe to have coffee with her friend round the corner. We'd have to wait and wait until she was ready to fetch us and then when we got home it was our fault that she was behind with the dinner. She'd tell us off and send us to our rooms and then she'd feel better. Matthew would build something out of Meccano and I would write letters to my Dad revealing all. But I never sent them. It wouldn't have made any difference.

MATTHEW

My Mother was stupid.

CHLOE

Mummy took me to the shop after school and bought me a Lucky Bag. That's because I was lucky. She said I was the luckiest thing to come to her. She bought me a giant Teddy and sometimes we would feed him through a hole in his side seam. His diet was quite limited: foam chunks with a side order of kapok. He turned into one fat bugger. I think we've still got him somewhere. My sister wanted a Tiny Tears doll, but Mummy said she never played with dolls so she never got one. But when she grew up, she had quite a lot of babies, so I think she might have liked a Tiny Tears doll after all.

ADDY

Margaret was the strangest neighbour I ever had; friendly as you like one moment and daggers drawn in an instant. It was a shame really, for she had a sweet family. Clive was a dream husband, more like a servant at her beck and call if you want the truth. He worked night and day to keep his family comfortable, and my husband held him in very high regard. He reckoned Clive was the best worker he ever employed and wished he would come to him on a full-time basis.

Of course, when all that trouble blew up with Margaret and her ridiculous tantrums, we felt it was just as well not to be any more involved than necessary. To be perfectly honest, it was a relief all round when they moved away, and the new neighbours were utterly normal which was quite refreshing. We didn't realise the strain of walking on eggshells until all that nonsense stopped. And the neighbours the other side were so pleased that they threw a party! Who could forget their home-made elderberry wine? It took us about a fortnight to recover. We stuck to lemonade the next time we were invited round there.

Dear Addy,

You may be interested to hear that we have completed our house move without any hitches. I have never in my life been so pleased to move away, just a shame that the distance could not have been further. You gave me a miserable time as your neighbour. I hope you welcome your new neighbours in a friendlier spirit, but I told them about you when their removal lorry arrived, so they are on the alert to treat you with caution. I thought it was the only fair thing to do for them.

I am relieved to have got myself and my children away from your malevolent influence. Goodness knows how your own children will turn out with you for a Mother. In closing, I'll offer a piece of advice that you really should heed. Keep your randy husband on a tighter leash. I'll say no more.

Our new address is written above. If ever you are passing, do feel free to carry right on going.

Wishing you everything you richly deserve,
Margaret

Two

MARGARET

The lovely old house we moved to was great. There were no
neighbours to speak of….the Grammar School over the road,
the Social Club to one side and an invalid on the other side
made for a quiet life on the neighbours' front. The house was
in a bit of a state though, and we seemed to never quite get to
grips with all the jobs that needed doing. After Chloe went into
the Juniors, we had to face facts, and my husband encouraged
me to apply for a job helping at the local school.

I'll be honest here, I didn't like the idea, but when I started,
they were such a likeable bunch of people that I couldn't help
enjoying it. It was a crummy old fashioned school but I made
some good friends and the Headmaster used to notice if I'd
got a new dress on or something and was really impressed
when I told him I made my own clothes. His wife thought that
suitable women's clothes were only available at Marks and
Spencer. I think she cost him a few bob one way and another.

They had a caravan which I was quite envious of. I wasn't
a keen camper and my heart used to sink a bit when we loaded
the tent onto the roof-rack each year but I kept quiet about
it. At least it meant we could afford to go abroad and I could
gloss over the camping part of our holidays when I was passing

the snaps around showing locations most people only saw on television. The kids came in handy; we trained them up to be pretty useful in setting up camp so as they got older it was less like hard work. Sometimes when we gave them watered wine at dinner time, they got a bit sloshed and then even silent Caroline would be entertaining.

Not that it would last. She'd be back to normal the next day, shrinking away like a shadow. She used to like to play Mother to Chloe back then and sometimes it was nice to have a break. I could send her for the shopping and tell her to take Chloe with her, then I could listen to Woman's Hour with my feet up and a nice cup of tea. Lovely! It's damned hard work bringing up three children let me tell you.

These days, Caroline's a bit of an Earth Mother. She used to exclaim to me about the never-ending laundry for her brood. Silly moo, you make a rod for your back if you let them use you like a servant. I wouldn't stand for it. I was expected to look after my own needs when I was growing up and once Caroline reached her teens, I saw no reason to wash anything except for her school uniform. It's what teaches kids to be self-sufficient and I know if I'd been fool enough to do everything for her, there would have been a giant heap of clothes for me to deal with every week. My sister Sandra used to laugh like a drain when she described how her daughter would tidy her room every Saturday and suddenly the floor would be clear but the laundry basket would be overflowing. What's funny about that? And the silly fool went ahead and washed the clothes for her...and ironed them *and* hung them up for her as well. She needed her head examining. And they were thick as thieves, the pair of them, practically lived in each other's pockets. Wherever Sandra was, there would be Claire. They were like best friends instead of Mother and daughter. It's not natural is it? And when the grandchildren came along, hell's bells, it was like the Second Coming. Sandra gave up her job and just *devoted* herself to those kids. I told Caroline the silly cow needed to get a life. I didn't want my daughter thinking I would give up everything to buzz around after her children. I sacrificed enough time bringing up my own tribe.

CAROLINE

I was no braver with my plans to run away from home than I was with sending letters to my Dad. I packed my duffel bag several times, but couldn't pluck up the courage to follow through.

I had several fantasy Mums. My lovely Aunty Sandra only lived round the corner when I was growing up, and I wanted to run away to her but I knew she wouldn't be able to keep me in real life. My cousin Claire was always smiling. I would be always smiling if Aunty Sandra was my Mum. One day when they were having a sisterly chat, Mum was grumbling about me and she said I had piggy eyes. My Aunty Sandra went "Oh Marg!" and gave me a cuddle, but she went home without me. Then we moved to the other side of town and I couldn't walk round to Aunty Sandra's house on Saturday mornings any more and read Claire's Bunty comic out of Mum's way. Claire and I used to swap. I had the Judy comic and when I'd read mine, we'd exchange them, not too dog-eared, and the whole morning would ooze away in the most luxurious slothful way. Bunty had tabbed clothes and a doll printed on the back cover that you could cut out and then dress up the paper doll with the paper clothes. But it meant that the story on the inside of the back page was all cut up so you couldn't read it any more. It was a big decision each week…should we cut up the back page or leave it intact? That was as big as dilemmas got in Claire's life. She taught me how to apply mascara and eyeshadow; oh and spot concealer too, which was less glamorous but a good skill to have in adolescence.

While I was happy with the Judy comic, Matthew's taste ran to the Whizzer and Chips and that was quite funny, but Chloe had baby stuff with a family of cats like Drag-a-Chair puss cat. I ask you. They don't print any of those titles any more. I think the internet's replaced all that, but there was such a frisson of excitement when we ran round to the newsagent on Saturday morning to fetch our comics.

Dad knew how we savoured our weekly comics. He always bought us an Annual at Christmas; such a minor gesture in the thrill of the day but oh! how I loved to turn the first page of a fresh new Judy Annual. I could pretend myself into any of the characters. There was Faye Farrell the nurse and she was my favourite but sometimes I wanted to be Sandra the prima ballerina or Chris who looked after children in an orphanage. But really I was more like Suzie who was always sent out with Baby in the pram. She never failed to return with Baby safe and sound despite the life and death experiences that had overtaken her on her trip round the block. Oddly, the artist never drew the Baby, who must be about 50 by now.

MATTHEW

My Mother was mean.

CHLOE

Mummy used to help me with colouring on Saturday mornings. We had to try and stay inside the lines and sometimes she was better than me and sometimes I would try really hard and I would be better than her! Then she would laugh and tickle me so we were both laughing until we nearly crapped our pants. Then she would make us both a mug of hot chocolate and we'd have two biscuits each, one plain and one fancy. She kept them in a tin with pictures of country cottages round the sides and a Tudor mansion on the lid. Sometimes she would open the tin and there wouldn't be as many biscuits as she thought there should be and she'd go "Matthew!" so loud it made me jump and Matthew would run down the garden and climb the tree. But he was godawful skinny so I don't think he could have stolen very many biscuits. His legs were so thin that his knees stood out like they belonged to someone else with much bigger legs. He looked better in long trousers.

ODE TO THE JOY OF TRAVELLING WITH CHILDREN

Are we nearly there yet?
The cry goes up again.
I already want to throttle them.
It's only half past ten.

Are we nearly there yet?
Why can't they shut their traps?
I'll have to crack, and hand to them
Their cheese and pickle baps.

Are we nearly there yet?
They whine and drum their feet.
Their patience only lasted to
The end of our own street.

By Caroline Johnson, Class 3 JF
Extract from "The Bishop's Mitre" school magazine.

3 School Road
Bedford

Jack's Newsagents
Franklyn Parade
Bedford

Dear Sirs

I was horrified by the outrageous bill you sent us. No wonder you can afford to holiday abroad every year. Cancel our order immediately, with the exception of "Playhour and Robin" which I wish to retain for its educational value. I refuse to pay through the nose for the other juvenile nonsense you supply to us.

Yours faithfully

M. Johnson

Margaret Johnson (Mrs)

Three

MARGARET

Sadly, our delightful little school was closed down and we were all scattered to the four winds. The fact that the school worked perfectly well cut no ice with the authorities. It didn't look the part so it had to go…and so did our merry little band.

The new school I transferred to just wasn't the same, so my husband suggested I should take up typing so I could progress up the ranks a bit. Bloody tough work though, studying at evening class as well as working 9am-3pm and all my domestic responsibilities. So he came up with a rota to ease the burden and on Friday evening, the kids had to muck in with the housework while Clive did the laundry. Then he cooked us bacon and eggs with tinned plum tomatoes to round off the evening, but at least we had a free weekend to look forward to. Apart from Clive of course, who still worked on Saturdays, oh and Caroline who had a paper round and then later a Saturday job in a local shop so Matthew took over her paper round.

Chloe was too little to have to earn herself extra pocket money but she would help me instead on Saturday mornings. We might bake cakes or sometimes we would make toffee. We could have done with a sugar thermometer really to be able to know just when the toffee was ready. There were days when we nearly cracked our teeth, the toffee was that rock solid. But they were enchanted leisure moments, just me and Chloe with a batch of toffee and an old film on BBC2 and no one grizzling or demanding attention. Then it was time for me to get ready to go out while Clive cooked boiled eggs for the kids' tea.

My Mother would come round every Saturday evening to babysit so that Clive and I could go out together. It's so important to be able to get away from the four walls and the demands of family. I think I would have gone mad without my Saturday escape. Mind you, I couldn't abide my Mother. She never did anything for me all my life and expected me to look after myself when I was growing up. She favoured my two brothers over me, absolutely idolised my older brother Simon. He repaid her adulation by emigrating to Australia with his wife Sue and their two young children. I don't think my Mother ever got over it. I got sick of hearing how well they were doing over there. It wouldn't matter to her if he became a roadside beggar, she would still regard him as a roaring success and a source of maternal pride. I could never compare with him or my younger brother Ted.

Luckily, I didn't have to talk to Mother on Saturdays. She would come on the bus to our house and then Clive would take her straight home when we got in. He seemed to get on with her a lot better than I did. He was considerably more tolerant of her selfish nature than I could ever be. She bought sweeties with her for the children every time. Always Smarties. None of them liked Smarties but she never got the message. They would eat the red ones then put the tubes away "for another day". They would never tell her they couldn't stand Smarties. I used to eat them in the end, blast it, just couldn't resist the temptation, then the GP used to say every time I visited him "you could do with losing some weight Mrs Johnson". Bastard.

CAROLINE

My wonderful Granny used to come every Saturday without fail and we always had to pretend to be pleased with the Smarties. She would ask what we had been doing all week and we could never remember anything interesting. She was just our Granny, always there and you don't think that one day she won't be there any more and maybe she had a really interesting life that you wish you'd asked her about. I'd love to talk to her now, but too late.

Mum didn't like her at all and wouldn't speak to her much, but Granny didn't seem to notice and that annoyed Mum even more. She just couldn't wait to get out the door. Granny would go and have a bath then because she didn't have a bathroom in her house, just a lavatory with a high-up cistern and a long chain in a lean-to at the back of her kitchen. This was in the 1970s; you wouldn't believe it would you? Then, at 8 o'clock, it was my job to make a cup of tea for her and sometimes I would be feeling creative so I made disgusting concoctions with the Rich Tea biscuits like putting salad cream on them and sprinkling on 100s and 1000s. Poor Granny! She always ate them and pretended they were delicious. A bit like us with the Smarties I suppose.

When she put us to bed, we always said a prayer which she taught us: "Now I lay me down to sleep…" then: "night night, God bless" and we knew we were safe and sound. When I was quite small, she bought me a yellow petticoat with frills for my birthday. I wasn't pretty, Chloe was the pretty one, and I didn't have frills on my clothes. But Granny knew I dreamed of frills and she came up trumps. She folded the petticoat up into a Basildon Bond Box (without the writing paper in of course) and then she wrote kisses all over the lid of the box like this xxxxxxxxxxxxxx. There were hundreds of them. She used to buy chocolate spread because I liked it on my bread and butter

15

when we went to tea at her house. She was a good Granny to have.

MATTHEW

My Mother hated my Granny.

CHLOE

Granny was good fun. She told us funny stories to make us laugh and wanted to look at the things we'd been doing. Sometimes there would be some toffee left to share, but mostly not. She was quite naughty and she'd let us stay up later than our bedtime but she would say keep it a secret from your Mother. I didn't keep secrets from Mummy, but I kept that one. Granny believed in the Bible like it was all true and thought Charles Darwin was a wicked man. She said "I didn't come from a monkey, I was made in God's image" and Matthew would say maybe God is a monkey. I think he was influenced too much by the Whizzer and Chips.

GRANNY

My grandchildren were a delight in every way. Margaret did not take naturally to motherhood, so it fell to me to do my best to fill the gap, and I was pleased to be so involved in their little lives. It is rather painful to relate, for Margaret is my own child, but oh dear! She was difficult sometimes. I saw a sign once in an office where I cleaned which put me in mind of Margaret every time I dusted it. "I'm not paranoid but they are out to get me" it said in Gothic font. I'm not saying Margaret is paranoid exactly, but she has a wondrous talent to see an insult where none was intended. She takes offence more readily than Mary Whitehouse ever did. And sometimes, the things she said were just beyond belief. It was like she couldn't bear it if everyone's attention left her for a moment. I was horrified to hear a tale from my sister Ruby that her daughter Harriet had confided in her. Some horrific nonsense about my husband interfering in a disgusting way with Margaret when she was a child. What complete codswallop! That dear man was the kindest, dearest, most loving Father any child could hope for.

Margaret and I had words about it, but she shrugged it off as if it was neither here nor there, just got angry that Harriet had betrayed her confidence. When I told my elder daughter Sandra about the whole saga, she just scoffed and told me to take no notice of Margaret's tricks. But the thought is rooted in my mind now. It's as though a little tarnish has smeared my memory of the poor man. And of course, he's no longer with us to defend himself. It's quite plain the whole thing is preposterous...but what if...? It's made my heart ache and that's a fact.

Dear Mother

I'm sorry to hear that you are unwell, but it has made me realise that you will not be with us forever, and I have a number of regrets I want to get off my chest before you go. I've thought long and hard about writing this letter, but this may be my last opportunity to say the things that have been on my mind for many years.

I know you never cared for me in the same way that you lavished love on my sister and brothers, and that is very hurtful to me. I have watched you treat their families with generosity while ignoring my own, and that hurts too. I was aware of your animosity towards me from early childhood, when I thoroughly resented being despatched by Pa to buy you flowers for Mother's Day. Such an empty gesture! You never bothered with me, yet I was supposed to offer you worship and adoration! When my brother Simon drank all the lemonade, did you remonstrate with him when I complained to you? Not you, he was the son whom you loved and I was the daughter you had no time for.

Pa's untimely death was extremely hard for me to come to terms with. He had got away scot-free with the depraved things he used to do to me, ignored by the rest of the family. Don't tell me you knew nothing about it, but you would never listen to me would you? It didn't fit the pretty picture *you held on to, so it couldn't be true in your eyes. Well let me tell you, it was true, every word. First Sandra, then me once she grew too old for his tastes. When he died, I didn't know whether to cry with relief or scream through the frustration of injustice. But all that mattered to you was that we should keep up appearances. No opportunity to air my grievances, oh no, all you wanted me to do was get a job so I could make a contribution to your household expenses. And you never had any time for me, you were always dashing off to one job or another. We were ships in the night, never exchanging a kind word as a normal Mother and daughter would do. I suppose your guilt got in the way.*

Your desire to keep control of me permeated every moment of my life. My wedding day was a farce, overseen in every detail by you. You made me the dress that you chose, you made the bridesmaids' outfits that you chose, we ate the food that you prepared at the venue where you cleaned. The only thing I chose for myself was my husband, and Thank God! at least he enabled me to escape from you.

I have learnt to set aside the hurts inflicted by you in the past, and can look with peace to a time in the future without you. I know that you have always hated me, but Mother, it may surprise you to know that I don't hate you in return. I am above all that. But I don't think I will attend your funeral.

Yours,
Margaret

Four

MARGARET

Caroline was not a feast for the eyes. She always looked like she was trying to hide, and would scurry about like a hunched up mouse when she was en route somewhere. She was skinny and ungainly all at once. I told her all the time to stand up properly and learn to be more graceful. Her father suggested ballet classes might help but I knew who would have to arrange that, so I ignored his proposal. But God, she was gawky! I hated to look at her.

She learnt to sew and made a few half decent clothes in her dressmaking lessons at school, so Clive thought it would be a good idea if we gave her a clothing allowance and I could take her clothes shopping. I shudder to think of it! The idea of trailing round the shops accompanying her long face was about as appealing as a pork pie in a synagogue so I told him I thought it would be more useful to her to learn to buy her clothes independently. He went quiet and looked at me for a bit but I held my ground. She wouldn't have been grateful anyway, she was always a sly little madam.

Clive thought that 50p a week would be a good sum to start and see how she managed on that. I thought about it and it occurred to me that it would be better to let her have

£2 a month because you can do more with £2 than 50p so that's how it went on. I'm not made of money. It's a lot more than I ever got from my Mother I can assure you. And Chloe was suddenly sprouting up, so she needed clothes as well and frankly she was more rewarding to dress up nicely.

But Caroline learnt to haggle at the market and used to manage a new skirt or sweater most months at my expense. Matthew didn't seem to care what clothes he put on, the more ragged the better seemed to be his watchword so his wardrobe wasn't costly. Bloody Mother sometimes used to say something, like "why hasn't Caroline got a nice coat to go out in?" I told her right out if she wanted to buy her a nice coat she could be my guest, but she'd have to buy the same for all three. I wouldn't put up with them being treated differently. That's the first route to sibling jealousy and I don't need that going on in my house.

CAROLINE

I was astonished when Mum told me she thought I was old enough to be responsible for buying my own clothes from now on and she had decided to let me have £2 a month allowance to learn how to budget. The first month I headed straight to Chelsea Girl but I couldn't afford anything so I went to the market instead. Even then, I had to plead with the stall holder and show him how much money I'd got until he gave in and said "OK OK take it and don't tell my brother". Of course, I couldn't go to the same stall every month, but it was quite a big market so I did all right although it was excruciatingly embarrassing. I always looked around first in case anyone from school might see me. It was a big relief when Primark opened in the High Street.

It was a bit of a blow when I realised I was expected to buy my own sanitary towels from now on though. Mum hadn't mentioned that part of the agreement. And tights. It gave me a broken heart every time I got a ladder. I don't know if you've ever tried to darn tights. It's just about impossible and they end up with nobbles all over or you have to find 15p for a new pair. Tights became the object of my worst nightmares. I came out in a cold sweat at the mention of Pretty Polly.

MATTHEW

My Mother bought me a blue shirt with flowers on once. It was revolting.

CHLOE

Mummy liked me to have nice clothes. I had curly hair and big eyes and people used to admire me wherever we went out. "Oh what a pretty girl" they'd say and give me their pack of Polos. That doesn't happen any more but I mostly wear black grunge now and I can afford to buy my own Polos. And fags. But don't tell Mummy.

ODE TO THE LADDERS IN MY TIGHTS

Like ladies everywhere I know
New nylons give us sheer delights,
But can a day pass by without
A blasted ladder in my tights?

We all have dreams of paradise
Where legs are always pretty sights:
No thorns, no nails, no rough-skinned palms
To cause us ladders in our tights.

The fairer sex appreciates
A gift to brighten days and nights.
A glut of hosiery supplies:
We scoff at ladders in our tights.

Till Kitty gets stuck up a tree
And we all have a thousand frights.
Oh yes! At last a use is found
For that long ladder in my tights.

By Caroline Johnson, Class 4JF
Extract from "The Bishop's Mitre" school magazine.

3 School Road
Bedford

Childhood Dreams Modelling Agency
Western Rise
Bedford

Dear Sirs

Please find enclosed some snaps of my young daughter Chloe. I am sure you will agree with me that she is quite gorgeous. Whenever we are out and about, strangers in the street will stop us to remark on her unusual beauty.

I would be very happy to allow you to use her as a model and I am in no doubt that she would be a very valuable asset to your agency. I can be contacted at the above address so that we can discuss suitable terms at your earliest convenience. I should tell you that I will be making a similar offer to other agencies so I would recommend a prompt response.

Yours faithfully

M. Johnson

Margaret Johnson (Mrs).

Five

MARGARET

As Caroline got older, she got more difficult to get along with. Thankfully, she spent a lot of time studying in her bedroom. She had a pretty room with a lovely big bay window which unfortunately meant the room could get a bit cold in the winter but she would bundle up and get in the bed if it was too bad. Her handwriting was atrocious but the little madam used to say it was because she didn't have a desk to work at. Did she think she was a bloody princess or something? I could only dream of a desk when I was her age. All my Mother wanted was for me to be old enough to leave school and start bringing in a wage. Desk my backside!

Matthew was studious too and his room had a very handy long alcove, so Clive fitted up a length of plywood which gave him a good big workspace. He just filled it with animals, not big things obviously, but crickets and stick insects and a gecko, yuck, that was truly repulsive. Its eyes never stopped watching you and quite often they were pointing in two different directions at once. The thing gave me the creeps. Matthew liked to catch caterpillars and fed them assiduously until they pupated. Chloe sometimes went in and wiggled the chrysallis to listen to the weird crackling noise it made. Of course, that was the sound of the developing butterfly being crushed to death and Matthew used to get furious with rage, but Chloe always had an enquiring mind which as a parent, you have to encourage.

At the weekends, Matthew would take himself off on long tramps in the woods and to the countryside and he'd come back with all sorts of weird fauna and flora which would all get catalogued. He was like a little old man before his time and took it all so seriously. Made his room smell a bit I can tell you. I refused to go in there any more. I told him if he caused the stink, he could clean the stink. Well he didn't, as you can imagine, so I just used to keep the window wide open and the door tight shut.

Mind you, it all came good in the end, because he earns a fortune now and is quite well known in celebrity circles. David Bellamy took him under his wing when he had a secondment to the BBC immediately after graduating and now I often see his name come up in the credits to some wildlife programme or other, and he always seems to have a new book on display in W H Smiths. I never buy them, I can assure you. He's quite rich enough without my contribution. But I understand he does a lot of good work with youngsters, so all my hard work during his upbringing must have rubbed off somehow.

CAROLINE

Mum was angry a lot. We learnt to recognise the signs of an impending rage storm. Mum would go into a silent reverie, staring inwards at a vision only she could see until there came a break-point. Then she would snap back into life, releasing fiery lashes of anger that whipped around our heads as we ducked for cover. The best thing we could hope for was that her attention might focus on someone else. But I was often the butt of her bad temper and found it difficult to please her. When I did the ironing, I folded it wrong. When I peeled the potatoes I cut them too small. That was when I hadn't cut them too big. Back then, I still thought that if I tried harder, she might come to like me.

One Mother's Day – I would have been 14 or 15 – I had saved my money since Christmas without buying one single thing I didn't absolutely need, and I bought her an earthenware dinner service from Argos. The thing nearly dislocated my arms carrying it home, but I thought surely this would make my Mother like me. But she didn't say anything, just put it away in the cupboard.

My Dad came upstairs afterwards and said she really loved it, it was just what she would have chosen herself, but I'm not so sure. Maybe she wanted something completely different and now she was stuck with what I'd picked out. She used to say she'd like some nice bone china but I couldn't afford that. She liked the gloves that Chloe gave her. They were really smart, with fur round the cuff but then Dad found out she'd nicked them and took her back to British Home Stores to confess. But he ended up paying for them himself, so Chloe still gave them to Mum and she still got a hug and a kiss for her nice gift.

Matthew gave some fantastic Christmas presents one year, even Mum was pleased with the pair of cut glass decanters he presented her with and got all flustered at the thought of how much money he'd spent on us all. But in January, she found the Green Shield Stamps savings books had all gone and his ruse unravelled in tears and ghastly recriminations, not to mention several lusty whacks on the behind. He had a gecko called Gerald that he loved and she made him sell it to pay her back. She still used the decanters though.

MATTHEW

My Mother was the most horrible Mother in the world.

My Dad didn't treat me as nicely as Mummy. Caroline and Matthew were both clever but I couldn't learn the mysterious art of reading very well at all. Now I think I would have been diagnosed as dyslexic but back then, you were just a lazy bastard if you couldn't read properly. I was OK with sums, but I couldn't always read the question so I fucked up the answer even though I knew the right way to work it out.

I didn't like going to school. Quite often on Monday I would have a tummy ache and Mummy let me stay in bed but Dad would say "how is she ever going to learn if she's not at school?" So by Tuesday, tummy ache or no tummy ache, I'd have to go to school and get my lessons wrong again.

Dad got two bedside chests from Texas Homecare and straddled a length of wood across them so I could sit and write my work neatly. Looking back, what I needed was not a trip to fucking Texas Homecare but a bit of help from a teacher who knew about kids like me. Things have come on a lot since those days. I don't think Dad had the first idea what to do with me. The Ladybird reading scheme had worked perfectly well with Caroline and Matthew and when I couldn't get the hang of Peter and Jane and their shitty lives, he didn't have an alternative plan. Mummy wasn't bothered as long as I was happy.

Oddly, although I couldn't read my ABC, the music stave was as clear as day to me. FACE stood for the notes in the spaces and for the notes on the lines, we recited "Every Good Boy Deserves Favour" or, as my cousin Roger used to say: "Eggs give boys deadly farts". He was very rude, but I always remembered the Egg version best.

For Sale

My Gecko

He is called Gerald

Please look after him

£ 10 please

Please call after School or at weekends

3 School road

3 School Road
Bedford

The Chief Executive
Argos Stores Ltd
Head Office
Avebury
Milton Keynes

Dear Sirs

I attempted to return a dinner service to your Bedford store today, but the staff there refused to accept it. They told me that because it was no longer in the original packaging and I was not in possession of the receipt, they could not assist me. The impression I was given was that they were actually suspicious of me and in the end I left, having been made to feel very uncomfortable. I am quite furious at the clear implication that your staff questioned my honesty. The dinner service could be easily viewed in your catalogue, so obviously I was not trying to palm off something which had not been purchased from yourselves.

Despite my protests, your staff remained adamant that they would not give me satisfaction, so I had to leave with my dinner service, which I might add is extremely heavy. No one had the common decency to offer to help me carry it to my car parked outside in the loading bay.

I must inform you that henceforth, I will be taking my custom elsewhere. Your intractability has cost you a customer forever.

Yours faithfully

M. Johnson

Margaret Johnson (Mrs)

Six

MARGARET

I don't think people realise what a hard job it is to be a Mother. You're always on duty, never a day off, nobody to say "hey, why don't you put your feet up for half an hour. Read your library book for a minute while I see to the dinner". What a dream.

Although to be fair, Clive has always done most of the cooking. He enjoyed it and he was much better than me. So in fact, I could read a chapter or two while he hummed away to himself in the kitchen. And I must say, whoever came up with the idea of public libraries should be knighted or something. I couldn't do without it.

I read all the greats: Catherine Cookson, Victoria Holt, Miss Read, Jean Plaidy. I like a bit of quality, something you can get your teeth into. I've always got a book on the go, I have to visit the library twice a week to keep stocked up. The librarians all say that I'm their best customer, or they look at their watch when I come in and go "Mrs Johnson! Goodness me, you're three minutes late!" We like our little joke, it's so companionable.

Caroline always fancied herself as a writer, but of course, it's a lot harder than you imagine. I had a go once or twice myself when I had a good idea that I thought I could work up into something worthwhile, but there were always so many calls on my time that I could never get very far. As for Caroline's efforts, they were so unpolished and immature and she wouldn't listen to my advice. She used to get so het up when I explained what she needed to do and then her eyes would start to go red and her voice get all strangled and the next thing you knew, there were the pages in the fire. She just didn't have the patience to stick at it. I told her over and over again, you need to persevere to get anywhere in this world. You want the best for your children, but sometimes they just won't listen no matter how hard you try.

Chloe was the one with the big talent, oh you would weep to hear her playing her violin. She'd draw the bow across the strings and it was like she could make that instrument sing. Now, music is a really difficult profession to break into, but we were determined not to let that talent go to waste, and we took her everywhere – literally, all over the country – to further her gift. And I daren't tell you how much a good violin will set you back, but when I listen to her, I can't regret one minute or one penny we gladly gave to support her. And with good cause, obviously, because it's what she does to this day. It's just a shame that it's such a poorly paid and unpredictable way to make a living. There's the great conundrum of our capitalist world: greedy bankers make millions for themselves while an artiste can move you to tears but will barely be able to keep body and soul together.

CAROLINE

I loved to write. When I was a kid in primary school, I used to dash off Famous Five knock-offs, fully believing they were the most original thing ever written. My teacher Mr Grainger used to read them to the class and made me feel like I was the cleverest writer the world had ever seen, but truthfully? They were puerile, derivative and basically rubbish.

Once I discovered proper writers, I realised how poor my efforts really were. I adored the Bronte sisters and just read those books until they nearly fell to pieces. But when I analysed the text, I got downhearted by the comprehension of how intricately constructed they were. The ambition of Jane Austen's little piece of ivory inspired me so, but when I tried to write something as good, I found I couldn't get the words to fall into place or the phrasing would be too clumsy. So I'd write it and rewrite it and every once in a while I thought I was getting on the right track, but Mum, who was always reading a book, would compare it with her latest and say it needed a more handsome hero or a more mysterious villain until I nearly wanted to scream. But if she's the average reader, then she's the target market, so her opinion counts.

When I read through my stuff again I would see all the glaring faults and realise my childhood home would never become a destination for a literary coach trip. Sometimes you have to face reality and let go of your impossible dreams.

At least I didn't tragically die of consumption.

MATTHEW

My Mother was an ignorant moron.

CHLOE

The best day of my life was when I got my gorgeous new Rodolpho Fredi violin. Actually, it was quite an old violin; the best ones are. Dad had to take a bank loan to pay for it, but it sounded so good, even my violin teacher looked like she'd crap herself with envy. It was more money than Dad had decided on, but Mummy found it when she wrote to the conductor of – get this – only the London Philharmonic Phucking Orchestra! She wrote to him quite a few times to tell him about me, but in the end I never got to actually meet him, in fact his secretary wrote to Mummy to ask her to stop harassing him. She was mad as hell with him and said he'd got completely the wrong end of the stick. But she always did her best for me…and my violin was definitely the best. I used to call it "my Strad" to see people gasp and ask how much it's worth, so I could say "oh this Strad? it varies". That was another one of my cousin Roger's jokes. He was a good violinist but not as good as me.

Mind you, he became a property developer instead and now he's a lot better off than I am.

MY VIOLIN

My Mom brought home a violin
So I could learn to play.
She told me if I practised hard
I'd play it well some day.

Without a single lesson,
I tried to play a song.
My fiddle squeaked, my fiddle squawked.
The notes came out all wrong.

My little brother fled the room.
Mom covered up her ears.
My puppy dog began to howl.
My sister was in tears.

My Dad pulled out his wallet.
He handed me a ten.
He made me swear I'd never play
That violin again.

Bruce Lansky

3 School Road
Bedford

The Editor
The Bedford Mercury
Market Square
Bedford

Dear Sir

Doubtless, you will be familiar with the Alexander Evans School of Music. You will be aware that it is highly renowned within the music industry and that only the most talented youngsters are accepted to be trained by the redoubtable Mr Evans.

My daughter Chloe is one of the star pupils at the school, and it occurred to me that as Editor, you might appreciate a "scoop" as I believe it is known in your trade. Chloe is destined to go far, and it would be quite something if one day you could point to the article in your newspaper which charted her first days of stardom.

The Alexander Evans School of Music is holding a recital at the Town Hall Annexe next Thursday evening at 7pm. I would advise you to send a member of your reporting team so you can be in the vanguard in recognising this phenomenon of talent.

I look forward to meeting you at next week's recital.

Yours faithfully

M. Johnson

Margaret Johnson (Mrs)

P.S. Silly me! I forgot to mention that Chloe is a violinist.

Seven

MARGARET

I wasn't allowed to keep up my education, just expected to get a job as soon as I was old enough to leave school. My Mother was widowed by then, and insisted she couldn't afford to keep me at school and anyway, I'd only end up getting married so further education would be a waste. So I wanted to prove to her that daughters could have careers just as well as sons, and we made sure Caroline stayed on into Sixth Form. She was clever enough to go to university, but she seemed to lose heart when her writing didn't go well and then she only wanted to get married and have a family. The irony! She wanted what I had to settle for instead of taking advantage of the opportunities we were willing to offer her. She was always the most ungrateful little twerp.

Well she got a dead end job, carrying on full time at the shop where she'd been working on Saturdays. She claimed she liked it; liked the other staff and liked the customers too. I felt like smacking her, but she was getting a bit too old for that. Still, she was earning a regular wage, which was a good thing. We felt it was only right that she should start contributing to her living expenses. Youngsters need to learn how to budget or they're at a disadvantage when they get out into the real world.

Clive thought that £5 a week should be adequate, but she was paid monthly, so to save her the inconvenience of weekly payments, I told her she could pay me £25 a month which of course was far too cheap, but it was a gesture in the right direction. Anyway, sure enough, she caught herself a husband, although I could have told her he was a waste of space. Far too good-looking for her, I knew his eye would wander once the honeymoon had worn off. He was in sales and moved round all over the place, first in charge of one area then moved to a bigger area, then troubleshooting in problem spots. Oh he got around in more ways than I can tell you, and they had to move house at the whim of his Managing Director.

I kept out of it, I thought the less involved I was the better. There are some things you don't want to know about your children's lives. And once they're off your hands, they have to learn to stand on their own two feet – and sort out their own mistakes for that matter. Pretty soon Matthew went off to university, and I felt like at last I'd got my life back. It was such a comfortable undemanding household with just the three of us.

CAROLINE

I thought I'd died and gone to heaven when Phil started courting me. I couldn't believe someone like him would be interested in someone like me, but he couldn't seem to tear himself away. He was a bit older than me, had a house and a car and all that, and a really good job with good prospects as long as he didn't mind moving around the country. Well, that didn't bother me. If you want the truth, I was so glad to get away from my Mother that if Phil had a wooden leg and a glass eye I wouldn't have cared.

No, but seriously, I adored and worshipped him and he made me feel so treasured, it was a feeling I'd never experienced before. I suddenly thought that all those trashy novels my Mother loved to read had come true and were happening to me! I suppose you would have to call it a whirlwind romance but I didn't have a single doubt that I was having the archetypal fairytale ending. "They all lived happily ever after". And my Mother was almost more smitten with him than I was! She used to hang on his every word and say "why can't Matthew be more like Phil?" I think the main attraction for her was probably that he was taking me away from her, but she was impressed by his flashy car and used to tell her friends quite loudly what a lovely house we were buying in a very exclusive new estate.

Well, it was nice, but the nicest thing about it was it was ours and we could do whatever we liked whenever we liked. Sometimes we didn't get out of bed on Sunday until the afternoon, and nobody gave us the death stare when we finally came downstairs. It was fantastic. I felt like a grown-up.

MATTHEW

My Mother was bearable from a distance. The further the better.

CHLOE

I missed my sister when she got married, a lot more than I expected. I hadn't realised how much she helped me out until she wasn't around any more. She understood that I was crap at making ends meet and she'd always pass me a fiver when I was short. She never made a fuss about it, just said you can make it up to me another time.

I couldn't work at weekends because there were always recitals or performances to attend somewhere. Mummy gave me an allowance, but it never stretched far enough. She somehow didn't understand how goddam expensive everything was. Smoking didn't help I must admit, but everyone in showbiz seems to think it's the natural thing to do and you feel like the odd one out if you go all saintly "oh no, not for me thank you" like you're too hoity toity to join in.

It's a great life, but I'll be the first to say we party hard. You only live once don't you? And some mornings when I woke up with a headache, a mouth tasting like old socks, and a complete stranger lying next to me, I wonder whether the one life might be too much for me.

Apartment 9
Mill House
Mill Road
Bedford

Dear Caroline and Phil

I'm sorry that Hilde and I are not able to join you for your wedding celebrations. We sincerely hope that you enjoy your day, and that you will have a long contented life together. You will be in our thoughts and we will be rejoicing with you in spirit if not in the flesh. I'm sure my Mother would have been very pleased and proud to see your happiness.

With our dearest love,

Uncle Ted and Tante Hilde

3 School Road
Bedford

The School of Biological Sciences
Zoology Building
Tillydrone Avenue
Aberdeen

Dear Sirs

I was astonished to receive the enclosed invoice for books evidently ordered by my son Matthew. I can't imagine why you have sent it here. He does not live here now and is unlikely to live here in the future. No doubt you will find him somewhere on campus. Probably he expected me to pay his bill and has given you this address in order to deliberately embarrass me.

Please ensure that my credit rating is not adversely affected by the non-payment of this bill. I would advise you to take more care in future to avoid potential ill-will against the University's good name.

Yours faithfully

M. Johnson

Margaret Johnson (Mrs)

Eight

MARGARET

We had such a lovely day for Caroline's wedding! All our good friends were present to see what a wonderful send off we gave her. Clive was a bit surprised that I hadn't got a fund stashed away to put towards it. He seemed to think we'd agreed that when she started paying for her keep, I would put it into a dedicated savings account to pay for her future wedding. Now please, does that sound likely? I'm quite sure I would have remembered discussing that outlandish arrangement.

Luckily, Clive had just made the last payment for Chloe's violin, so he was able quite simply to take out a new bank loan for the wedding. Not that we went mad. We decided on a budget of £1000 and we stuck to it; I was proud that I spent exactly what we planned and not one penny more. I certainly don't agree with fancy celebrations where the bride gets ideas above her station, but on the other hand, I never forgot how my Mother orchestrated my wedding and foisted the day that she wanted upon me. My own wishes were the last thing on her mind and I was determined not to repeat her mistake.

Mind you, I had to put my foot down where some of the guests were concerned. The Function Room we'd hired had space for 90 people, and no way was I paying for my brother

43

Ted to be included at the expense of my good natured colleague Mary. Caroline got a bit upset because she wanted her Uncle Ted and she complained that she didn't know Mary at all. She just didn't get it. I loathed my brother with a passion. He was such a user and never stopped taking advantage of my Mother; lived in her house well into his thirties instead of getting off his backside and having the guts to pay his own way. Just scrounge, scrounge, scrounge all his life. And Mother let him get away with it, justifying the situation because he was in training and wouldn't get the benefit until he was qualified. He's a snooty barrister now, rolling in money, and I can tell you I was not prepared to pay for him to sit eating roast chicken and guzzling Asti Spumante at my expense thank you very much.

It was a good job we'd reconciled with my sister Sandra after a nasty spat a couple of years before when Claire got married. Claire wanted a small private affair with just close family and friends but no children. We hit the roof when we realised we were invited but not our kids. I told Sandra straight: if the kids don't come, nor do we. I was surprised at her allowing Claire to get away with it to be honest; as if her friends were more important than her family. She knows how important we regard family bonds to be. It was utterly impossible to imagine an event of such huge significance as a wedding without all the blood relatives being present. It wouldn't seem like a proper marriage otherwise. There was a big upset over it all, but I stood firm. Some principles can't be compromised.

I think Sandra secretly knew I was in the right, because although we never spoke of it afterwards, she never stopped sending cards for birthdays and Christmas and anniversaries and dropped off sweet peas from her garden, and tomatoes when she had a glut, so eventually, I decided to be the mature one here and I accepted her back into my life.

Not Claire though. I want nothing more to do with her. That caused another little sniffle from bride Caroline. She kept reminiscing about all the things she reckoned they'd done together and please, please could she come to the wedding. Nearly did my head in. But I refuse to have anything more to do with the selfish madam and the fact of the matter was, I was footing the bill so I had the final decision on the guest list.

We had a bit of a tussle over the wedding cake as well. Caroline didn't seem to realise we had a budget to stick to. She wanted the full three tiers but we said two would be plenty. That's all I had at my wedding and it was perfectly adequate. Thing was, she wanted to keep the top tier to be a christening cake sometime in the future, but that wasn't my main consideration right then. I'd seen a beautiful hat that I knew would set off my outfit to perfection and no matter how I did the sums, something had to give. I reasoned that the cake would just get eaten, whereas I would always have the hat. Clive wanted to surprise his daughter with the three tiers, but it made no sense to me, so I rang up the caterer and told her we'd decided on the top two tiers only. So it ended up being Clive who got the surprise when he went to fetch the cake and found it wasn't all there. He got quite cross with the caterer apparently and she had the nerve to blame it on me. I thought discretion was the better part of valour on that one and kept out of it.

The hat was glorious, everyone commented on it. Unfortunately, the cake ran out by the time the waitress reached the last table where Clive's brother Ron was sitting with his family but he just told her they didn't like cake, so everything worked out fine. I knew it would.

CAROLINE

In the end I just decided to enjoy my wedding day and not think about the things I couldn't have. When I had imagined my wedding – every girl daydreams about the big day, don't they? – I never thought my cousin Claire wouldn't be there, in fact I thought she'd come and do my make-up for me and we'd have a lovely girly time. As it was, my Mother allocated me a 20 minute slot in the bathroom because there were other people to consider as well as me. The most important thing was I was about to set off on a lifetime with Phil and I really didn't need anything else to make me happy.

My Mother loved the whole day, although she had difficulty keeping control of her hat. It was the most extraordinary thing, as big as our garden gate and just about as attractive. Nobody could take their eyes off it. Goodness knows what possessed her to buy the thing, still, if she ever finds herself in need of a bucket, it might come in handy.

After the event, I ordered some extra photographs and sent them to Claire and to Uncle Ted because I missed them being there and that seemed like the best thing I could do. I didn't tell Mum though. I didn't need any more lectures from her... and now I had my own life, I didn't need to bow to her needs again. I was like the French Revolution: Liberte! Egalite! Fraternite! And I'd escaped Madame Guillotine!

MATTHEW

Caroline's wedding was a lot of fun. For Mum.

CHLOE

Mummy was good at organising. She had a picture in her head and never stopped until she'd made it reality. I was a bridesmaid of course and Caroline had to choose one of her friends. She wanted three but Mummy said that would be too many and detract from the bride. So it was me and Louise on the day. Mummy said pink dresses would be pretty and suit my colouring, but it was a shame about Louise who had bright ginger hair which clashed disastrously. Caroline suggested green, but Mummy pointed out that green was an unlucky colour and nobody wants to bring bad luck to their wedding day.

Caroline wanted me to play the violin for her to come down the aisle, but how the fuck was I supposed to play and follow behind her at the same time, so she had the Trumpet Voluntary played on the piano instead. It was a shame they didn't get the piano tuned but never mind, it's only a short moment, gone in a flash.

Caroline looked really happy and Phil was the most handsome groom you've ever seen. I wasn't too sure whether he was wearing mascara, but if not, he has the most amazing eyelashes. He ought to be a model. I suspect he thinks the same thing.

Uncle Ron was ticked off when he got no cake. He loves fruit cake, but Aunty Honor said she'd bake him one when they got home. He brightened up then, because he could have an entire cake instead of just a slice, which anyone can work out is a better deal. Aunty Honor is a marvellous cook, which is probably why Uncle Ron is quite a bit larger round the middle than Dad. They were admiring Dad's youthful figure dressed in his best suit, and Uncle Ron said "that's because if he doesn't cook, he doesn't eat" and Aunty Honor gave him a quelling look and said "Now then Ron" in a way that made him shut the fuck up for the next half hour.

PHIL

I married Caroline and got Margaret for a Mother-in-law. But I got married despite that. I didn't have to live with the old witch myself after all. I could cope with brief visits. All I had to do was turn on the charm (every salesman can do that) and I would have her eating out of my palm. She was the most gullible fool you could ever hope to meet. Sometimes I used to amuse myself by thinking up new compliments to pay her, and the more ridiculous they were, the more she lapped them up. "Oh Margy-Mum, your hair is looking so sleek today. Have you been to the hairdresser?" "Oh no, Phil, it just looks like this naturally. Let me help you to another slice of cake." Silly old bat. Her hair was like a toilet brush.

Dear Mrs Grant

I was very disappointed at your outrageous efforts to place the blame on my shoulders for the unfortunate misunderstanding with my daughter's wedding cake. My husband was most upset to find an incomplete cake when he collected it from you but he is a charitable man and could accept the human error on your part. What really compounded his dissatisfaction were your attempts to suggest that his own wife was somehow responsible. If there is one thing guaranteed to annoy my husband, it is an unwarranted attack on me.

I have thought long and hard about this sad incident, and I can only conclude that you got the wrong end of the stick when we spoke on the telephone to discuss the finer details of the cake. I realise now that I should have written to you, then we would have had the irrefutable truth in black and white before us.

The inadequacy of the cake you supplied left my husband and I in a very awkward position on a day that should have been a joy for everybody. One table received no cake at all, which as you can imagine, was embarrassing in the extreme. The only saving grace was the good humour with which our guests greeted their empty plates. You should be eternally grateful for the kind understanding of those people.

Needless to say, I will not be recommending your services to anyone in my wide circle of friends.

Yours sincerely,

M. Johnson

Margaret Johnson (Mrs).

Nine

MARGARET

With Caroline gone and Matthew at university, my life was just fine and dandy. But there's always something round the corner isn't there? I had a bit of a bust-up with the new Head at school.

The trouble with new people is they think their ideas will work better, even though the old ways are working perfectly well. As I like to say "if it ain't broke, don't fix it" but Mrs Edgerton ("do call me Judith" simper simper) thinks that computers are the future and my paper systems need throwing out. I told her "you're as good as saying I need throwing out then" and I told her straight I wasn't paid enough to start re-training now. Next thing I know, she's gone behind my back and arranged someone from the education authority to visit to "bring me up to speed" on the new systems coming into force. My blood boiled! Who does she think she is? But it's like talking to a brick wall.

I was very disappointed in my friend Mary. I honestly thought she would see through the façade of Mrs Sweetness and Light Edgerton, but she said "oh come on Marg, look on it as an opportunity to hone your skills". She seems to think we're lucky to get Do-call-me-Judith. She's so naïve, doesn't see the true character behind the honeyed words, but when I tried to help her understand the true picture, she went odd and said "sometimes you can be very cruel Marg". I'm only trying to make her see the truth, she ought to be thanking me but suddenly she's always "busy" when I suggest coffee, while Pollyanna Judith just never stops smiling, like she's the bloody Cheshire cat or something. Nobody can really be that nice can they? I'm the only one who can see through her act. She's got everyone else, including Mary, eating out of her hand like little lapdogs, bow-wow. Well, I'm not taken in and I shan't forget. Once I'm trained up, I'll look for another school with nicer staff members.

In the meantime, I'm enjoying my personal freedom. I've got the plumber coming round later to look at my plans to update the ancient bathroom. I love all these new colours you can get now, and they're surprisingly inexpensive. I'll be glad to see the back of the monstrous enamel tub with the ridiculous claw feet. I've fallen in love with Sun-king; the most gorgeous peachy shade. I bet the manufacturers will end up abandoning production of white bathroom suites because no one will want them any more when they've got so many attractive alternatives to choose from. And while I'm at it, I'll try and persuade Clive to stump up for a professional treatment for the floor as well. Who in this day and age would put up with wooden boards when we could have a nice bit of easy-clean lino? Time to bring this house into the modern era, I think.

CAROLINE

I've got everything I want... except a baby. I can't stop thinking about it. Phil doesn't know but I went into Mothercare when I was in town and picked up their catalogue. I've hidden it in my underwear drawer and I get it out when Phil goes to work and leaf through the pages imagining myself pushing this pram or that stroller. Then I pull myself together and rush round with the vacuum cleaner or wash the windows. I love being domestic. Nothing pleases me so much as a clean loo. Crikey, I sound like I've lost my marbles! But every day is perfect and then the weekends are better still. I wouldn't swap my life with anyone.

I even get on with Mum now. I don't see her much obviously, she's 150 miles away, but I ring up a couple of times a week and what I do is, I ask her a question. You know, advice like the best way to cook fish maybe or which are the best potatoes for chips? What a laugh, we all know it's Dad who does the cooking and anyway, I've got plenty of cookery books to look at. But she's pleased to be asked, I can almost see her preening herself as she laughs and goes "Oh Caroline, you are hopeless". A small price to pay for peace in our time I believe. Mind you, it backfired on me when I asked her a genuine question: how do you cook roast potatoes? I've never actually done them before and Phil suddenly expressed this out-of-the-blue desire for a traditional roast. So she told me to put them in a hot oven for three-quarters of an hour with a good dollop of lard. They were dreadful, just like rocks. When I told Dad about my raw roasties, he said "didn't you parboil them first?" Parboil?! What the heck is that? There's no parboiling in my Hamlyn Recipes for Two.

Never mind, Phil didn't complain, just said "Ahah, I feel an early night coming on" so that's what happened and the washing up was all still piled in the kitchen the next morning, what a disgrace.

MATTHEW

My Mother chose the grottiest bathroom suite invented. It was orange.

CHLOE

I was glad when I was old enough to leave school. I hated it to the very last day. I was only any good at music and everything else was a waste of time. I didn't pass any exams, I didn't even bother going to most of them, but it didn't matter because I could play the violin in the pit at the local repertory theatre so that kept me going. It was great actually, if there wasn't a performance or a practice I didn't have to go in so I could stay in bed all morning then mooch around the shops. It was like being on fucking holiday every day.

My friend Fizz plays the clarinet and we like to make plans to go to London and seek fame and fortune. But Mummy shrieks when we talk about it and starts clutching her chest. She thinks we'll get raped and murdered if we leave our cosy home town. She doesn't know the half of it. If she had any idea what we get up to in the orchestra pit, or more particularly out of it, she really would have good reason to clutch her chest. Come to think of it, there is a lot of chest clutching involved in our nocturnal activities, and other parts of the anatomy as well, but it's all a good lark.

MRS JUDITH EDGERTON

Margaret was a very tricky member of staff to manage. "Kid gloves" is the phrase which comes to mind when I think of her. Even when I was doing my best to help her keep her position, she made me feel like it was she who was doing me the favour. She resolutely refused to accept that if she wasn't trained up to required standards, she would be replaced by someone who would be able to do her job in half the time and with half the number of errors as well. She always seemed to be on the verge of walking out, and to tell the truth, that would have been quite a relief. But we persevered between us and I hope I made the right decision in investing the budget for her training.

3 School Road
Bedford

Dear Mary

This is a sad letter for me to write, and I have thought long and hard before putting pen to paper. You have been a fairweather friend to me, but despite that, I will do my duty by you and then never expect to have further contact in future.

I regarded you as a good friend, and can rest in the knowledge that I was certainly a good friend to you. Who did you turn to when you needed help? Me. Who did you turn to when you wanted coffee in the staff room at break time? Me. Who did you turn to when your car wouldn't start and you needed to ring your husband? My office. Who did you turn to when your newspaper hadn't been delivered and you wanted something to read at lunchtime? Me. Who did you turn to when the hem on your trouser leg came down? Me.

Then you repay all my many favours by taking up with that two faced smarmy bitch and simply dropping me. You would not accept that I did not wish to accompany you on outings if she was included. You refused to listen to my warnings about her true nature, so please don't come running to me when she betrays you – which I promise you, she will. Then you will know how I feel right now, having to recognise that you have never cared for me as a true friend should. It was all pretence with you, wasn't it? Well, I've got the measure of you now, and I assure you that people like you never prosper. I hope you sleep well in your bed. And I wonder what you will do next time your hem comes down?

Yours in disappointment
Margaret

12 Park Lane
Bedford

Dear Margaret

Wundaweb

Mary

Ten

MARGARET

I got a phone call this week from Sandra, absolutely bursting to tell me that she's going to be a Granny. Well, I'm pleased for her, but I hope her Claire doesn't expect me to show an interest in her progeny. It'll be a cold day in hell before I have anything more to do with her.

Sandra said she hopes I won't have to wait too long before I have the same good news from Caroline, but I'm in two minds about it if I'm honest. Sandra's already given notice to take early retirement so she can help Claire as much as possible, but I really wouldn't fancy that. Early retirement, fine, helping bring up a new batch of kids? No thank you very much. When the day comes, I'll have to make the position very clear or if I'm not careful I'll find myself on call for babysitting duties. I'm just not doing it. I had no help bringing up my lot and frankly, they've worn me out. I've got too much else going on in my life right now.

I've moved to a brand new school, so all the staff are new and it seems to be going well. We're all finding our feet together, and my purpose built office is so easy to run. I've got a place for everything and everything in its place, and woe betide anyone who comes in and disturbs anything. The computerised system makes the administrative processes so much simpler, I can't think why they weren't introduced years before. All that training that Judith Edgerton arranged for me did me a good turn as it happened, because I don't think I would have got this position without my training record being up to date.

I can't say I miss the woman though, and certainly not Mary either. What a turncoat she turned out to be! Her and Judith have become firm friends, their families even went on holiday together last summer. It made it a bit awkward really, because I didn't mince my words when I was trying to get Mary to see sense about our wonderful new Head, otherwise known as The Great Pretender. So when they got so pally, I thought it's only a matter of time before she splits on me and I don't want to hang around waiting for that day. That would test those never-ending smiles. So I was pleased when I heard about this position, and to do her justice, Judith wrote me a glowing reference, calling me the most efficient secretary any school could be blessed with, which was quite gratifying. Only the truth though.

CAROLINE

When I spoke to Mum and she told me Claire was pregnant, it was on the tip of my tongue to tell her that we were trying for a baby too. But I thought better of it, I didn't want to put a jinx on our attempts, and I didn't want her to build up her hopes either. She said twice that I wasn't to think that just because Aunty Sandra was going to be a Granny, she wanted to be one as well. I know she was trying to ensure I didn't feel under pressure to please her, which was actually quite kind of her, wasn't it? Of course, everyone would be pleased with the news of a new baby in the family, but I appreciated that she was playing it cool. Hopefully, I'll be able to give her some exciting news very soon!

Bit of a fly in the ointment, though, Phil came home last night and told me we were being moved, but I always knew that was on the cards. We're off to Sussex, which might be quite nice because I could get to see Uncle Ron and Aunty Honor a bit more depending where we settle. Anyway, it'll be lovely to be a bit closer to them.

Aunty Honor was one of my many fantasy Mums when I was growing up. Of course it's a bit different now that I get along with my Mum, but back in the day, I used to see the things that Aunty Honor did for her boys and wonder why some Mothers loved all their children and some Mothers didn't. When they used to come and stay with us for Easter or Christmas, Uncle Ron and Aunty Honor had my bedroom while I shared with Chloe. One time, after they'd gone home, I found Aunty Honor's handkerchief under the bed and I kept it. I should have given it back, I know, but I hid it under the mattress and when I'd done something naughty and got sent to my room with a smack, I'd get the handkerchief out and stroke my cheek with it. Good Lord, how pathetic I was.

But I loved my Aunty Honor and she was always kind to me. You know that phrase about a home ringing with laughter? Well, if you want to know what that sounds like, you only have to visit Aunty Honor's house. She had three boys, Richard, Robert and Roger. I always wondered what happened when the postman delivered a letter addressed to Mr R Johnson. Matthew said it was a good thing their surname wasn't Sole. Rude boy.

MATTHEW

My Mother was extra grumpy when Aunty Sandra told her she was going to be a Granny.

Mummy was never cross with me, but she took a very deep breath when I had to go and ask her to help me out with some money. I was paid fuck all for playing my violin in our tin-pot little provincial theatre, and I got zilch if there was nothing in production. She gave me an allowance, but it never lasted long enough. I didn't want to ask her for extra and I knew it would be no use asking Dad, so I'd blagged some money off Fizz's brother. When it was my round at the bar, I pretended I'd left my purse at home and he lent me a twenty and I got a couple of fags off him as well, but then I had to avoid him which got more and more difficult. In the end, Fizz asked me and she was all embarrassed about it and so was I, but I pretended it had just slipped my mind.

I didn't know what to do but in the end there was only one thing I could do: ask Mummy. After she'd done some deep breathing and goggled her eyes a bit, she sighed and said "how much?" so I told her fifty quid to give me a bit of leeway. She let out a little squeak, but then she went and fetched her purse and doled out the tenners. As she gave me the last one, she held on to it and looked me square in the eye. "My one condition is you stop that filthy smoking," she said in the firmest tone I'd ever heard her use towards me. "You'll ruin your health and it makes you stink. So no more. Understood?"

It was a shock to hear her being so stern. I just nodded. I wasn't in any position to bargain with her. And at the time I meant it. Really.

Greenfields Primary School
Abbey Road
Bedford

To *whom it may concern:*

I am pleased to be able to furnish Mrs Johnson with a reference as requested. Her work has always been carried out to her own exacting standards. She is tenacious and dogged in her determination to follow the path she has set before her. She has recently completed the latest training course as recommended by the local Education Authority and having done so, is now equipped with the skills required to competently manage the day to day running of a school office.

She will be a hard act to follow and her absence will be felt to an immense degree by staff, parents and children.

Should you have any further queries concerning her ability, please have no hesitation in contacting me personally at the address above.

Yours truly

Judith Edgerton

Judith Edgerton
(Headteacher)

Dear Claire

I've thought long and hard about writing you this letter, but I have come to the conclusion that it is time someone set the record straight.

As an only child, you have always been spoilt rotten by my foolish sister who has chosen to indulge your every whim. As a result, you have grown up to be a thoroughly self-centred young woman, with no thought for how your actions impact on the family beyond your own cosy little circle.

Your decision to exclude me and my family from your wedding celebrations perfectly illustrated your selfishness, and since then, Uncle Clive and I have never been able to think of you without pain and sorrow. We had imagined our affection for you was returned in equal measure, but plainly we were mistaken. The many acts of kindness we showed towards you over the years appear to have been wasted, as you now think you can ignore us to the extent that you have caused a sad rift between us.

I am sure you are as pleased about your pregnancy as your Mother is. However, do not expect cards and gifts of congratulation from Uncle Clive and myself. That is the cost of your continued display of haughty disregard. You have no one but yourself to blame.

I sincerely hope you do not bring up your own children with the same lack of discipline that you enjoyed.

Yours,
Aunt Margaret

Eleven

MARGARET

I suppose I shouldn't have been surprised when Caroline announced she was pregnant but it did take my breath away for a moment. She and Phil are so unsettled right now that I thought she'd wait until a more practical time. They were all set to go to Sussex when Phil was told they'd be moving again, this time down to Devon.

Luckily for them, Phil's firm pays for the moving expenses or it would be costing them a packet and now there's a baby on the way, there's no chance of madam Caroline contributing towards the household bills. My heart goes out to Phil with all the pressures he's under between her and his employers but he keeps soldiering on without a word of complaint, doing his best for his family. Caroline really fell on her feet with him! I don't know how keen I am on this move to Devon though. I can't help feeling what a long way it is, I suspect my grandchildren will grow up as strangers to me.

Anyway, the first thing I did was ring Sandra to tell her we were both going to be Grannies and she sounded so thrilled. She thinks we'll be able to share the experience. How's that going to happen? Her daughter lives a mile away and mine lives the other end of the country. Sandra had just been to buy the new pram, which is her gift to Claire for the new baby. Her in-laws are buying the cot, she tells me this is the accepted norm in these situations. First I've heard of it, let's hope Caroline isn't expecting the same. Her Phil's got a lot more money than we have, and anyway, it's nicer for her to choose her own things.

As it happens, I'm a bit stretched just now, with having to give Chloe a helping hand. She gets paid a pittance and she's so generous she gets herself into trouble. I just hope she sorts herself out because I can't afford to bail her out too often or Clive will realise something's going on and then sparks will fly. She's on my mind all the time, I'm quite worried about her to tell the truth. You never stop looking out for your kids do you?

CAROLINE

Suddenly, everything seemed to happen at once. Phil was given notice that the company were moving him to manage the sales team in East Sussex, then there was some big problem with Devon and Cornwall and the manager got fired.

Fortunately the news came through the day before we exchanged contracts on our new house. I might have been a bit upset if it was the day after. So off we went to a rented house in Plymouth instead and before I'd even finished unpacking the boxes I got the call from the GP's surgery to say my pregnancy test was positive. I thought all my birthdays had come at once. I rang Phil that instant, I couldn't wait for him to get home, but when I dialled his office number, it turned out that he had transposed two digits when he wrote it down for me. When the phone finally picked up, I screamed "I'm pregnant!!!!" and there was a long pause before some guy said "Well done love. Do you know this is a public phone box?" I could have died but we had a good laugh later and Phil never let me forget that the first person I told about our new baby was a passing stranger.

I wasn't sure what to make of Mum's reaction. She seemed a bit muted, saying what a long way she would be from her grandchildren, but I said there will always be a spare room for you and you can come as often as you want. Then she changed the subject so I don't know if she's a bit upset but I'll try to keep her as involved as possible. Granny was always on hand for us, and it would be great if my children could have the same relationship with Mum.

Anyway, it's going to be a busy old time, that's for sure. Our 6 month rental finishes a week before my due date, so we've got to find a suitable house ready to move into within a pretty tight timeframe. I always liked a challenge!

MATTHEW

My Mother seemed to think she had single-handedly created Caroline's new sprog.

CHLOE

Hell's bells, I was in some deep shit. Thank Christ for Barclaycard. In the nick of time, Fizz showed me an ad for a completely new touring orchestra being set up with a base in Hackney. It offered a much better financial package which I needed, like, yesterday. We both auditioned and we both got in so London here we come. I haven't told Mummy yet because we all know she will go ape-shit.

We're on the look-out for something affordable to rent and I think we're going to settle on a tiny one-bedder we viewed just off the High Street. We won't tell the landlord but we reckon we can stick a sofa bed in the lounge and he'll never know there are two of us in there. It's a great location for us to be part of the life of the city, and convenient for all the transport links; just teensy weensy like a doll's house. Lucky we haven't got a cat, because we certainly couldn't swing it if we had.

When we're rich and famous we can trade up to a penthouse looking out over a sweeping panorama of the Thames. In the meantime we have a nice view of the Co op delivery yard, but it's handy if we run out of milk.

SANDRA

My sister and I becoming Grannies both together seems like fate at work. We'd shared plenty together as children, and it felt so right to be able to share the pleasure of this new big experience.

I've been busy decorating our small bedroom as a nursery so that we can have Clare's little one to stay whenever she needs a break. It looks grand. I chose a teddy-bear wallpaper and a toning yellow and white stripe for the curtains and then I had them make up a quilted cot coverlet in the same stuff so it all looks quite beautiful. Claire and I picked out a comfortable nursing chair for her and I secretly bought another one for our nursery too so she can be just as much at ease wherever she finds herself. The musical mobile is set up over the rocking crib and this afternoon I bought one of those new intercom systems from Mothercare. You can put the baby to bed and still listen in to be on the alert as soon as he wakes. Such a good idea! But everything seems so up to date and clever compared to how we managed in the bad old days!

I've told Margaret we'll go out together one day to get all the baby equipment she'll be needing, but so far we haven't been able to settle on a suitable date. I don't think she realises how the time creeps by. She doesn't want to be leaving it all to the last minute and then not be ready on time. But these things have a way of sorting themselves out. If needs must, I've got enough stuff to spare some for her. She knows she only has to call but I'm not going to press her. She gets in a tizz if we're not careful and then she lashes out so unpredictably. Sometimes it's hard not to take her hurtful comments to heart. I've learnt to ignore her when she's having one of her turns. I'm sure she'll soften when she holds her new grandchild in her arms. There's nothing like a new baby to melt the heart!

Dear Caroline

Daddy and I enjoyed all our anniversary celebrations very much. Malta is a lovely place for a visit, though I was glad to get back to home, sweet home.

While I was away, I had time to mull over a few things that have been niggling in the back of my mind, and having thought long and hard, I feel I should give you some advice.

At our celebration dinner, it struck me that Phil is looking very tired. When he described his average day, with all that travelling, I felt exhausted just listening to him. It is obvious to me that your thoughts are all about your expectant condition, but you must remember to take proper care of your husband. He works so hard for you, and is always so attentive and caring towards all of us. And so gallant! He always notices when I've had my perm freshened up. A husband like him is quite simply gold-dust, and you of all people will have to work hard to keep him. I suggest you spend less time thinking about yourself and instead, pay more attention to your poor husband. I'm sure his own family have noticed that you are not always a mindful wife, and it would be a shame to alienate such lovely people. Take my advice before it's too late, and you too will be able to share a celebration dinner to mark thirty years of marital bliss!

Thank you for organising our anniversary dinner for us. It was quite a shock to see all those faces when we arrived! I don't really like that restaurant, we had a bad experience there once, when we received very poor service. And I'm sure they water the drinks down. But it was a kind thought.

Love from
Mum

Twelve

MARGARET

Caroline had a baby girl, so dainty and much prettier than the great lummox that Sandra coos over like it's the Dalai Lama or something. We didn't get to see her until she was nearly three weeks old, but the house move was such a complication. Caroline had only been out of hospital three days when they moved in, so we said we'd keep out of the way until they'd got themselves settled.

It worked out well as it happened, because it came at the end of the long slog up to the school summer holiday, so I was really feeling in need of a break. I will say this about Caroline, she's turned into a fine cook and she treated us like royalty. I had a lovely week's rest with no domestic cares although a couple of nights I heard the baby cry which was a bit of a disturbance but we didn't like to complain.

On the last night, Clive said he'd treat us to a meal out, but Caroline said it would be difficult with breast-feeding, so she did us a casserole in the slow cooker. She said she was feeling a bit off. I told her that breast-feeding is a mug's game, really knocks the stuffing out of you and you can't ever give the baby to someone else for a break. She's so determined to get everything just right, wants to be the best Mother ever. Don't we all but you have to realistic.

Anyway I was proved right, because the day we left, she had to call in the doctor, she was feeling that rough, and it turned out she'd got a raging infection and needed complete bed-rest. Phil's sister dropped everything and went down for a week to look after things so Caroline got herself a nice few days of being fussed over which I'm sure would be lovely.

We couldn't have stayed on anyway. We had to get back in time to help Chloe with her move to London. That was a very bitter-sweet experience I can tell you. I really don't know how she'll cope but I know I can't try to hold her back. Clive hired a van and we'd bought her a sofa bed, and a few odds and ends for the kitchen, and linens and so on that she'd be needing for life on her own, well not quite on her own, she's got Fizz of course. Still, we saw her settled and that put my mind at ease because I could picture her and imagine what she might be doing each day. Before we came away, we went to the Co op and bought her a trolley load of groceries so I knew she wouldn't starve, and a big box of Milk Tray that she loves.

It was a wrench to leave her though and I'll admit I had a little weep in the car going home. I hope she'll manage all right without me.

CAROLINE

What a beautiful baby I've got! I was quite ill for a while but Phil's sister Karen was just wonderful and let me stay in bed with my little baby while she looked after everything and let me get back on my feet. The doctor just said I'd been overdoing it after the birth, gave me a bit of a telling off actually and a lecture about the body needing rest and so on. I told him I'll try and remember next time I have a baby, ha ha.

Anyway, my little Olivia is so gorgeous that when I look at other people's babies I feel quite sorry for them. She's lovely when she's awake and she's lovely when she's asleep. Karen kept telling me to have a nap whenever she slept, but I can't stop myself from gazing at her. I can hardly believe that Phil and I made something so perfect. When I look at her, I wonder how anyone can harm a child and I've made a pledge in my mind to be the sort of Mother I would have liked to have. I survived my childhood and I'm sure it did me good and helped me to be self sufficient but my Olivia will know every day she is loved.

Karen stayed a fortnight then she had to get back because she'd taken unpaid leave from work and she didn't want to jeopardise her job. Well neither did I, but I felt myself welling up when it was time for her to go. I've turned into a big baby myself! I don't know what I would have done without her. I asked her whether she would be Godmother to Olivia and then she started blubbing as well. What a pair of ninnies! Let's put it down to hormones.

MATTHEW

Mother is a Grandmother now. Whoop-de-doo.

CHLOE

London is wild! My life is wild! We don't do mornings any more, can't see the point of them. There's a party every night and quite a few of them seem to be at our place. We spend more on booze than we do on food, that's what I call a balanced diet. Vodka and tonic and a Cadbury's Crème Egg, what more can you want at dinner time? It's wall to wall fun here. Oh and work as well, but even that's good.

We go on tour next month, away for three months and then back as a support for a performance at the Albert Hall.

Oh we move in exalted circles these days, darlings! Even tried a little bit of weed the other night but I'm not making a habit of it. I'm telling you, everyone does it and worse; you wouldn't believe it but I've turned into the sensible one now. I called for a bit of restraint the other night and fucking Geraint (saxophone) asked me whether I was into bondage. What a wanker. He thinks I fancy him. I so do not. I heard him calling me a fat arse when he thought I'd gone to the loo. I couldn't help wondering if he has any mirrors in his house because he's no oil painting himself. And he thinks it's hilarious when he says he plays the sex-ophone. Oh ha-bloody-ha, I split my sides.

I've got a new niece. Olive! What were they thinking? Will they give her a brother called Popeye?

KAREN

My poor sister-in-law! I was nearly scared to death when I saw her, she looked so white and ill, but still she thought she needed to put the kettle on for me. The doctor was very concerned, came twice a day for three days and told me confidentially that she was lucky he wasn't hospitalising her, in fact he would if he couldn't trust me to keep her in her bed and not allow her to do anything remotely strenuous.

When I asked her why she hadn't rested while Margaret was visiting, she got quite distressed and said something about her Mother being traumatised and exhausted from a busy term at school and I am proud to say that I bit back what I wanted to reply. I am confident when I say that if there was an award for most selfish woman in Britain, there would be no competition.

My half-soaked brother isn't much better either, but at least he goes out to work and does his bit to support his family.

And now he knows how the washing machine works because I made sure to show him, so that will be a little something to ease the load when I go home. All I need to do now is to convince Caroline that she won't be failing in her duties by allowing her lazy husband to muck in. As I told her, it's his dirty laundry too!

Dear Karen

Just a quick note to thank you for looking after Caroline following her recent confinement. I feel I need to clear up a silly misunderstanding. I suspect you may have been led to believe that I refused to offer any assistance to my daughter, but I do assure you that is a dreadful misconception. Like any Mother, I am ready and willing to drop everything at any moment to rush to the side of any of my children who might need me. That I was not present in this instance was entirely due to Caroline's lack of communication with me.

This is a problem that reappears throughout our history. She is not an easy daughter, and sometimes she sets out to deliberately cause ill-feeling by making some unreasonable request, mostly at short notice or without any real need. For their own good, we have always tried to encourage our children to be independent and have therefore judged requests from them on the basis of priority. As you well know, it is impossible to be in two places at the same time! The calls on our time are such that you would find it difficult to comprehend. Clive works hard every day, and my own job is remarkably demanding in its diverse challenges. I never know what I will be doing from one day to the next! Coupled with our busy social engagements and the requirements of our other children, we hardly have a

73

moment to ourselves. Sometimes I joke with Clive that one day we will meet ourselves on the doorstep as we come and go in a head-spinning whirl of activity!

Anyway, while I have no doubt that Caroline has shown proper gratitude for your ministrations, I assure you that your presence was entirely unnecessary. In future, I would request that you do not interfere in our family concerns, and we will not interfere with yours.

Yours sincerely
Margaret

Thirteen

MARGARET

My poor Chloe has been so ill we had to bring her home to recover. She collapsed while she was on tour, she'd obviously been working far too hard and pushed herself too far. I was dreading it was her kidneys that were giving out, so it was actually quite a relief when it turned out to be diabetes. At least it's treatable, though not very pleasant at all.

She's had to learn to inject herself with insulin and she's going to have to be more careful about what she eats. She's got a sweet tooth just like me and if I'm honest, she has got a bit chunky.

This has been a wake-up call I suppose but I know she's going to be a brave girl and get herself back on track. I'm feeding her up with all the right things and I've substituted honey in her diet instead of sugar so her fondness for sweet things is still satisfied without the harmful side effects. A Mummy knows best!

She's so dedicated though that all she wants to do is get back to her London life. I've told her she must be patient and let us get her completely better before she puts herself through that punishing regime again. I gather Fizz is bothering her a bit because she's struggling to pay the rent on her own. What does the girl think Chloe can do about it? She's not being paid while she's off sick and what's more, she's not using the flat either. Why should she pay for it? She's got enough to worry about as it is. I always thought Fizz was a good friend and I'm usually a good judge of character, but I can't be right all the time obviously.

Caroline was going to bring Olivia up for a visit while Phil's at a conference in Nottingham, but I had to put her off. At times like this, Chloe has to be my priority. Now Caroline's experiencing motherhood, I'm sure she understands a lot better how the worries and responsibilities weigh on you without cease.

CAROLINE

It was a bit of a shock to find out that Chloe had diabetes. Without meaning to be unkind, I hope it will be the motivation she needs to lose a bit of weight. She was always such a pretty child, but her lovely face seems to have disappeared into a blob. Maybe this will turn out to be a blessing in disguise.

Not that she'll ever be as pretty as Olivia needless to say. Speaking of whom, my best girl is the sweetest thing. She's got several little friends from Mother and Baby group, which has given me some good friends too. They're all entering the crawling stage now so we're all having to make our houses baby proof and suddenly the most fascinating subject seems to be stair gates. We'll be having an earnest conversation when we'll suddenly go "what's happened to us?" and have a good laugh.

We have to keep in mind that all this baby stuff is only temporary, in fact I said the same thing to Phil the other night. Olivia has been teething and she was being a bit fractious. I was trying to settle her and Phil went "can't you come to bed woman?" which was a silly question because that's exactly where I wanted to be at midnight, not pacing round the nursery trying to soothe a grizzly baby. But that's quite rare, she's slept through since she was two months old so we've been very lucky. And all she has to do is give her Daddy one of her big grins and he goes to mush. She'll be able to wrap him round her finger when she's older. I bet I won't get a look-in with her then!

Poor Phil's a bit worn out I think. He's got a big area to oversee and is out on the road quite a bit which of course is very tiring. Then there have been a lot of expenses with the house and baby equipment. Why does someone so small need so much stuff? So I know the credit card has taken a hammering lately though I've got my doubts whether Phil really needed a new suit for Olivia's christening. It was a bit difficult to grumble at him though because he bought me a new dress as well, what a cunning strategy. It was bad luck that the washing machine broke the same month but hopefully he's in line for a bonus at the end of the year which will be useful for paying off the credit card.

I think it's hard for everyone at this stage of their lives, but at the weekend I made a picnic and we went a lovely walk on Dartmoor with Olivia in a harness on Phil's back. We enjoyed ourselves so much and it didn't cost a penny.

MATTHEW

My Mother seems to have forgotten about me. Good.

CHLOE

Frigging diabetes is a bummer. That's official. I'm on a diet forever and that's about the best part of the situation. I finally managed to escape from Mummy's clutches and got back to London before Fizz went completely mental at me. She's behind on the rent and the landlord is on the rampage so we're in a bit of trouble basically. I'm so lucky that my place in the orchestra was kept open for me but I got no pay while I was away. Fair enough I guess, they had to pay the girl who filled in for me, but now my bank account is bled dry, a bit like my fingertips when I have to keep doing my blood sugar tests. My friend Barclaycard is keeping the show on the road at present but I'm going to have to be mighty careful. Partying is over!

Well sort of.

Counting the pennies is a very boring way to live. I've even gone on to roll-your-own ciggies. Yes, it is that bad ladies and gentlemen, but no one can accuse me of not trying. And a little bit of the naughty stuff in with the tobacco helps it along nicely I must say.

Caroline's baby's christening was at the weekend but I opted out. Number one, I don't like babies, Number two, I don't like churches, Number three, I don't like train fares. But I did find out the kid's name is Olivia not Olive, so that's a relief.

FIZZ

I'm beginning to wonder whether Chloe is more trouble than she's worth. She's a big load of fun when we're partying – and boy does she party. But when mumsy wumsy calls, she drops me like a hot potato and if I have to clear up this place once more while she's resting in bed because her condition causes her to fall into a torpor of fatigue ….grrrr. And the worst transgression of all – my fags have started disappearing. So I keep them in my back pocket to stop her nicking them then I forgot and sat down and snapped off a whole new pack of Benson and Hedges. So now I've got 40 titchy fags instead of 20 regulars. The effing milk of effing kindness is fast running dry.

Dear Fizz

You are a remarkably silly little girl with a remarkably silly little name. I believed you to be a good friend to Chloe, but you have revealed yourself in your true colours, and I for one, will never speak to you again.

You will be aware of how ill Chloe has been. I can't begin to describe the strain I have been under as I have nursed her through her difficulties. As her friend, your only concern should have been to offer her your absolute and unremitting support. Instead, you chase her for money! Is there something the matter with you?

Let me state this plainly to you, since you obviously do not possess the brain power to work it out for yourself: Chloe has no money. While she is not working, she is not being paid. It is your selfish belief that she should continue to contribute her share of the rent for the flat where you are the sole occupant. Why should she pay for your flat? I might as well ask you to pay for her accommodation with us. How would you like that? So I hope that scenario demonstrates how ridiculous your demands truly are.

Chloe cannot pay. Chloe will not pay. I hope you do not imagine that you can blackmail myself and my husband into paying you anything. You will not see one brass farthing from us. If you do not immediately discontinue your harassment of our family, I will have no option but to report you to the police.

I trust that is the end of the matter.

Yours sincerely

M. Johnson

Margaret Johnson (Mrs).

Fourteen

MARGARET

I shouldn't have been surprised when Caroline announced she was expecting again, though I hope she's making time for that poor husband of hers. He looks a little bit frazzled to me, like his mind is somewhere else. I know as well as anyone how demanding madam Caroline can be and I hope she realises there's more to life than producing babies.

And she mustn't neglect little Olivia either, she's at a very delicate age. She'll be just two and a bit when the new baby arrives, the same gap I had with Caroline and Matthew. So I know better than anyone how hard it is to give proper attention to everyone's needs. Caroline will have to learn that her own needs are absolutely bottom of the pile.

I seem to remember having to drag myself through the days, I was that worn out. It was as much as I could do to keep going until Clive got in from work, then he would give them a bath while I had a little lie-down. Oh, how he loved their bath-time, he would sing to them and make up adventures with the rubber ducks and then read them a lovely story for bedtime. As often as not, I'd nodded off myself by then and he would have to wake me up when the dinner was ready.

I can't ever look back on that period of my life without feeling a wave of exhaustion. I think it's probably the hardest time of your life, being a Mother of small children. Caroline seems to be thriving on it just now and certainly Olivia is a credit to us all. Let's hope there isn't a backlash.

By coincidence, Claire's pregnant again, but when I told Caroline, she seemed to know already. I've got a suspicion that she's back in touch with her cousin after all her offensive behaviour towards us. Caroline's just a doormat, let's anyone walk over her. I've told her plenty of times, she should have a bit of self respect but she just carries on in her own sweet way. She'll learn the hard way one day and I suppose I'll be the one who has to pick up the pieces.

CAROLINE

One of us was thrilled to be having baby number two, but I began to realise that Phil didn't seem so keen this time round. He was working really hard, even having overnight stays sometimes when he was visiting agents right down in the foot of Cornwall. I worried that he seemed to be growing away from us, not quite interested in the things Olivia was doing and a bit short with her sometimes as well. I thought the best thing was to keep going and wait for it to blow over.

In the meantime, I tried to make sure everything was running smoothly so he didn't come home to chores not done and a list of jobs for him to complete. His energy just seemed to have evaporated and I began to wonder if he was suffering from depression, but when I suggested he go to the doctor, he got quite shirty with me so I shut up.

I was nearly eight months pregnant when I had my bombshell moment. Putting away the laundry, I found a vending pack of Durex rolled up with his socks. I had to sit down with my head between my knees for a minute and that's not easy when you've got an eight month bump in the way.

Well, no matter how I reasoned it out, he didn't need any Durex packs for my benefit did he? I felt really sick. Should I confront him? But I was pregnant! What if I drove him away and I'm left with a new baby and Olivia? With one expectant month to go last time, I was so excited I could barely keep still, but this time I was scared out of my wits. I just didn't know what to do for the best.

Then out of the blue, he said we needed to move further west because the travelling was killing him and if we lived in a more convenient spot he'd be able to spend more time with us. He said he was feeling guilty about leaving me with all the responsibility for home and the babies and it would make us all happier if his commute was less demanding. I was a bit confused by it all really, but what he said made sense, so once again with a baby about to be born, I was preparing to move. Still, I could see his point and I wanted to be sure to do the best thing for the whole family. Round to the estate agent I trotted and we very quickly had interested viewers and then a lovely older couple, cash buyers no less, agreed to pay the asking price so happy smiles all round. It was a bit difficult for me to go house-hunting, so Phil scouted around a bit, but no luck immediately.

By now, I had more pressing matters on my mind with the baby's arrival being imminent. It wasn't quite so simple now I'd got Olivia to consider, but I'd spoken to Mum when I first knew my due date and as it fell in school holiday time, she'd agreed to come and hold the fort while I went into hospital. But I was in for a shock when I asked her what day she was planning to come because she'd plainly forgotten all about it and was quite indignant. "I have got a home and a family of my own to look after" she said and I must say, I was a bit taken aback because I thought I *was* part of her family. Silly mistake.

So I was pretty much up the creek without a paddle and I had a bit of a panic attack. As luck would have it, Phil's sister Karen chose that moment to ring me and she could tell I'd been having a bit of a cry. Of course, when I told her what had happened she just said "oh don't be silly, I can be down there in a tick and everything will be fine". Which it was. Baby Hannah was born safe and sound, Olivia had a lovely time with Aunty Karen, the house sale went through without a hitch, we'd got a rental all lined up to move into.

Then Phil left me.

MATTHEW

Caroline was in a right mess. Mother helpfully said she'd brought it on herself.

CHLOE

I know I should have been stressing about Caroline. But I was having enough stresses of my own. Fizz and I had to do a moonlight flit with the help of some delivery guy she knew. He "borrowed" a van from work and we just chucked our stuff in the back any old how and moved it all to a complete shit hole a good ten miles away. We hoped that was far enough that the landlord wouldn't trace us. We certainly didn't bother leaving a forwarding address.

The new place was fucking disgusting but at least we didn't owe back rent and we could try and make a fresh start. The orchestra had quite a few touring dates anyway, so home conditions didn't seem so important when most of the time instead of living in a crummy flat we were living in a crummy B&B, que sera sera. Hey, we had to make a living.

And Caroline was in trouble but she did have a new baby and she loved babies so it wasn't all bad. I think it was another girl.

PHIL

Just couldn't hack it. I'm not that kind of guy. Family, prams, nappies, teething rings, no thanks. The first one was just beginning to get interesting, but doing it all over again, Jeez. And meeting my little squeeze Susie didn't help, yes, I admit it. But what do you want from me? Sackcloth and ashes? I prefer a bit of Ted Baker as it happens. Susie is such a doll. No stretch marks, great in the sack, thinks I'm God. Hey, I'm human! OK? Give it a rest for Chrissake.

3 School Road
Bedford

Dear Caroline

Well, I must say, you've got yourself into a fine old mess now. I wish you'd listened to my advice. I always told you what a waster you were marrying, but you were determined to have your own way. I could have predicted this result from the first moment I met the man. To be honest with you, I had difficulty being civil to him throughout your marriage and when he turned up on our doorstep, so smarmy and self-satisfied, I wanted to scratch his eyes out. There will always be men like him, who think they can take what they want, confident in the knowledge that the poor old parents will pick up the pieces.

I am feeling somewhat recovered now after the debilitation brought on from caring for you and your children. I had almost forgotten how much hard work is required for proper childcare. And you were so vague and helpless, you were no use at all in upholding your parenting duties. Your Father and I were quite concerned that you wouldn't be able to manage and the children might have to be taken into care. Fortunately, we were able to guide you through the storm and you seem to be coping now. That's what families are for! But in future, I think you should concentrate on caring for those dear little mites. You don't want to risk Social Services getting involved. You'll have to be sensible and accept that with two small children, you're no catch for a man, so that will give you ample time to devote to your girls. It's a shame you didn't settle closer to us, I could have been such a help to you if only you were just around the corner. But no doubt Karen and Jack are at your beck and call, and I'm glad to have a little rest from childminding for now.

Love from
Mum

Fifteen

MARGARET

Caroline's fairytale marriage ended up with her homeless and penniless. We had no option but to take her in when the new buyers moved into her house. You'd think they could have delayed while she got herself sorted out, but they said they couldn't legally hold up the chain so they needed to proceed. You can't believe the selfishness of some people. I'm sure it wouldn't have hurt them to come to some arrangement to help her.

She was in such a state when she came to us, it gave me a pain to look at her. She seemed to be sleepwalking through every day, thoroughly grief-stricken like Phil had died or something. I always knew he was trouble, but she never listened to me. It made me pretty angry in the end. It was obvious that she needed to get a divorce and take him to the cleaners with a good financial package. Would she listen? Not her, kept saying he was her children's father and all that drivel. As far as I was concerned, he'd forfeited all rights to his family the instant he got his leg over the Bodmin bimbo.

I realised I'd have to take matters into my own hands so I rang up a solicitor in the Yellow Pages and made an appointment for her so she could call time on the wasteground of her marriage. I suppose it was my own fault for not going with her, but when she got back, she hadn't done anything useful at all, certainly not begun divorce proceedings. All she'd agreed was that the solicitor should contact his solicitor to arrange financial support while poor old Phil had some breathing space. My heart bleeds!

Then Clive told her she needed to freeze the bank account or her waster husband would empty it and she'd be left with nothing. Of course it had all the money from the house sale (although that turned out to be a lot less than we expected) and Clive was worried it would disappear never to be seen again, so he was right to err on the safe side. She was wishy washy about the whole thing but no way was I risking her sponging off us permanently, so I found her chequebook and rang the phone number printed on it and more or less hustled her into making the arrangements.

Which turned out to be a bit stupid actually, because then she had no access to any money at all, which left us to carry the can. When I pointed this out to Clive, he looked at me like I'd said something a bit loopy. "We just need to protect her while she gets herself organised," said he. "It won't be long." I suppose so, but I don't go to work in order to support my grown-up daughter thank you very much. It's not natural for goodness sake.

The solicitors needed to have some idea of an outline financial package and she invited Phil over to discuss what they should do. When he turned up on my doorstep I could have scratched his eyes out, but instead I just blanked him. Completely. I behaved as though I couldn't even see him and I wouldn't reply when he greeted me. Bloody cheek of the man. But I was chuffed with myself for acting with such restraint. Sometimes the quiet, discreet method says so much more than overt rage and I knew I'd got my point across. So much so that he never returned. And Caroline got on the train the next day and took the kiddies to visit their Aunty Karen and Uncle Jack so peace was restored.

While they were there, they found a little terraced house that she could just about afford and it was only a five minute walk from Karen's house. I knew that would please them because they're the type of people who always get involved in other people's lives. The interfering type if you ask me, but Caroline probably needed some interfering to make her see sense. And Jack being a solicitor would come in useful I've no doubt if Caroline played her cards right.

CAROLINE

I could hardly get my breath. It was as bad as it gets. When people talk about feeling hurt, I'd never known before that there is an actual physical pain to having your heart broken. If it hadn't been for the children I would have got under the duvet and never come out again.

My Dad came and fetched me home while the removers took everything away into storage leaving my empty house feeling just like I did: a desolate shell of nothingness. Baby Hannah kept me going because I had to tend to her needs no matter what and as for poor little Olivia, she cried over the slightest thing which wasn't like her at all. I had to try and keep her with me because I could see Mum was getting irritated with her and I worried that she'd lose her temper and shout at her or even smack her. She had no patience with her distress, and it was heart rending when poor Olivia asked several times a day when her Daddy was coming back.

In the end I phoned Phil and told him he needed to come and talk to her and we'd got some financial matters to figure out as well, so he reluctantly drove up one day. It was a disaster. Mum wouldn't speak to him, wouldn't acknowledge him in any way, nearly gave herself a cricked neck by looking in the opposite direction. It was like she was three years old, completely embarrassing. All the problems I was facing and I had to try to appease my husband over her behaviour. Can you believe it! He'd left me in the lurch, literally holding the baby, and I was apologising to him!

The upshot was, he refused to come back and told me all future meetings would have to take place elsewhere. Oh and I was only allowed to ring him in an emergency because it upset his girlfriend when he talked to me! By the time he left, we hadn't arranged anything, I'd just had to defend myself and the situation I found myself in as if it was all my fault.

When he left, I burst into tears and Mum told me to pull myself together. That was the last straw. I thought if I stayed another day under her roof, I might do her a mischief and I wouldn't be any use to my children if I was in prison. So the next morning, I called a taxi to take us to the train station and we got ourselves to Karen's. I hadn't even let her know I was coming but she took one look at me and gave me the biggest hug.

Thank God. I could rest at last. I went to pieces a bit with the relief but she just took over and let me do my grieving without carping on. And it was her own brother who was the other side of the tale, so it was more than I had any right to ask of her. Sometimes, blood isn't thicker than water after all. She and Jack held me together through it all. Everyone needs someone like her. And Matthew was a brick.

MATTHEW

I was doing well and I could give Caroline the 1000 quid she was short for her new house. Mother told her she needed to stand on her own two feet. Sympathetic as ever.

London got a bit too hot to handle. The landlord managed to track us down and he was going to sue us so I took out a bank loan for the arrears but then I couldn't afford the rent for the place we were in. Fizz got fed up because she said they were my bleedin' arrears and she'd already contributed towards them when I was ill and living back home, and we ended up having a big barney. Fuck knows what the 40 miniature B&H had to do with it, but we both said things that suggest to me we won't be speaking again this side of death.

So now I'm in Edinburgh which is fab but it's cold in winter. I've got a lot more hats and scarves than I used to have. I'm in the Royal Scottish National Orchestra hurray but lowliest second violin boo, very unimportant indeed, in fact if there was a third violin, that would be me.

Inevitably and as you have already guessed, I'm not very well paid either so no change there then. I've got a bedsit, I wish I could say on Princes Street but it's not even on Pauper's Street, it's that bad. But it's a start, and when I've paid off the bank loan, I can look for somewhere better. At least I've lost six pounds, thanks to being unable to afford take-aways any more.

I wish I had a bastard ex-husband to give me an unearned monthly hand-out, that would solve my problems. Caroline's got herself a little house and she's invited us all to squeeze in for Christmas Day but I don't think I'll go. I'll just tell her I've got performances that I'm committed to. I don't fancy the idea of being compared with her and not coming up to the mark. Plus I would miss all the Christmas parties up here and I can't possibly be away for Hogmanay which I've been told is an unmissable spectacle.

And I would have to buy them all fucking presents. I'll stay here.

SUSIE

My lovely Philly-boy is so scwummy and yummy I could lick him all over until he was all licked away. We have sexy games in our sweetest tiny cottage. It's our very own ickle love nest, it is. I light a whooshing fire in the living room and when he comes home, we start in there and then we get so hot we go in the kitchen and once we even went in the garden but a spider crawled on me and I simply screamed. They are just so scary, eek, I don't even want to think about them, they make me so shivery. Philly-boy makes me shivery too but a different way to spiders, more like a Tiger, roar! We are so special! I am the luckiest little girl in the whole wide world! I love him, oh I do.

Dear Phil

You plainly thought it perfectly acceptable to decide that
your wife was too old (ten years your junior), had too many
babies (yours), and was now only fit to be put out to grass
(ours).

Of course, as our daughter, she was welcomed home
with open arms and I have naturally cared for her and your
children as though they were my own. You did not recognise
any responsibility on your part to pay us anything towards
their upkeep, and I assure you they cost us a pretty packet.
But that's exactly the kind of low-down, inconsiderate
behaviour I would expect from a snake in the grass like you.
I don't know how you sleep at night.

So here's a little piece of advice from your ex-Mother-
in-law.

Keep your trousers zipped in future.

Yours sincerely
Margaret

Sixteen

MARGARET

I was quite surprised to learn that Chloe had moved to Edinburgh but when I heard that she was now a member of the Royal Scottish National Orchestra, I understood immediately. I always knew she would go far. I'm sure she was glad to get away from Fizz who had turned out to be a very poor sort of friend to her, completely unsupportive and unsympathetic.

She was unable to join us for Christmas at Caroline's. Mind you, it was probably just as well, because it was such a tight squeeze. It's a tiny house but she would insist on having Karen and Jack as well as their daughter and son-in-law when really there was only room for me and Clive. She put on a good spread and Jack was joking that we'd have to choreograph the cracker pulling or we'd end up in the fireplace. I'm sure he thought it was funny, but he wasn't sitting in my place with the table leg jammed up between my legs in a thoroughly unladylike and uncomfortable manner.

Luckily for us, Caroline managed to bag the dishwasher in the marital property negotiations. You should have seen the mountain of washing up stacked in the kitchen. I would still be there now if we'd had to do it the old-fashioned way.

It didn't really matter anyway, because Karen said she'd give her a hand when we left. It's nice to visit but it's nice to leave. Pandemonium is the word that springs to mind: Olivia getting too excited and Jack being uproarious with his supposedly hilarious humour.

I began to feel a headache coming on after lunch so Clive brought me home and I put my feet up with a nice cup of tea. Then he made us some ham sandwiches with a bit of salad for tea and I think I really enjoyed that the most out of the whole day. And a drop of Christmas cheer: a good malt whisky for Clive and a snowball for me. Lovely! Sometimes the simple things are the best.

We were hoping to visit Chloe to see in a proper Scottish New Year, but unfortunately, she's performing over the holiday period, so she had to put us off. It would have been nice to see her new home but I'll have to wait for a more convenient time. I hope she's taking proper care of herself and not missing any injections. The trouble with having a creative streak is that she's not always very practical but that's the price she pays for her art.

It's a bit sad to think of her missing out on all the celebrations up there. We raised our glasses to her at midnight on New Year's Eve but I expect she would have been tucked up in bed by then, conserving her energy for the next performance in her busy schedule.

CAROLINE

I wasn't sure how our first Christmas without Phil would go, so I just made it as busy as possible and we had a truly good time. Hannah is far too young to understand, but Olivia is just about old enough to get excited by the idea of Father Christmas. Jack's got a whole Santa outfit and he brought it round on Christmas Eve when he and Karen popped in to give me a hand with the last preparations.

While Karen and I peeled the endless sprouts, he went into the tiny bathroom and struggled his way into the Santa clothes. He was a bit put out when we told him he didn't need a cushion up his front, his round belly was quite adequate au naturelle. Then he obliged by taking the stockings upstairs. I think he was hoping that Olivia would wake and see him but I warned him that he could take her back to his house if he got her all excited when she should be sleeping. Anyway, it all went off smoothly and Jack enjoyed himself at least.

Christmas Day was just the ticket. I couldn't afford a lot for the stockings, but the girls are so little that it didn't matter to them, and before we knew it Karen and Jack arrived with Rosie and Jago and it was all as merry as I could hope for. Mum and Dad arrived in time for dinner and she grumped a bit when she saw how crowded the table was. It was true that the highchair takes up more space than an ordinary chair but that's just too bad and I'd given Mum the best carver chair as it was. She tucked into her dinner like a trooper and had three helpings of pudding so she must have enjoyed it in the end.

She told us all about Chloe, who seems to have done really well for herself: lead violin in the Royal Scottish National Orchestra. I know she's talented but wow! I guess I didn't realise just how talented she is.

Jack was on top form throughout and had us all in stitches. I just love the way he manages to be talking to the adults and entertaining the children all at the same time. He's going to be a brilliant Granddad one day, ha ha no pressure Rosie and Jago!

Mum and Dad went home straight after lunch. She never likes to hang around, in fact the first time she came to visit when I'd just moved in and there was still a heap of boxes to unpack, she didn't even take her coat off. "Can't stay long" she cried and drank her cup of tea and went home again! An hour's drive for a cup of tea! That's Mum for you.

Once they'd left, Jack drove round to fetch Karen's Mum and Dad so they could see the grandchildren on Christmas Day. I didn't like to invite them earlier, because Mum is so unpredictable and sometimes she can be a bit snotty with them. The way I see it, it's not their fault that Phil didn't do the decent thing, so why should they be deprived of their grandchildren? And they've really helped me since I've been on my own, paying for the carpets upstairs and then putting their hands in their pockets again when the ancient dishwasher broke down.

We all settled down and had a cosy evening playing Cluedo which Father-in-law could not get the hang of at all. We laughed till we cried. It was a perfect day.

I had hoped Phil would come and see the children over the Christmas holidays, but he went to Lanzarote with his girlfriend. He said they'd been super busy and just needed to take the opportunity to relax. He came to see them the second week in January instead, and brought masses of presents. You've never seen anything like it. I don't know where I'm going to put them all and the girls began to get overwhelmed and fractious which he didn't like.

I thought perhaps he could keep some of their toys at his house for when they come to visit, but he's in the rental that we were originally going to move to, and he says it's not suitable for children, so we'll arrange something when he moves somewhere more permanent.

He looks well but I do not like his funky new leather jacket. Makes him look like a Hell's Angel. A Hell's Angel that's past its prime. A Hell's Angel that's past its prime and isn't very angelic. I will not be bitter. A Hell's Angel that's past its prime, isn't very angelic and is beginning to develop a paunch.

MATTHEW

Caroline invited me for Christmas, but I was on an expedition. Even if I wasn't, I would not spend Christmas Day in my Mother's company, not for a million pounds.

CHLOE

Wow! Christmas stroke New Year was a blast. My bedsit is a heap of crap but it didn't matter because I was never there. I just went from one party to another and went home when I needed to change my clothes.

I won't tell you about all the things I got up to, mainly because I can't remember all of them, but I have made an important discovery. Snow-white and the Seven Dwarves is on at the Edinburgh Playhouse and I have found out that dwarves are very good for having sex standing up. I hope this information will be useful to you at some point in your life.

Had a bit of a blip with the buggery insulin dose and had to take a trip to A&E on 2nd January where I got lectured at by some old geezer in a white coat, but it's all sorted now and I'll just be more careful in the future. The main thing is that Mummy never hears about it.

Finances as usual are a sore subject. I cannot figure where all my money goes. I'm thinking I maybe need to advertise for pupils to bring in some extra cash but they'll probably be spoilt brats and I will want to snap their bow. Which won't help. Sod it.

Caroline did well at Christmas. I don't think Jack and I have enjoyed the big day so much since Rosie was small and still believed in Santa.

My cretin brother came to stay for one night in January while he visited the girls but it wasn't a comfortable experience. He left his young lady with us while he went round to Caroline's and even Jack couldn't keep the conversation going. Jack being Jack, he couldn't help himself observing afterwards what a remarkable coincidence that Susie rhymes so neatly with floosie.

She appears to have a mental age of about three, and one topic of conversation – Philly-boy. Ye Gods! I don't want to lose touch with my brother, and it would break my Mother's heart if he stopped seeing us, but I foresee a lot of hard work if his Susie-poosie sticks around.

Please excuse me while I fetch a sick-bucket.

 Dear Santa

My Mummy gave me your book to choose
from. It says Argos on the front. Is
that where you live? I liked your book.
Please look at page 96 number (a) and (d).
page 99. number (f) and (g).
Those are the things I don't want.
Happy Christmas Santa

love from
Olivia
+ x + x + + x

Seventeen

MARGARET

Poor Chloe is finding things tight just now and I've had to give her a helping hand. It's so difficult for her now there's only her to pay the rent and even though she's got a good position, the pay is hopeless.

I've decided that I will apply for a bank loan so I can clear everything for Chloe and give her a fresh start. She'll have a chance then. She's just never been able to get back on her feet after she fell behind with her rent when she first got ill. It's all just spiralled out of control from there and with the disgraceful interest charges, she's just working to pay the blasted bank. I reckon if I can give her a couple of grand, she can get herself clear and then she'll be all right again.

Clive need never know. I'm well aware he wouldn't approve, but he's never had the same bond that Chloe and I have. Caroline has always been his clear favourite, and I've never thought it right that he made so much of her. A parent should never show favouritism amongst their children, that's the first thing you learn when you become a Mother and I've always lived by that golden rule.

Clive wanted us to help Caroline when she had to replace her bath, but I told him straight, that's a slippery slope to go down. If we help her once, she'll come to us every time she has a problem and I won't have her expecting us to bail her out every five minutes. She's got an independent life and she needs to learn to manage for herself. And it really irritates me to think back to the educational opportunities we wanted for her but she rejected. As a direct consequence, she's stuck now doing menial cleaning jobs, taking in ironing, looking after other people's kids to help pay the bills. Waste your school years and inevitably you'll end up in a hand-to-mouth existence.

Now look at Chloe: she's holding down an important position and coping with a serious illness far from home and we don't have to replace her bath do we? You have to treat them fairly, however hard that decision might be. And as for Matthew, he's never asked for anything. Come to think of it, I'm not too sure where he is.

CAROLINE

My little brother is getting married! What a turn up for the books! I didn't even know he was courting. I can't wait to meet his fiancée, Evie is her name and he met her in Patagonia but it turned out she grew up about ten miles away from us. Isn't that just the way things go?

I don't know what Evie has done to him, but he seems quite happy to have the whole traditional white wedding shindig and Olivia is to be a bridesmaid so she's very excited. Hannah is only two, so we decided it would be too much for her and she wouldn't understand what she was supposed to do. But as for Olivia, it's the thrill of her life. She can't wait to see what her dress will be like. Evie's Mum has a friend who is doing all the dresses and I should think she's got her work cut out because there are six bridesmaids altogether as well as the bride.

But there's plenty of time, they're planning to get married next spring so they can go trekking on their honeymoon. Can't think of anything worse personally but on the other hand Evie sounds like the perfect match for Matthew. I expect they will be happiest when they're covered in mud and comparing crickets or something more exotic probably.

It always seems odd to me that he lives in urban Bristol instead of being somewhere in the remote wilds. But he does a lot of work with the BBC and he assures me that there is a lot more wildlife in the cities than everyone realises. And I don't think he means the wildlife in Bristol's red light district either. So we're all looking forward to a grand family wedding and he's told me to make sure I'm present when Mum chooses her hat. Like she's going to listen to me!

I think Mum was pleased with the news, but she obviously knows who Evie's Mother is and she didn't take to her, so some diplomacy will be required I think. I wonder whether Chloe will be able to make it to the wedding. I don't think I've actually set eyes on her for at least a couple of years. She always seems to be busy performing whenever I invite her down, but she's doing well for herself, and happy too, so that's the main thing.

MATTHEW

I've chosen a wife who is the polar opposite of my Mother.

CHLOE

I wasn't planning on attending my brother's wedding, but I seem to have got myself into hot water up in Edinburgh. Same old trouble, my salary would be perfectly adequate if only

I received it weekly, but it will not stretch to the end of the month. I sat down and wrote out everything I spent and it made no sense so I threw away the piece of paper and cried instead. That didn't help, I know you'll be surprised to hear that, but what can I say. Shit shit shit.

Mummy hadn't finished paying back the last bank loan, so we had to own up to Dad and now I've got to go home and live under his nose until I "learn to behave like a responsible adult". He's very harsh and says it's time for me to learn some essential life lessons or I'll be a dependent forever. And since he won't allow me to be dependent on him forever, I need a budget or a Sugar Daddy. I know which option my money's on. Except I haven't got any money.

As a consequence, I'm going to be at home for my brother's wedding so I'll be attending alongside the aged parents. Be still my beating heart! I'll probably have to wear a dress as well. It just can't get any worse. I might as well become a nun. Oh yes; also I don't know a single dealer back home. Bollocks to it.

I am going to be a brisemade
That's like a princess for 1 day

I think I will
hav a crown and
I hav to tell the
brise wat to do. So I
am in charg. Usully my
Mummy is in charg. But
she can hav the day of
and I will do it insted.
If I can keep my crown
I mit be in charg forever.

I think I will give it back acterly

Dear Evie

I'm so thrilled to hear the news that you and Matthew are to be married. I hope you know what you're letting yourself in for! I'm looking forward to meeting you so I can tell you all the stories of his youth that he will have been keeping secret. Like the time he put a worm down his teacher's boot when he was in primary school – he was a hero to his whole class from that day on. Though he did get the slipper from the headmaster, but he thought it was worth it. His only regret was that the worm came to a sticky end. Literally.

Olivia is beside herself with excitement, and loves the picture of her bridesmaid's dress that you sent to her. She can't wait for the big day, and neither can I!

With best wishes,

Love from

Caroline, Olivia and Hannah

Eighteen

MARGARET

We got through the wedding as best we could. As luck would have it, Evie's Mum turned out to be the Education Authority trainer who came to show me how to operate the new computerised administrative system.

We didn't hit it off from the very beginning. I got the distinct impression that she regarded a simple school secretary as being very much below her on her personal scale of importance, so I'm afraid that I didn't rush myself when she arrived for a training session. I had work of my own to complete, and I strongly believe that it's a mark of inefficiency to break off from one job in order to skip onto another. So she would have to wait for me and she didn't always take kindly to the delay in her precious schedule.

One time, she said she'd have to go on to her next appointment if I couldn't be ready for her more promptly. I simply pointed out that she was being paid out of my school's budget and as such, she was duty bound to fulfil her contractual obligation to my school. That shut her up and after that she moved to a different training section so I had a new trainer.

Not that that did me much good, I ended up giving training to the trainer, but I got my certificate and that led to my new job, so all's well that ends well. But it didn't make for an easy atmosphere between the families on the wedding day.

We were very much second fiddle aside from being at the top table. Evie's family and friends outnumbered ours by about five to one, which I thought was severely unreasonable, but Matthew would never fight his corner, just clams up and lets everything happen around him. He seems to get on very well with his new in-laws so I don't suppose I'll get much of a look-in now he's a married man.

Evie has obviously got him well and truly in her pocket. If you ask me, she's just after his money, anyone can see what a successful man he is and that, I think, is the attraction. She's got a dozen sisters so her inheritance won't be much. She's latched on to my son to ensure her future security I reckon. Not a good harbinger for a happy marriage to my mind. But I can't say anything to him, he's never taken kindly to my advice. It's out of my hands now, but no one can accuse me of not trying my best.

CAROLINE

Olivia had the best time of her life the day Matthew married Evie. She felt so special, even though the bridal entourage nearly filled the aisle, there were that many of them. Evie has four sisters who were all fully involved. The three married ones were matrons-of-honour and the other one was chief bridesmaid and she looked after Olivia like she was a Princess. When it was time to go to the reception, Evie hoisted Olivia up into the horse-drawn carriage with her and Matthew. She nearly burst with excitement, trotting down the road and waving to all the passers-by. She loved her day.

Evie's family were all so friendly and made us amazingly welcome. Matthew adores them and has been swallowed up like he's a fully fledged member of the family. He says he's gone from two sisters to six just by saying "I will". And a nice Mother-in-law as well which he truly appreciates. He says it's so refreshing to be able to have a conversation without worrying that he might say the wrong thing and cause a big upset. He goes climbing with his Father-in-law and they are clearly firm friends so I think he's got a life of contentment in front of him.

And I wouldn't be surprised if Evie doesn't announce a happy event quite soon. She was really taken with little Hannah, who is so merry and sweet. She's nearly three now, and is growing into a real character. It worries me sometimes that the girls have no father figure in their lives, but their Uncle Jack does a pretty good job of filling the void.

Phil doesn't seem to feel any commitment to his daughters which is sad because he's missing so much. I wonder if his girlfriend prevents him from visiting? But he would come to see them if he really wanted to wouldn't he? I find it difficult to understand his mindset, it's like he wants to set them aside and enjoy his new life without having them as an unnecessary complication. Or a reminder of his past life maybe?

He keeps missing maintenance payments and gets cross with me when I object. I hate that every conversation now seems to degenerate into an argument over his reluctance to visit or offer financial support. This is the man I expected to spend the rest of my life with but I don't feel as though we have anything in common any more. I've reached the conclusion that no matter what happens now, we have no future, so I've told him he can have his divorce if he wants. So I think that's all about to happen but I'm not going to dwell on that at Matthew's wedding. Much better to enjoy the day and remember that more marriages succeed than fail.

It was a surprise to see Chloe. Even more of a surprise to see her legs! She was looking good in a very simple dress with a vivid purple jacket that really caught the eye. Mum kept well in the background and didn't wear a hat of any description so that was a big relief.

MATTHEW

On our wedding day, my bitch Mother told me and Evie we were making a big mistake.

CHLOE

Matthew got married. I went with Mummy and Dad. I've still got no money, so Dad paid for me to have a new outfit but he had to approve it. So you can imagine what it was like. I felt like a 50 year old, nearly went to get a shampoo and set with a lavender rinse to achieve the full effect.

He's enrolled me at college so I can get a teaching certificate and earn a living teaching fucking brats how to make a caterwauling noise on a naff Education Authority violin or vile-in as they were always known. So that's my days taken care of, then in the evening I'm back in the pit at the Repertory Theatre in town so I can earn some money which immediately vanishes into the black hole that is my bank account and let's not even talk about the credit card company.

I can barely believe what's happened. It's like a game of snakes and ladders. I was in the Royal Scottish National Orchestra then I've gone from the snake at square number 99 right down slither slither to square number 2 in one move. Starting over from scratch is a tough call which I'd never planned on.

What's really hard is being treated like a child. Dad doles out weekly pocket money like I'm 5 not 25. I can tell he's thinking this is exactly what I deserve although he's never said anything more on the subject after the first lecture. He is in charge of every item associated with my finances, and will continue to control my every waking minute until I'm clear again. I'm on such a tight rein, I'm nearly strangled. I hate it. I don't have any fun any more.

This is my life: go to college, go home, give myself insulin injection, eat dinner, go to the Theatre, go home, go to bed, get up, go to college and repeat ad nauseum. I am not allowed to go to the pub which to my way of thinking negates the whole purpose of going to work. What kind of shitty life is this for someone my age? The minute I see a way, I'm out of here.

EVIE

My new Mother-in-law chose my wedding day to give me the dubious benefit of her advice. She evidently has me down as a scheming harpy who is marrying for money. If she had any interest whatever in anyone except Margaret Johnson she might have noticed that my family is not on its uppers. I find it hard to believe that she has lived in this area all her life and has no idea who my Father is but maybe she only reads the Problem Page when she gets the newspaper. In fact, she's probably the prime correspondent.

Matthew said I mustn't give her the satisfaction of allowing her to spoil our day so I'm trying to put her out of my mind. I've told my new husband that I don't feel like seeing her very frequently and he laughed and said if it's up to him, we'll never see her at all. Suits me. I've come across some slimy insects in my life, but she beats the lot.

3 School Road
Bedford

Dear Matthew

This is a difficult letter to write, but as a Mother I must do the best I can for my children even though the message I have to relate is not an easy one for you to hear.

I tried very hard to speak to you on this subject on your wedding day, but you were too busy entertaining your wife's family members to spare the time to pay any attention to your own Mother. I'm sorry that you haven't been able to see that family in their true colours, but sadly, I fear for your future. I was unfortunate enough to have professional dealings with your new Mother-in-law and I assure you, she is not a pleasant woman. This will become apparent to you as time goes by. As you will know by now, I have a very sensitive nature, and I am able to accurately assess people's characters immediately upon meeting them. I have never been wrong yet, and I know in my heart that you and your wife are not suited. In fact, I can foresee a terrible marriage before you unless you take steps to disentangle yourself as soon as possible.

I have thought long and hard on this matter and have concluded that it is only fair to you to tell you the whole truth. Your wife has no affection for you. She has married you for your money and your future prospects and I implore you not to be further entrapped by her and her scheming family. Whatever you do, don't make the mistake of having children with her, as this will entrench her marital rights and will enable her to ruin you financially when she divorces you.

I suspect that you will not listen to my warnings. You and Caroline have never appreciated my efforts on your behalf. However, I can rest easy, in the knowledge that I have done my duty as a Mother.

Yours,
Mother

Nineteen

MARGARET

I don't think I've ever been so angry in my life. My poor Chloe has run away! Clive just drove her to breaking point and I am at my wits' end. I kept telling him he was being too hard on her and then he had the bare faced nerve to turn on me and accuse me of being the cause of all the trouble.

Me! I'm the one who has had to support her and encourage her in all her endeavours while he just wanted to bring her down. Yes, she struggled financially, but what did he honestly expect of her? Consider her problems; being so ill, being let down by that Fizz girl, being hounded by her litigious landlord threatening her with God knows what, the stress of Caroline's marriage breakdown. Good Lord, it's astonishing that she's done so well for herself under the circumstances.

Clive has never appreciated that poor child and now we've lost her. I could murder the man. I won't even sleep in the same bed, in fact I'm using Chloe's bedroom now, it makes me feel closer to her. I keep her nightshirt under my pillow and I concentrate my mind on her until sometimes I get a feeling deep inside that reassures me that wherever she is, she's OK. It's a soothing sensation and gives me comfort, but that disappears when I set eyes on Clive so I avoid him as much as possible. I don't want anything to do with him at the moment. He's taken my girl and he's broken my heart. I never thought I'd say it but I hate my own husband. I don't think I will ever be able to forgive him.

CAROLINE

What a mess! Dad is distraught and blaming himself which is pretty bad, but don't worry, Mum is blaming him even more. For goodness sake, Chloe is 25! It can hardly be described as running away from home at her age, but Mum thinks the national police force should be mobilised to find her precious girl. I keep telling Dad that Chloe has been on a collision course with catastrophe for years now, and the only person who can help her is herself. He's tried so hard to teach her to be properly responsible for herself, but Mum keeps undermining all his efforts and has convinced Chloe that she's a special case and the world owes her a living.

The thing is that I know where she is but I'm sworn to secrecy so I can only keep reassuring Dad and try to smooth things over. Matthew managed to trace Chloe, he's got so many contacts within the BBC you wouldn't believe.

Anyway she's all right, I think by that he means she's still alive; and he's keeping a watchful eye on her so we're ready to act as soon as she needs help. She doesn't seem to be doing anything officially. I think she's trying to slip under the radar and so she's not got a proper job. She's living in a squat with a crowd of other people somewhere in North London. It sounds pretty grim, but she's a grown-up and has to make her own choices sooner or later.

In amongst all the drama, I hardly noticed that my divorce had gone through. The marriage I entered with such a flourish ended in a whimper as the 16th case in the list last Wednesday at the magistrates' court in town. And that was that. I'm a divorcee. I don't think I like that description very much, it smacks too much of failure.

It seems to have given the all-clear to my good friend Jenny who thinks I need fixing up with a replacement. She can't accept that I'm not keen on going down that route again, and trots out that old joke that she's married so why should I be happy? The thing is, I've found I can manage to be self-sufficient and that is a surprisingly satisfying achievement. I've got a variety of menial little jobs, but they fit well around the girls' needs and mean I can afford to buy them new shoes and so on without depriving them of my time.

Sadly, they still only have one parent as Phil has continued to be absent from their lives and months go by with no contact from him. So we've made a life without him and we've got a great little routine that we really enjoy, so the last thing I need is to go rocking the boat. To be honest, I like being able to make my own decisions – and, admittedly, my own mistakes – so maybe I'm growing too selfish to fit my wishes around some bloke who probably has no idea that his mates have decided to fix him up whether he likes it or not. Although it would be nice if someone brought me a cup of tea in bed each morning. Or I could always get a teasmaid.

MATTHEW

My Mother ruined Chloe.

CHLOE

I'm free! I couldn't hack it and I left. It's a free world and I couldn't live the way Dad wanted me to. I thought I'd take off to London with my trusty violin and simply busk for a living. Did I get a shock! It's like big business, if you trespass on someone else's pitch, you need to know how to run fast or you can expect a fucking black eye. Which is what I got actually, but it's better now.

But I was desperate, so I didn't let up despite risk to life and limb and eventually this guy Jimmy took pity on me. So he got me fixed up with a pitch near Macdonalds in Fulham which is mine for two hours every other day and I pay him 25% of my takings. I learnt it's best to be honest, because he weirdly knows just how much to expect and when I tried to keep more than my agreed share, he just took the whole lot and advised me in the kindliest tones (ha ha) not to try it on again or I'd have no pitch and no violin either. But it's a good spot I've got, and I earn as much as I used to get in the Royal Scottish.

Jimmy sent me to this house I'm living in as well. At first I thought it was his house because I have to pay him rent, but evidently it's actually an arrangement fee. The other residents have explained that I need to keep paying him if I want to live here, otherwise I won't be living here any longer and quite possibly won't be living full stop. I hope they're just scare stories but I'm not going to push my luck. For now this will do while I get back on my feet.

The main problem is that it's getting pretty cold and I will be the first to admit the amenities here are not fully operational. In fact I think if we called in the Council, the place would be condemned, but we won't be doing that because we have a strong suspicion that it belongs to the Council so inviting them in might not be a good plan. For a start, they might want to know where their boiler has gone and I'd like to know that too because heating is a luxury you really miss when you haven't got it. In truth, we're all a bit grubby, but washing in cold water is too medieval for this life.

I've learnt that the best way to keep warm is to wear all your clothes at once which has the added bonus that it prevents them getting nicked. The secondary problem is that it's hard to play the violin when your fingers are frozen and it's equally hard to play the violin with gloves on. I believe this is called "between a rock and a hard place". But the other two girls living here earn their money at a pole dancing club and that is something I will not do. For a number of reasons. My big boobs might be popular but the other big bits: maybe not so good.

I'm having to be super careful with food because insulin is a problem. Jimmy is supplying me right now but it's expensive and I'm not sure about the quality. I need to get myself registered with a doctor, but I'm worried about proof of ID.

Come to think of it, why am I here? This is about as shitty as anything I've ever done. By Christ! Have I gone off my head?

JIMMY

There's one born evry minute. Hey, you wanna watch yerself pal. That canal's cold and it's mighty deep.

The Chief Constable
Bedfordshire Police

Dear Sir

I am at my wits' end. I have reported this matter to your plods who continue to take no effective action. My daughter has run away, probably to London, and your lazy idiots sit behind their desks, playing cards I suspect. Certainly they are not following up leads or making enquiries as to her whereabouts. She is a gentle, artistic and vulnerable young girl, who is like a lamb to the slaughter in that depraved city. If she should come to any harm, the blame will fall on your shoulders. How will you be able to sleep at night?

The dereliction of duty displayed by yourself and your police force is shocking. The public ought to know about the real face of policing. I believe your job would be in jeopardy if the truth came out. My husband is a personal friend of a friend of the Deputy Mayor of Bedford. I don't think I need to elucidate.

Yours sincerely

M. Johnson

Margaret Johnson (Mrs).

Twenty

MARGARET

She came back, thank God forever and ever Amen. It turned out that Matthew had some contacts in London so he managed to keep an eye on her, and he was on hand to rescue her when she got desperate. We don't see eye to eye on a lot of things but I will say, Matthew has inherited my caring nature. She's staying in Bristol with him for now.

Clive has been up a couple of times but says it's best if I don't see her just yet. He thinks I'll be upset at the state of her and so I've agreed to wait until she's feeling better. I'll just have to trust Matthew and his wife to care for her as well as I would. Clive says she's spending most of her time sleeping and the doctor has told them she needs complete rest because her body was on the verge of a complete breakdown, she'd neglected herself so badly.

The other shock was learning she's acquired a regular drug habit, soft stuff by all accounts, but it only goes to show that she's been living in a den of iniquity. I hate to think what she must have gone through and can't wait to get her safely home. She obviously needs to be under my eye because she's such an innocent soul she'll get sucked into all the worst snake pits. Clive tells me she's being very well cared for and I must trust

Matthew and his wife, whose praises he cannot sing highly enough.

Well, I'll be patient for now but a Mother knows the best place for her child is at home and that's where she'll be at the earliest opportunity. I should be grateful that everything's turned out well in the end and Clive and I are back on speaking terms. I don't think I can ever forget the dreadful trouble his behaviour caused but my heart is big enough that I can find it within me to forgive him and put this dreadful experience behind us. At least he must be aware now that I was right all along, though I'm not going to rub his nose in it. That would be plain spiteful, and that's just not me as anyone who knows me would tell you. But oh! the relief!

CAROLINE

Chloe is at Matthew and Evie's, and he's not planning on letting her go back to Mum any time soon.

Dad's been to visit, and he's in complete agreement that she's in the best place. He's so happy to have found her that he nearly wept when he told me the whole sordid tale. For better or worse, he's decided to pay off the outstanding rent that her ex-landlord is still pursuing so that she can have a fresh start once she's recovered. He's concerned that if she still has the same financial pressures, she'll fall into the same bad habits and it'll be a vicious circle. Thankfully, dearest Dad doesn't have the remotest suspicion about her credit card bills or the poor soul would be plunged into fresh despair.

I suppose my big worry is that Chloe is already conditioned to repeat the same cycle again and again. But everyone's doing everything they possibly can to help her out of the hole she's dug herself into, so let's hope this time she'll make good. When she's feeling a bit better, I'll invite her to stay here and she can reconnect with the simple things of life, playing with the girls, eating some good food and living peacefully. No excitement here.

Although that's not strictly true I confess. Jenny's intrigue prevailed and I took the girls to a barbecue at her house to find myself being introduced to a tall dark handsome stranger. Well, tall and dark at least. The whole thing was so obviously a set-up that I almost felt as though I should apologise on her behalf for being so transparent. I think the embarrassment factor between him and me was about equal but she was completely brazen about the whole thing and didn't seem to think she had anything to be ashamed of.

Well, she got the result she wanted, because he turned out to be just a real nice guy who looks after us all as though we are precious jewels. I don't have any idea where the whole thing will end up, but we're having good fun in the meantime. I'm determined I'm not going to plunge in, it's too risky both for me and the girls, so I'm taking it one step at a time. There's certainly no rush to make any big decisions. I'm still relying on the teasmaid at the moment.

MATTHEW

Chloe's not a bad kid really.

CHLOE

I love Matthew. I love Evie. I even love my Dad. I hate myself but only some of the time, then Evie gives me a good talking to and I feel better again. I got myself into the biggest mess ever, and given my history, that's saying quite something.

I'm not exaggerating when I say they saved my life and I feel now as though I mustn't let them down. I've got to get myself back together and I think with their support, I might just do that. This is the first day of the rest of my life and all that motivational guff!

It's early days, but Matthew is fairly confident he can call in a couple of favours and get me some work at the BBC once I'm back on my feet. He must be the best brother! Sometimes I just sit and cry because I'm so grateful. Then they laugh and tell me to buck up and we get the Jenga out and I'm so happy to play a kiddies game and have a drink of lemonade without any vodka. Oh for a simple life always! It's a little bit scary to think of going out into the big wide world again, but I really think I can do it. Give me a fiddle and the world's my oyster. Either that or Rome burns.

JIMMY

I'll find her. She owes me. I never forget. I mean NEVER.

TRADITIONAL RULES FOR JENGA

Select a jenga brick and with a soft touch, manipulate the brick out of the stack without toppling the remaining bricks. The tiniest of gentle movements make for the most successful results.

OUR RULES FOR JENGA

Hammer it!!!!!!!

Twenty-One

MARGARET

What can I say about my darling daughter? They must think I'm completely stupid. Do they imagine I don't know they're deliberately keeping us apart? I never trusted that wife of his from the start and Matthew was always a manipulative character from the word go. They have turned Chloe into their special project and my input is clearly not required. Clive just says that Chloe is happy and doing well, so we should leave her to get herself established in her new life.

It's hard to argue when she's done so well for herself. I always knew her talent would stand her in good stead, though no doubt Matthew will take all the credit for her success. She's got a place with the BBC Concert Orchestra, which is not something every musician can boast of. I would love to see her just to set my mind at rest. It's all very well them telling me she's fine, but I need to assure myself that she's being cared for to my standard.

She's still living with Matthew and that wife of his, so I can only hope they're not taking advantage of her. Knowing that pair, I wouldn't be surprised to hear they're charging extortionate rent and making her do all the cleaning like a Philippine immigrant. I'm really worried about the whole situation and seriously afraid that they'll just drop her when they get bored. Her artistic temperament makes her so fragile and I'm the only one who understands how to handle her.

Matthew has never understood the importance of nurturing the family and I was never able to impart to him my ability to care for everyone according to their needs. I sorely fear that I will need to be alert and ready to pick up the pieces when their pet project doesn't suit them any more.

The other daughter has been busy as well, too busy to bother herself with her sister's predicament. As usual, it's just left to me to deal with everything while she plans another wedding. She needn't think we're financing this one. How many more will there be before she's finished? Not that she's consulted me, she's just making all the arrangements herself without seeking my advice. Well, let her make as many mistakes as she likes, none of my children care about my feelings any more, so why should I worry about them?

When I think how hard I worked bringing them up with all the opportunities I never had, I could just weep with frustration. I'll probably end up dying alone and no one will find my rotting body for weeks because my own children will be too busy with their important lives to give a thought to the poor old Mother who gave them everything.

CAROLINE

I know what you're thinking; so much for taking things slowly. But one day Geoffrey and I looked at each another and seemed to simultaneously think "What are we waiting for?" We're happy, the children are happy, we don't need to save for a house or to establish our careers and, most important of all, Jenny would be thrilled to learn that her plotting had been successful. So we took ourselves off to choose a nice ring and came home engaged.

When we broke the news to Jenny, she gave a scream which caused a stampede amongst wildebeest in Africa and made her little daughter burst into tears. Hugs and kisses ensued all round (but not amongst the wildebeest), little Amelia dried her tears, Jenny dried her's, Geoffrey looked bemused and I basked in the glow of my diamond. Basically, I've been basking ever since, and we've been having fun making plans for the rest of our lives.

Decision number one revolved around where to live but resolution was simple enough. Bishop's Rourke is halfway between my house and his so we found ourselves a new house there, enabling us both to keep up with the lives we already have. Karen and Jack were relieved that we wouldn't be taking the children miles away because they see so much of them that it would be a real wrench. But the fifteen minute drive is perfectly manageable and the girls are so entranced by all the enthralling changes in their lives that they are like a pair of kettles about to boil over.

Just as thrilling is choosing their bridesmaid's dresses for the big day. I thought it might be best to keep the celebrations simple but Geoffrey thinks we should let Olivia and Hannah direct the whole shebang. He'll learn. If they had their way we'd be travelling in a pink My Little Pony carriage to a beachside ceremony with hula hula girls to serenade us. I think not. Still, at least Mum isn't directing on this occasion, in fact she made it very clear that she would not take kindly to any calls on her time. Not that I mind, planning a wedding is a very pleasant occupation when all I need to consider is what do we want to do. The liberation!

Here's a perfect example: neither of us like champagne, so bingo! We're not having any! Who needs bubbles up their nose to drink the toasts? But we are having a humungous cake so Uncle Ron can have third helpings if he wants. Under Evie's and Matthew's care, Chloe has been doing so well and I've asked her to play for me. Not that I'm any expert on processional violin music, but she's advised Canon in D by Pachelbel and I think it sounds pretty impressive, better than Geoffrey's suggestion: the theme tune from Match of the Day. Ha ha very funny. Can't wait to hear his speech.

I speak to Chloe every weekend and never miss "Friday Night is Music Night" on the radio, imagining her ensconced in the studio with her mates and her music. Although sometimes I'm enthusing about a piece they played and then she tells me she wasn't there this week. But she sounds like she's loving every minute with the Concert Orchestra. I'd never realised what a variety of things they do, but on Monday she might be recording short infills for a TV programme and by Friday she'll be doing a full blown concert in Hull or somewhere. She sounds like she's having the time of her life.

MATTHEW

My new mantra: just keep Chloe away from Mother.

CHLOE

It's quite exciting to have Caroline's wedding to look forward to, but a bit nerve-wracking at the same time. I haven't actually seen most of the family for some years, certainly no one since I had my breakdown. I can dare to call it that now that I'm in recovery.

Mummy wants me to go and stay with her for the week prior to the wedding as I've got a week off and nowhere particular to go. My debts are being paid off rapidly now that Matthew has taken over my finances, but I don't have enough spare money to afford a proper holiday. I haven't seen Mummy for ages and Matthew doesn't like to talk about her, just starts to get riled if I mention her. Evie's no better, I can talk to her about anything at all except Mummy. She gets upset and says Mummy tried to spoil her wedding day, but I'm sure there must have been some misunderstanding.

At any rate, I don't think I'll tell them where I'm going for my visit, just let them think I'm looking up some old friends on my week off. Which will be true. Sort of. And it will give me plenty of practise time for the Pachelbel piece. I want it to be perfect. I don't want to let Caroline down.

JENNY

I knew it! Just call me the fairy Matchmaker. Geoffrey's been a good mate to my husband Stu for years, ever since good old Geoffrey rebuilt the garden wall at my parents-in-law's house after Stu crashed his newly restored E-type into it. I sometimes wonder if he did it on purpose just so he could start work all over again on the resulting wreck. I think Geoffrey spent as much time with his head under the bonnet as he did laying bricks, but as every woman knows, blokes need toys to play with or who knows what the fools would do. Anyway, a bond was forged that has gone from strength to strength with every purchase of Classic Car magazine. And when you live in a house as old as ours, it's jolly handy having a reliable builder on speed dial.

3 School Road
Bedford

The Bishop of Bedford
Bishop's Lodge
Cardington
Bedford

Reverend Sir

It was my questionable pleasure to attend a wedding recently which caused me distinct concerns. As a lifelong church-goer, I pride myself on having some idea of what is and isn't acceptable within the walls of a consecrated place of worship. Saint Peter's Church at Bishop's Rourke gives me grave misgivings.

The congregation treat the place as though it is a home. There is no solemnity in evidence, children are encouraged to join in with the proceedings and the congregants seem to make no effort to wear their best clothes. The songs are sung as though they are being performed on Top of the Pops, and by the way, I do not appreciate the actions that we are expected to join in with. I left kindergarten many years ago and that was the last time I made hand gestures to accompany nursery rhymes. There seems to be a total lack of respect on display in this particular Church, and indeed, it seems to be symptomatic of many ills of society today.

What I am most worried about is the presence of a woman taking on the duties of a normal vicar. I am sure you are familiar with the teachings of Jesus' favourite disciple Peter, in which case you will be aware that women should not occupy a place of authority in the Church. I am therefore doubtful that the bride and groom are properly married in the sight of God. In your shoes, I would be launching a thorough investigation of Saint Peter's Church without hesitation.

I trust that you will be guided by God to follow the right course of action in this unfortunate case.

Yours sincerely

M. Johnson

Margaret Johnson (Mrs).

Twenty-Two

MARGARET

It wasn't like any wedding I'd ever been to, complete shambles more like. But standards today being what they are, the guests seemed to love it. What's wrong with the old hymns that everyone knows? They belted out these new-fangled songs with guitars twanging and drums hammering and no organ at all, everyone singing at the tops of their voices with no respect for the dignity of the church. And it wasn't even a real vicar; a woman with a dog collar presided instead. I just hope they are properly married, though at least it will make the divorce easier if they're not.

Absolutely everyone was there whether they'd earned that honour or not: my feckless brother Ted and his German wife (don't mention the war!), Sandra's snooty daughter with her husband and their pair of hooligans. They all smiled at me like we're the best of friends but I just gave them a dignified nod and moved on. And would you believe, they'd invited all Karen and Jack's family including her parents, which I felt was quite inappropriate. Who in their right minds asks their ex-husband's relatives to their next wedding? I'm surprised at Geoffrey putting up with such an insult and I'm sure his family must have felt it, although his Mother Sarah was having a good chin-wag with Jack. Probably asking his legal advice on how to protect the family assets.

Once we got to the reception, Olivia and Hannah tore round the garden like mad savages, mind you, every child present seemed to have a singular lack of manners. Inevitably, Hannah managed to rip her dress on the slide and Caroline didn't seem in the least bit bothered. As for Geoffrey, he just encourages them to be outrageous, so I foresee that discipline in their household will be non-existent and my grandchildren will be brought up to be unruly thugs.

As you can imagine, he and Jack get on like a house on fire and between them, they got the children thoroughly worked up with their Olympics competitions: Bishop's Rourke versus the rest of the world. Did you ever hear such nonsense? It was as much as we could do to get them to come indoors for the speeches.

Poor Chloe wasn't able to make it in the end, I think she came home to me in the nick of time. She's completely overwrought, obviously been living on her nerves for too long. I knew she was being pushed too far too fast. She just isn't as strong as everyone thinks and having her in my care for a week has been a real eye opener. I've thought long and hard about the situation and I can only come to the conclusion that Matthew and his wife have been brainwashing her. I find it quite sinister.

I've told Clive that she goes back to them over my dead body, but he doesn't seem to appreciate how serious the matter is. He was still trying to make her come to the wedding with us right to the moment we left, and I got quite cross with him in the car. He doesn't see how her brother and sister just want to use her, why, Caroline even asked her to play her up the aisle. She couldn't see that for someone in Chloe's fragile state, the pressure was totally unfair. How dare she expect her to perform in front of all those people? But she only ever thinks of herself and as a consequence, she's set Chloe right back. At least she's back under my roof now and I can look after her properly until she's able to cope better.

CAROLINE

We had the best day ever! It was just one long party and I think everyone enjoyed it as much as we did. Of course there were one or two hiccups, but nothing we couldn't manage. It was a bit of a surprise when Dad said "Now don't worry…." What's the first thing you do when someone says that? Worry of course.

Anyway, Chloe had been taken ill and couldn't make it after all so small panic about the music but Pachelbel's Canon can be played on the guitar also and luckily the vicar's daughter was able to oblige at short notice, well absolutely no notice actually; so well done Lydia for saving the day. For a moment, I thought Dad meant that Chloe had fallen back into a depressive state again, but he reassured me that it was just a blip and she would be fine in no time. Mum just said "oh you know what Chloe's like, you mustn't blame her." Not that I was. I just don't want her to get ill again.

Anyway, it all looks under control. Dad and Matthew had their heads together for a while, then Matthew and Evie left to fetch Chloe back to their place. They have been so dedicated to her, I can't tell you how much I admire them. But I wish Chloe had been able to share our lovely day.

The girls made the most of their day of stardom although Hannah will never be able to wear her pretty dress again. She looked like a proper ragamuffin with her net petticoat wildly escaping from the shredded taffeta skirt but Karen found a pair of scissors and cut the skirt off completely. Hannah pranced around in her billowing petticoat and said she preferred it like that so who could disagree?

I would be hard pressed to choose the best moment of the day but when Olivia and Hannah came sidling up to us at the end of the evening and called Geoffrey "Dad" I nearly cried. But I didn't. What a cliché that would be. I waited till I got home instead.

MATTHEW

We had to miss most of Caroline's wedding so we could kidnap Chloe.

CHLOE

I sort of enjoyed my week with Mummy, but I got so confused. She fusses over me and makes me feel so special. But she told me a lot of things I didn't know about and I kind of wish I still didn't know about.

She confided that Caroline is just getting married to put a roof over her head and have someone to help look after the girls. I can't figure it out. She's got a roof over her head hasn't she? But I know better than anyone how easy it is to lose control of your finances, so maybe she's in some trouble but she hasn't told me. And when I've been talking to her on the phone, she's seemed totally gone on Geoffrey. She bores me sometimes with the gooey mush of it all, but I let her witter on while I update my Filofax. But Mummy says she's not always truthful and I shouldn't take what she says at face value. I don't know what to make of it.

And as for Evie and Matthew, Mummy thinks that Evie is having an affair... but I live in their house, I'm sure I would know if that was true. Mummy says I'm too innocent for my own good, letting them all take advantage of me. When I told

134

her that Matthew is managing my finances she gave a great snort of disbelief and said did I need my head testing which was a bit near the knuckle in actual fact. I told her he'd nearly got me debt free and she said she'd believe it when she saw it, more likely he'd got himself debt free. But he wasn't the one with the debt. I can't think about it any more.

I thought I'd have some quiet time and practised Pachelbel which Mummy enjoyed until I told her Caroline wanted me to play it for her to process up the aisle. Then I thought she might have a heart attack, she went so red in the face and couldn't seem to get her breath and I thought I might have to call for an ambulance. It made me cry a bit, I was that frightened, but when Mummy saw I was getting upset, she pulled herself together and we had a snuggle until I felt better.

She apologised and said she just couldn't help herself getting angry when she saw how my brother and sister used me. She said Caroline could easily afford a proper violinist at her wedding but just wanted me on the cheap. I said I thought she wanted me because I was her sister but Mummy went Ha! like a pantomime villain and I wondered whether I was being taken for a ride after all. When the morning of the wedding came, I felt so muddled in my head, I didn't want to get out of bed. I just felt I couldn't face everyone. I tried to explain to Dad, but he said I would be letting Caroline down and that made me feel about a bazillion times more guilt-stricken. Mummy kept telling him to leave me alone, couldn't he see he was making things worse as usual, he'd never understood me.

I just lay there between them like I wasn't really there at all while they argued about what was the best thing to do with me. I thought I might shrink away into nothing and they wouldn't notice me evaporating before their eyes. Then Dad said, look we've got to get going or we'll be late, are you coming or not? and I pulled the duvet over my head and kept silent while little tears began to seep down my cheeks. Dad huffed and stomped downstairs and Mummy nipped down to the kitchen and got me a big bag of Maltesers and told me to have a nice rest while they were gone.

I had my little cry and then I had the Maltesers and then I fell asleep. The last thing I was expecting was to find Evie shaking me awake and before I could draw breath I was in the car with them and heading back towards Bristol. Evie just laughed about it all and called me a Silly Billy and prattled about the wedding and I began to feel better. I think my imagination must have run away with me. I wish I'd gone to the wedding now. I can play Pachelbel with one hand tied behind my back. It would all have been fine.

GEOFFREY

I find with some surprise that I am now a Dad! I blame it all on Stu. He offered us the infamous E-type as our wedding car, but we decided that we wanted to get to the Church on time and graciously declined his offer. Well Caroline graciously declined, I told him in a more direct way. What a plonker.

He turned up on time with Jenny and Amelia in his BMW which tells you everything you need to know about the E-type. They are all very pleased with themselves and Stu gatecrashed the speeches with his usual discretion. Nobody minded, except Margaret of course. But she wouldn't be happy if we'd had pomp and ceremony at Westminster Cathedral. Thank God my wife is nothing like Mrs Sour-puss. My wife! Did you hear that? My wife Caroline and my daughters Olivia and Hannah! That's my family. Thanks to Stu. Grudging thanks obviously, but thanks all the same Stu you twonk.

Dear Matthew

I hope you are proud of yourself.

You and your wife ruined your sister's wedding day by your precipitate actions in kidnapping Chloe. I believe your clearly premeditated scheme will cause lasting damage to a child who is more vulnerable than you will ever understand. How will you sleep at night with the knowledge that you have been the ruination of your own sister? She was safe in my care, recovering her faculties and coming to terms with the true facts of her family status. Now, without doubt, you will try to mould her in your image and encourage her to expunge me from her life. As for her career, I realise that will be the last thing to concern you. I suppose all her God-given talent will now go to waste while you take advantage of her good nature. Does she skivvy for you? How much rent do you charge her? What are her duties in the running of your home? Oh yes, I have the measure of you, and always have done. You don't fool me with your pretence of "care" for your sister. I am well aware there is an ulterior motive.

It has been difficult for your Father and I to face the reality of your utter disrespect towards us, but neither of us is surprised by your behaviour. Hurt, yes, but history provides ample evidence of your disregard for our feelings. Just as one example, you joked about offering a second hand

137

car to me that your wife had finished with. You called it a death trap but seemed to think it would be ideal for me. To know that my own son would like to see me dead left me speechless with agony, and your Father has never forgotten your "joking" comments. I would never dream of saying something hurtful to you, so why should I be subjected to your unfunny "jokes"? I could relate many more instances of your arrogant contempt towards us, but what would be the use? You have never listened to my opinion or taken my advice. I wash my hands of you.

Mother

Twenty-Three

MARGARET

I'm so livid. I will never speak to that conniving pair as long as I live. Luckily Chloe doesn't seem to have come off too badly in the end. My pep talks through the week must have bolstered her enough to face the world again, because she seems to be surviving back in Bristol even though she's still under the influence of her two-faced brother and his double dealing wife. She'll see them in their true colours one day and then I'll have her back again. I can be as patient as it takes.

It just seems to be one thing after another right now. I'm having a bit of an argument, no, let's call it a debate at school, where everyone seems to think I'm being unreasonable in refusing to attend evening meetings for the great privilege of taking the minutes. I've explained I'm quite prepared to type the minutes up during my working hours, but I am not paid to work in the evenings. The Head has sanctimoniously claimed that all the teachers do extracurricular duties and that the school would be a lot poorer without the voluntary input from so many staff members but I pointed out that my salary is not the same as a teacher's and I have a husband to care for.

It had slipped my mind for a moment that the Head has a severely disabled wife whose care requirements are pretty all-encompassing but I ignored his glare and stood my ground. If I once give way on this principle, I know how it will be: "Oh Margaret, would you kindly do the teas for the PTA's annual general meeting? Oh Margaret, will you help the children at the Nativity? Oh Margaret, will you paint the white lines on the football pitch?" It would be the thin end of the wedge so it will have to be "Oh Margaret, are you going home bang on time?" "Yes I am and you can stick that dark and gloomy expression somewhere darker and gloomier."

And just when I think it can't get any worse, I'm told I'm going to be a Grandmother again. Twice over. Caroline hasn't let the grass grown under her, does she think that husbands are just baby manufacturers? This one will end up going the same way as the last one, you mark my words.

And Matthew had a happy announcement to make as well. I expect the baby will be the subject of a biological case study and will be sold to the BBC for an astronomical fee. It will put the cat amongst the pigeons, that's for sure. I don't suppose they're going to want poor Chloe in the way. Unless they think she'll be a handy babysitter. I wonder who the father is?

CAROLINE

Geoffrey was so keen to get a family under way, and I've never been one to hesitate about babies. I was a bit nervous about repeating the mistake I made last time round. Looking back, it was obvious that Phil really wasn't ready for a family, so I deliberately kept quiet on the subject this time. So much so that ironically, Geoffrey began to think I wasn't interested and had to pluck up courage to broach the question, fearing that I might say I felt my family was already complete. The reality was quite different, needless to say, and fortunately it wasn't long before I was looking at a positive line on the pregnancy tester.

And now we're speculating: girl or boy? Geoffrey comes from a family of boys, well not the wives obviously, so his Mother is positive it will be another one, but I'm sure I've read some research that says once you've had two babies of the same sex, the subsequent babies are likely to be more of the same. In which case, we're going to need more bathrooms.

Olivia is already displaying a high personal grooming instinct and she's only 9. Hannah is still unconvinced that soap has any relevance in her life, but it's only a matter of time before she needs unguents and lotions to slather. I've had my first scan and everything is fine but we've opted to wait till the birth to find out the baby's sex. How old fashioned! Evie and Matthew already know they're expecting a boy, but they're approaching the whole thing from a scientific viewpoint. They're so cerebral, it's scary. When they start talking about genomes or something, I confess I glaze over and think "leave it to nature".

Chloe is nearly as excited as they are, Mum a little underwhelmed I would say. She's already told me that as my due date falls during term time, she's sorry but much as she'd like to, she'll be unable to come and give me a hand. Well I'm sorry to be mean-minded, but that's a relief then. And the spare room is now being transformed into a nursery so sadly, she'd not find the comfort factor up to her standards. Goodness! Now I'm being nasty and I must think tranquil thoughts or it's bad for the baby. Though Matthew would say that as a theory, that's an unproven concept which should be dismissed as an old wives' tale.

I'm sure he and Evie will be great parents. I know it's not quite the same thing, but Chloe has flourished under their care. She's managing her diabetes efficiently, continues to enjoy her career with the Concert Orchestra, and is very settled in Bristol with them. She has a lot of commuting to do, but she's managing to put a bit of money aside each month into a savings account so she will be able to afford to rent a modest place of her own when she feels ready to take that step.

But for now, she is more comfortable with the security where she is, so one step at a time is the best way for her.

Mum and Dad have been to see quite a few of the concerts she's played at, but strictly on a visiting-only basis. Matthew's relationship with Mum remains frigid and she is not welcome in their home which I think Evie finds a perfectly acceptable arrangement. Luckily for Geoffrey, Mum is only a half hour drive away from us, so the question of her staying over has never arisen. I suspect his views would coincide with Evie's, which is sad but understandable.

Mum doesn't seem to relish my husband's company. The only time she's ever shown any interest in him was when she was enquiring about the family business that he is a small cog in. When she found out just how small, she decided she'd got one of her heads coming on and "Clive!", it was time to go home.

MATTHEW

We're having a baby. I think I might finally get over the loss of my gecko.

CHLOE

So much excitement! Evie and I have been painting the nursery which now resembles a jungle although Evie says some of the animals are not indigenous. However, we've decided to overlook that crime in view of the fact that the baby won't be aware of the true facts. Also, this particular jungle is situated in a three bed suburban semi so the general habitat is not entirely convincing anyway.

I worried that Matthew and Evie might want me to move out to make way for the new addition but there has been no question of them removing the welcome mat. Truthfully, they've given me back my life. Not only am I debt-free, I've actually got savings at the bank for the first time in my life. I do go out, mostly with work colleagues, but I hardly drink at all, certainly getting bladdered is a thing of the past. And I'm down to a steady five cigarettes a day and really, I could give them up completely if I wanted to. I've lost two stones, my diabetes is under control, I won't say I've never had a hypo, but it's been such a long time I can't remember when it was exactly. The Orchestra work is good, even though it involves a lot of travelling, but I don't mind, as I find train journeys strangely relaxing. So it's all good!

Oh
My
God,
I'm
So
Bored!!!!

EVIE

I'm having a baby. Lots of people have them, too many in fact, but it still feels like a very special thing, no matter how scientific I'm trying to be about the whole thing. I know important things are going on, minor things like a General Election for example but who cares?

Chloe has been so good, helping me with baby preparations and insisting I rest even when I'm honestly not weary at all. Sometimes, it's like having two husbands in the house. No, I'm joking, she's turned into a really good friend. I wouldn't have believed her transformation was possible when she first came to us, but now I can't imagine life without her. I hope she stays forever.

3 School Road
Bedford

Dear Chloe

*Just a quick note to make sure you are all right at your
brother's house. I was so sorry when you were summarily
removed from our home where you were receiving such
devoted care. Matthew was always a presumptuous child,
always thought he knew best, and I should have known
you wouldn't be safe if you weren't under my eye. I don't
blame you of course, my darling girl, I know how you trust
everyone to act in your best interests. It's so shameful to see
you taken in by your brother and that wife of his.*

*Do be careful that they don't put upon you. Remember
that you need your rest. It isn't good for you to have too
many demands on your time. Your condition dictates that
you put yourself first, never mind what that pair tell you.
And you must find time for sufficient practise, so make sure
you plan your day to suit your needs, not theirs.*

*Dearest Chloe, I know it must be hard for you be away
from me. I am thinking of you all the time. Be brave and
try not to miss home too much. If things get on top of you,
you only have to ring me and I will send Daddy to fetch you
immediately.*

Best love to you,
Mummy

Twenty-Four

MARGARET

I've got two new grandsons which makes a change I suppose. I haven't seen Matthew's little Rueben yet, and don't expect I will any time soon. Doubtless my devoted son intends to exclude me from the life of the little mite but I'll have to grin and bear it. It's no use dwelling on what I'm missing, I'll only get upset and then Clive will get uncomfortable and start his fidgeting which scuffs the carpet.

I spent a couple of days with Caroline and baby Nathaniel which I understand is a family name (not ours of course, we're not that important) but family name or not, it's still a ridiculous mouthful to saddle a baby with.

It was quite a surprise to be able to get away in term time, but when I announced I'd become a Grandmother again, the Head said "you'll be needing some compassionate leave then" and gave me a week off. It was the last thing I was expecting, and of course, it meant I had to visit Caroline or what would I have told everyone when I went back to school? But Caroline certainly didn't need me, she'd got that many people buzzing round her I felt quite left out. I sometimes wonder whether her friend Jenny lives in her house, she seems to be always there. Maybe it's a ménage-a-trois, you hear such goings on about the Yummy Mummy set.

Karen and Jack brought her parents over to see the new baby, which, let's face it, is just plain weird. All that nicey-nicey stuff can't be genuine can it? I'd like to be a fly on the wall when they got home. I wonder what they really think of sweetie Caroline and darling baby Nat, yuck, it made me feel ill to listen to it. Geoffrey's Mother Sarah was centre stage, needless to say, even though she's got four other grandchildren, but you'd think this was her first, the fuss she was making over him. Dear Lord, it's only a baby!

I barely got a look-in but at least I didn't get baby-sick on my shoulder like some people I could mention. Geoffrey was dispensing tea like a Lyon's House waitress. I can see he's being put upon left right and centre, I just hope he doesn't go the same way as that rat-bag ex of hers.

And I had to sleep on Hannah's bed while she went on a Z-Bed in her sister's room. Hannah's bed might be all right for a little princess but my back needs a firmer mattress so I was glad to get on my way the next morning, with plenty of photographs to show off in the staff room. And I was able to have the unexpected bonus of a nice rest at home to recuperate, so I caught up on a couple of books I'd been saving from Christmas. What a treat!

CAROLINE

Another beautiful baby, aren't I the lucky one! And a boy this time, just as Mother-in-law Sarah predicted. The pipework makes nappy changing a new adventure every time so I've had to learn to be a quick mover at the changing table. I've been surrounded with so many helpers that I haven't needed to lift a finger. Such luxury!

Even Mum came to my aid which I wasn't expecting at all. Shame she broke the iron when she dropped it fetching it out of the cupboard which was a bit of a nuisance but Sarah popped into Woolworths on her way home and picked up a new one for me. And actually it's better than the old one, so Mum did me a favour as it turned out. Domestic duties have never been Mum's forte so it was probably as well that she didn't embark on the ironing. Jenny did it instead the next day and made such a beautiful job of it that I've requested her permanent services. Ha ha fat chance.

She takes all the credit for little Nat, saying if it wasn't for her, Geoffrey and I would never have met so she expects Nat to grow up and be her protector in her old age. I said "what about my old age?" but she said either I'll have to give birth to another son or I'll have to learn to share. Her daughter Amelia is firm friends with Olivia and Hannah which is the nicest thing as they amuse one another endlessly with girly stuff, dressing up their dolls although Hannah prefers to dress up the dog but that's Hannah for you.

We're expecting Evie and Matthew at the weekend so we're looking forward to meeting our new nephew Reuben. I suppose it will be a madhouse but on the other hand, I always think it's an advantage if babies learn to sleep through a raucous din. There's no time for shushing in our household. No one would be able to hear it.

MATTHEW

In the immortal words of Del-boy Trotter, "it's a baby!"

CHLOE

The eagle has landed. I mean Reuben has been born. I don't like babies. I'd forgotten. But I don't, not even when it belongs to Evie. And our lovely cosy chats aren't the same with a baby gumming away ferociously at her boobs. Gross!

I like my life here, I like my bedroom, I like my routine, but... London would be easier to be honest. Isla (cello) and Lucy (oboe) have got the box room in their flat-share coming vacant next month, and they are encouraging me to take it. I haven't discussed it with Evie and Matthew yet, but I'm really tempted. I've been warned that the room is seriously tiny, but then again I play the violin not the grand piano so I think I could cope. In all senses of the word.

Evie and Matthew have set me back on my feet and I'm so grateful I could cry, but maybe it's time for me to move on; a natural progression in my life. Sometimes I almost feel like a grown-up. I think I'll take a look at Isla and Lucy's place and then make up my mind. Who am I kidding? Anyone can tell my mind is already made up. Oh London! Here I come! Batten down the hatches.

GEOFFREY

I thought I was a Dad already, but this is something else! I saw him born and everything. It made me feel a bit light headed for a minute but don't tell Caroline. I think he's a handsome chap but what do I know? Mum tells me he's a good lad, but she may be equally biased. Anyway, he's three days old now and I think he's used approximately 500 nappies. I told Dad to buy shares in Pampers. I'm off to wet the baby's head this evening with Stu. We're taking the E-type. It's OK. We'll be needing to walk home anyway.

Turn gently, Earth, while Baby's new.
Fall softly, Rain, like drops of dew.
Shine warmly, Sun, and light the sky.
Swing sweetly, Birds, a lullaby.
Then Baby will be unafraid
And learn to love the world God made.

Twenty-Five

MARGARET

At last Chloe has escaped the shackles of her brother and his wife. She's back in London and seems to be having a whale of a time. Matthew and that woman held her back and completely stifled her. I'm only thankful they didn't manage to squash her artistic temperament which would have been devastating.

Mind you, you wouldn't believe the fuss when she announced she'd found herself somewhere to live in the big bad city. Clive was beside himself, on the phone to Matthew all hours of the day and night. I told him straight, if the girl is capable of organising a move to London, she's capable of living there. He's full of gloom and doom, wittering on about how things were last time, but as I said, she's older and wiser now. If we expect her to fail, how will she ever have the confidence in herself to be independent? Or what has it all been in aid of? Matthew doesn't own her and he has to learn to let her go, just like I had to.

Geoffrey took one of his company's vans down to Bristol and between them, he and Matthew got her moved into her new place, not that there was a lot to take. I took the train up to see her in half term and her room is not what you'd call spacious. I've seen bigger wardrobes. But I will say that Geoffrey had some very ingenious storage ideas and his carpenter knocked her up a long shelving unit above her bed so she's got space for her odds and ends. Her flatmates Isla and Lucy seem very nice girls indeed, but let's face it, the BBC Concert Orchestra doesn't take on any old riff-raff does it? I can picture them playing their instruments together as an ensemble during the winter evenings, what a delight for the neighbours.

Not like my new neighbours in our downsized empty nester's home. Unfortunately, the people next door haven't emptied their particular nest and their hulking great son plays popular music at top volume with the window open when in my opinion he should be going to work. No need to work though when our generous government dishes out my taxes to support work-shy louts like him. He tries to help me unload the shopping from the car, as if I don't know full well he's looking for an opportunity to nick my purse. In fact I thought he'd done just that the other week and he got quite tetchy with me but I don't think he'll be offering any more of his "help". Anyway, it was all right in the end because I remembered I'd put the purse safely in the glove box so he wouldn't be able to see it.

Clive went round to apologise, what is the matter with the man? Just because he hadn't stolen anything this time does not mean he won't try again. These people need putting in their place. You only have to read the Daily Mail to know the truth of this wicked world. I feel quite sorry for my poor little grandsons being brought up in today's lawless society.

CAROLINE

My little chap is coming on a bundle and turning into a big bruiser. (I mean Nat not Geoffrey). I'm pleased to report that the girls adore him which is extremely handy because they keep him amused while I run round like something demented.

Geoffrey is busy busy busy with work, juggling two small builds and a pensioners' bungalow courtyard development which means he has to be in two places at the same time quite frequently. His Dad's scary heart attack, which came soon after Nat's birth, has meant that Sarah has been occupied caring for George so I've been trying to keep up with the books while Geoffrey has taken over the day to day running of the business. All very challenging, but really it's time that Sarah and George began to take things a bit easier. If a heart attack isn't a big enough warning to slow down, what is?

I'm trying to fit in a City and Guild's book keeping course to help me keep business records accurately, and I've been getting through a shocking number of pencil erasers. Hopefully, I'll get the hang of it, as long as I can stay awake through my classes. But whoever came up with the principle of double-entry should be stood against a wall and shot without mercy. Twice. That really would be double-entry.

Chloe has taken the giant step of leaving Evie and Matthew's house and taking on a flat share with a couple of the girls in the Orchestra. So far it seems to be working out, so we're all hopeful that she will cope this time. Whenever I speak to her on the phone, she seems very upbeat and so glad to be back in London. I think it's her spiritual home. Personally speaking, I couldn't bear to live there but she seems to thrive in the bright lights and there's no doubt that her work situation is simplified without quite so much travelling involved.

Isla and Lucy sound like a racy pair but I've no doubt that Chloe will give them a run for their money. She always did like living at Party Central but she promises me she's being sensible and I'm sure she's learnt her lesson after the last muddle she got herself into. And now you'll have to excuse me: I've got to wash some stubborn paint out of Hannah's hair – somehow it's always Hannah! She's obviously had art today, but she doesn't know how she got so much paint in her hair. I wondered whether she had absent-mindedly run the paintbrush through it while she was busy thinking but she assured me she doesn't think at school.

She's such a pickle, always in one scrape or another. Mum wants to know why she can't be as dainty as Olivia because whenever she sees her, Hannah seems to be hanging upside down from a tree with a dirty face and torn trousers. I'm just glad she's so full of life, but Mum thinks she's going to grow up a lesbian. Which of course would be dreadful! I just said "well as long as she does grow up we'll be thankful for that" which did not go down well at all, so now Mum regards me as an uncaring Mother.

I wish she could just enjoy them, but she grumbles at them for being childish. They're children for goodness sake! How are they supposed to behave? And why does she have to be such hard work? I can never please her.

MATTHEW

We missed Chloe when she left.

CHLOE

Woo-hoo! London is fab! We have parties! We go places! There are a hundred different options every time we decide to go out on our free evenings. I didn't realise how much I missed it until I came back.

I don't even mind that I have such a tiny room. You should see how Geoffrey got it fitted up for me. I've got the niftiest drop down desk which folds up against the wall when I don't need it and with a poster stuck on the back of it, you don't even know it's there. Mind you, when it's folded down you can't open the door but that is almost the most attractive element of it.

Isla keeps saying she wants to swap rooms with me and I don't think she means it but it certainly goes to prove that size doesn't matter, ha ha. It's so good to be home!

JIMMY

The bitch is back. I knew it. I'm watching her. No one gets away from Jimmy Fullerton.

The Department for Work and Pensions
Main Street
Bedford

Dear Sirs

I've thought long and hard about writing this letter but I believe it is my civic duty to report a fraud when I see one.

I have a neighbour who I understand to be in receipt of Unemployment Benefit when he is plainly capable of working. He appears to be fit and healthy and is compos mentis. So why does he loaf around all day playing his music until the windows rattle? His parents seem perfectly normal, so I cannot imagine why he is allowed to get away with his idle lifestyle. It pains me to think that the tax which is taken out of my salary is providing an income for the workshy and lazy.

I do not wish to give my personal details as I would be worried about possible reprisals. These people live right next door, so it would be very handy for them to heave a brick through my window.

I would urge you therefore to follow up my information and investigate this young man. His name is Tim Chater of 5 Bellevue Gardens.

Yours sincerely
Anonymous

Twenty-Six

MARGARET

We've had a busy old time of it, back and forth on the motorway for hours attending to family duties. First there was Nat's christening, the most ostentatious event you could ever imagine. Caroline does like these odd jolly services where the congregation seem to be having too much fun to respect the old ways. After Nat had been jiggled all around the Church, we went back to Caroline's and he got jiggled all around the garden. I expect he was ill the next day.

As for the crowd of people that were invited, it was like the first day at the January sales. Olivia and Hannah had been given the task of looking after Clive and me in the unfortunate absence of Chloe who had to pull out at the last minute. Olivia escorted us to a place to sit in the shade and Hannah kept our plates full all afternoon, so we didn't have to stir from our seats. In fact, she kept our plates so well filled that we had to surreptitiously beckon the dog to come and help us. I hope Caroline's looking after dear little Hannah properly. She sounded like she'd got a sore throat coming on.

There was masses of traditional home cooking, which Caroline had obviously been preparing for days although she kept telling everyone how Jenny and Karen had helped her, as well as a couple of friends from the girls' school. She was always good at getting other people to jump to her bidding. Geoffrey had laid on waiting staff, borrowed from the local pub and they kept our glasses topped up although Clive was on lemonade because he had to drive.

Sarah was parading George around like he was a sideshow, but everyone seemed pleased to see him up and about, and I must say he looked remarkably chipper bearing in mind he was at death's door just six months ago. Sarah has just devoted herself entirely to him ever since his heart attack and has left my girl to do all the company's administrative work as if she didn't have enough to do with her growing family. If only I lived a bit closer I could give her a helping hand but it's out of the question given the daily grind of my life.

Matthew had brought his family along but our paths didn't seem to cross. Evidently, his wife took one look at all the work Caroline had expended on the event and decided that Reuben's christening will be celebrated at a hotel. Except it isn't a christening, it's a "naming ceremony", all new age amongst the trees. Pagan in other words, but nothing surprises me from that pair. I expect she practises witchcraft in private; probably has a doll that looks like me and is stuck through with pins. I wish I could get my hands on a doll that looks like her, I think I'd throw it on the fire or something as painful as possible.

As the day wore on, Caroline looked quite exhausted, though she never stopped for a moment. Her trouble is she always feels the need to milk favour, I can see it clear as day. She was always the same and I have to confess, it worries me sometimes. No one could deny that she's the most generous person alive, but I can see she tries to buy people's friendship and approval by her acts of kindness. She doesn't understand that's not the way life works.

In this world, you need to be tough and stand up for yourself. I was always trying to teach her that lesson since her childhood, but she was a hard nut to crack. She has such unrealistic expectations, and she'll regret her ways when she is betrayed by a fair-weather friend.

The reality is that friendships come and go, it's a natural part of life, but if you make a doormat of yourself, you'll only get trampled on. I know I've lost friends over the years, and it's tough, but you just have to pick yourself up and carry on. Better to have a few real friends than a horde of fly-by-nights taking advantage of you. Every gardener knows that a vigorous pruning is good for healthy growth.

CAROLINE

We had a lovely day for Nat's christening. I think even Mum enjoyed it, she certainly seemed to appreciate the place of honour we'd designated for her and sat in splendour on her cushioned chair while her faithful granddaughter plied her with food in an admirable display of zealous loyalty.

You should have just seen the face Hannah pulled when I gave her the job of looking after her Granny, but she's been studying the Victorian age at school and she decided to be John Brown to Granny's Queen Victoria, because "she's just like Queen Victoria. She is not amused". Once she was in character, she enjoyed her duties to the full but we had to tell her to lay off with the gruff Scottish accent.

We had some terrific photographs, a lovely one with George surrounded by his grandchildren who are all quite oblivious to how close we were to losing him so recently. He has recovered so well under Sarah's loving care and he seems almost back to full strength now, though they are still taking a back seat with the business. Karen and Jack had Rosie and Jago with them along with their two little boys, and a big bulge in the front of Rosie's dress suggests a new playmate for Jack is well on the way. Jack and Geoffrey were in charge of the bouncy castle. Karen and I knew they would hog it anyway, so we thought we might as well get them to be useful in shepherding the children.

Little Reuben is such a jolly chap and the girls wheeled him around very proudly in the doll's pram. I didn't like to tell Evie that the usual occupant is the dog but since Reuben is generally surrounded by a variety of vertebrates and invertebrates, it probably doesn't matter. Aunty Honor and Uncle Ron made the trip as well as my cousins Roger and Robert with their families. I was glad the weather stayed sunny otherwise the house would have been bulging at the seams.

Karen and Jenny came over the day before to join me and my friends Mandy and Denise for a working party in the kitchen. We prepared a mountain of food which we felt sure we'd be eating for the rest of the week but I was thankful that we'd made so much because everyone had a very healthy appetite. Although the dog was very very sick later that evening, much to Nat's fascination.

MATTHEW

I avoided Mother at Nat's christening. Like the plague. Which is what she is.

CHLOE

I missed Caroline's christening party in the end, just didn't fancy it if I'm honest. I'm not that turned on by family events, and catching up with long-lost relatives sounds about as appealing as catching up with the Kray twins. But by coincidence, it turned out the Orchestra was due to play at Bristol's Colston Hall the week after Reuben's naming ceremony, so I got the train down and stayed in my bedroom at Evie and Matthew's house. It was just like the old days.

We had a lovely meal in the Avon Gorge Hotel which I always used to love. The view over the suspension bridge is pretty spectacular. As every Bristolian knows, it was built by Isambard Kingdom Brunel, which must be the best name ever. Why don't people call their kids Isambard Kingdom any more? I really think they should but Evie didn't seem convinced. She told me I should save it in case I ever had a child of my own. As if.

Actually she doesn't know I had to have an abortion three months ago, and I have no intention of telling her about it. The wonderful NHS just vacuumed it all up, no questions asked, and it was as if it never happened. I didn't even need to take any time off, just worked it around my free days, so I don't know why anyone makes a big deal about it. It was lovely to see those guys though, and to revisit a few old haunts but I can't tell you how pleased I was to get home again.

UNCLE RON

My charming niece Caroline does make a lovely fruit cake. Honor is good at baking cakes as well, but I think Caroline has the edge when it comes to a traditional fruit cake. I look at our growing families and I think my brother and I have done a decent job. That's not to say I haven't had an easier go of it than Clive. I married Honor. He married Margaret. And that is all I am going to say on the subject because Honor is giving me one of her looks.

Again.

HANNAH'S DO'S AND DON'TS WHEN
LOOKING AFTER GRANDPARENTS

Do:

- Ask whether Granny wants ice in her drink. If you give her ice without asking, she won't want it. If you don't give her ice, she does want it. Doh!
- Make sure Granny always has something on her plate. While she's eating, her mouth is occupied so she can't complain I mean talk.
- Look after Grampa. He has to go home with her.

DON'T

- Tie Grampa's shoelaces together.
- Spit in Granny's drink (or don't get caught at least).
- Let the dog lick their plates.

Twenty-Seven

MARGARET

Holy Christ and back again! Another baby! That girl pops them out like there's a shortage. I've had to think long and hard and I came to the conclusion that I would have to give her some timely advice. Not that she wanted to hear, in fact she put the phone down, claiming that the baby was crying. I couldn't hear anything but she always was a sly one.

I've told her straight I am not going to be at her beck and call. If she wants a football team she can do her own refereeing. With our retirement just a year away, Clive and I want to enjoy a bit of hard earned freedom from family responsibilities and I felt I needed to state our case very firmly before anyone gets the wrong idea. The last thing we want is to find that we are somehow expected to be more involved once we've got more time to spare. I can assure you, our spare time will be for our own benefit, 60 is more than old enough to be able to finally down tools and enjoy a bit of liberty.

Luckily, Clive has always been very sensible with his money and has carefully salted away a healthy pension pot. He's planning a travel itinerary so we can see the world! You're never too old is what I say, and the smaller house we're in now is very easy to lock and leave. As long as the ghastly neighbours

162

don't want to interfere. They're constantly peering in the front window as they pass, giving a wave as if we're best mates, or going "coo-ee" over the fence like a Brooke Bond chimpanzee. I like privacy in my own home, but Clive does insist on chatting with them which just encourages their unwelcome attentions. Well, it will be a relief to be able to wave them goodbye as we leave on a lengthy expedition.

And Clive will certainly be glad to be released from the straightjacket of work. Sometimes when he gets in, he looks quite ill and I tell him something simple like beans on toast will be fine this evening. Every so often he gives such a grimace as though he's in pain so I tell him he should go to the doctor and get checked out, just look what happened to George! But he grumbles at me not to nag and isn't George just fine now? He's the most stubborn man on Earth. Sometimes the thought of him being home all day long gives me a shiver of apprehension. Some of his habits are quite annoying, like clearing his throat every three and a half minutes for example. You can practically set your watch by it. Actually, I never noticed it until Chloe pointed it out, but now I find myself listening out for it. I wish she hadn't told me.

CAROLINE

I wonder whether Mum knows how upsetting she can be? Sometimes I feel like giving her a piece of my mind right back, but I know the sort of ructions that causes so I have to bite my tongue.

But sometimes she goes too far, telling me I expect too much of her with all my babies and the demands that places on her. Ha! What a joke, she's never offered any help with my children and I wouldn't dare to ask. Yet somehow she manages to take the shine off any nice occasion. Lucky she didn't marry a milkman, or she would curdle all the milk.

Frankly, I don't give a monkeys what she thinks about me bringing another child into this over-populated world to be a burden on precious resources and yet another worry to poor old Mum with all the numerous concerns she has to bear. Goodness knows what she's going to say when she finds out that Evie is expecting again. I'm glad to report that the rest of the family is chuffed to bits with our new little Josh who we are all going to love to pieces. I almost feel like immediately getting pregnant again just as revenge for Mum's rant, but Geoffrey and I have decided that four is enough.

As it is, we're going to put an extension on the side of the house to give us a bit more space. Olivia and Hannah have always shared a room since our early days before Geoffrey came along. They get along really well, but they have very different interests so they could do with a room each. Olivia gets a bit fed up when her ballet leotard is used to wipe the mud from Hannah's BMX bike. Chalk and cheese sums them up well I think. Olivia is like a little fairy flittering about from ballet class to tap to drama while Hannah ploughs her bike through muddy trails with gay abandon and really needs a washing machine all to herself.

Nat is growing like a weed and is the tallest in his pre-school class, in fact he's taller than most of the children in reception class, which he is due to enter in September. George will miss him. He has made it his daily duty to collect Nat when he finishes pre-school each lunchtime. He brings him home and we have a bowl of soup and they go upstairs to play for hours with the train set or the Scalextric track, until sometimes Sarah has to ring up and order her AWOL husband home. Then Hannah will take his place and that's when the train becomes derailed or the cars crash and the emergency services have to attend to remove the corpses. And baby Josh sleeps through it all.

MATTHEW

Life is good.

CHLOE

Cigarettes are ridiculously expensive. I don't know why I don't give them up. Some Orchestras go touring abroad where fags, and booze for that matter, are much cheaper. Maybe I'll think about looking around for another position. I have to face facts. I'm a competent musician within the Concert Orchestra, but I'm never going to rise through the ranks any further than I am, which is bottom of the heap basically.

I'm not saying I don't enjoy what we do, but sometimes, I'm just plain bored. But when I analyse my life, what do I have to complain about? Yes, I've got diabetes, but that's completely manageable and I've learnt to live with it. If you want the truth, most of the time I forget about it, it's such an automatic part of my daily routine that I don't give it a second thought. I've got a job which, on paper at least, is any violinist's dream. I live in the best city in the world, with good mates and a fantastic social life.

Caroline rings me up for a chat and I feel utterly sorry for her and her banal existence which she seems inexplicably to love. She's had another baby, I've lost count now how many children she's got, but at least I'm under no pressure to provide any grandchildren for the ancient parents. Just as well, I expect I'd lose it or break it or accidentally put it in the microwave. Maybe I could go on X Factor. They could autotune me and I'd sound like Vanessa Mae. Or more likely Vanessa Feltz.

I recently received an extraordinary report concerning a small pupil who is supposedly being molested by his grandfather. Of course, we must take these matters seriously, but we were all dumbfounded. The letter suggested that this activity has been going on since before the child came into our care, which hardly rang true when one of the teaching assistants recalled that the grandfather had been seriously ill following a heart attack. I was almost tempted to ignore the allegations, but you never know. Sometimes it's the most unlikely families that turn out to have dark secrets. So with a heavy heart, I passed on the letter to Social Services, but it turned out that they were already familiar with the person who had written the letter. She's made similar accusations in the past, always groundless, so they advised that I should monitor the situation in the normal way, but expect to take no further action. We hear all sorts in this business, but when I look at this particular family I feel quite upset.

7 Bellevue Gardens
Bedford

Dear Caroline

I've thought long and hard about writing this letter to you, but someone needs to warn you about the mistakes you are repeating. You know how important family ties are to me, and it would break my heart to see a re-run of your sad history as you rush headlong towards another catastrophe. You drove one husband away with your irresponsible desire to procreate. It is not as though you were raised in the Roman Catholic faith. Nor is the world so under-populated that women have a duty to continuously give birth.

For once in your life, you need to give consideration to other members of your family. I am certainly getting too old for you to expect me to give up the enjoyment of my activities in order to dance attendance on you. This constant flow of babies puts an unimaginable strain on my inner resources and I worry continually about what will happen when your marriage falters. The thought of you once again turning up on our doorstep with four children in tow is quite simply too much for me to contemplate. Sometimes I feel quite ill thinking about it, and your Father worries about my health.

Your husband looks quite worn out. I don't suppose you notice it, but you never had my sensitivity. You need to heed my advice unless you want yet another failed marriage. When I became a Mother, I quickly understood that every waking hour would have to be devoted to my family but you don't seem to have learnt that lesson yet and I am worried that you never will. I am gravely concerned for you. For everyone's sake, you must teach yourself to be less selfish.

Love from
Mum

Twenty-Eight

MARGARET

How can life be so cruel? My husband had cancer. I'm sure he could have been cured if the hospital hadn't made such a hash of things. I did lots of research, and there were all sorts of treatments that I suggested to the specialist but he wouldn't try anything new, just said that all they could do now was try and make him comfortable. I think he was trying to imply it was my fault for not calling the doctor sooner. But Clive kept insisting he would be fine, and sucked another Rennie lozenge while cancer was rampaging through his intestines and sending out reconnaissance teams to his organs.

So we never got to travel the world after all, and one day when we got back from a hospital appointment, we found the house had been broken into and my jewellery was gone. I knew exactly where it could be found: next door under their lad's mattress but the police didn't want to know.

I can tell you, it was the last straw and I admit I went to pieces. I simply couldn't get out of bed for a week, and Geoffrey had to come down and he sorted out the new front door and installed a security system for us. Made a right mess of the plaster in the hall by which time I'd had enough and I told him so when he said he couldn't spare the plasterer until the following week.

Clive couldn't manage anything by now so all the clearing up fell on my shoulders, although at least Matthew dealt with the insurance company for us when they started getting mealy-mouthed about the claim. I don't know what he did, but they went from saying we were making things up and inflating the claim to meekly sending a cheque for the whole amount without any further quibble. But we changed insurers when the policy came up for renewal.

Well, I did. There was no "we" by then. Clive went very suddenly and unexpectedly in the hospice with no one beside him, when we thought he'd still got a couple of weeks, maybe even a month. The Macmillan nurse explained that some patients just seem to reach a point where they've had enough and they decide the time is right to let go and we should be pleased that he is at peace. Well! I went straight home and packed up his clothes and took them round to the Heart Foundation shop. Macmillan is getting nothing from me.

So I retire in six months from a job I hate, working with people I hate, in order to......what? No travelling, no companionship, no point basically. I'm a bit frightened if you want to know the truth. I don't know how to pay a bill or put petrol in the car or how the lawn mower works or anything like that. And my children are so far away and too busy to spare time for me.

Matthew has sorted out the will and all the financial arrangements but he wouldn't spend precious moments with me to listen to my worries. No, he just couldn't wait to get back home to be with his pregnant wife who's about to give birth any day now so I'll revert to bottom on his list of importance. He's written me an accounts journal to follow so I know what I have to do each week, each month and so on, but he can't understand that I need someone here alongside me not a blasted ready reckoner. You bring your children up with loving care and then when you need them, they're nowhere to be seen.

Or they make a nuisance of themselves. Caroline keeps inviting me for Sunday lunch which is always very tasty, but it's such a faff driving all that way. It wouldn't occur to her to come to me and cook me a nice meal. And her house is so noisy, always full of visitors as if her own family isn't bad enough. Her friend Jenny is always kind to me, I bet if she was my daughter, she'd drop everything to take care of me. Caroline has never liked me.

CAROLINE

Oh! Dad's funeral was a woeful thing! Mum didn't want the neighbours "gawping" so the hearse went directly from the undertakers to the crematorium. I don't think I've ever seen a lonelier sight than my Dad arriving all on his own in a solitary car to save a neighbourhood spectacle. It was difficult at that moment to keep from breaking down, but Mum was steely and insisted on no unseemly fuss. Except she had a dreadful wail when the undertakers brought the coffin in and Chloe had to nuzzle up and soothe her as best she could.

She'd arranged a nice hotel buffet lunch, but Evie and I had received our strict edict: no breastfeeding, people don't like it. Apparently. It wasn't so bad for me, Josh only has a bedtime feed now, but Heidi is just a tiny baby who feeds on demand and with a new-born's frequency. Matthew just shrugged and paid for a room in the hotel which Evie stayed in for the duration.

Poor Uncle Ron was totally devastated by the loss of Dad. Of course, no one expects their younger brother to go first, it's not the natural order, and he can't get to grips with it at all. He looks ten years older.

Mum is not good at being on her own and is in need of some careful handling. Matthew has visited a few times to help with her financial arrangements but he has a battle every time to get away. She seems to think he should be making her his priority and can't comprehend that he has a family at home that needs him. Geoffrey ended up taking his plasterer and his painter off a job so she could get her odd jobs done, then she went and put the house up for sale as soon as the work was finished. Said she hated the house, she'd always hated the house and it would never be a home to her now, oh but would we all have a last family meal with her on her 60th birthday to say farewell to this epoch of her life.

We weren't too sure whether to take the invitation seriously, particularly as she never brought the subject up again. I was nervous that she might think I was pressurising her when I mentioned it, but she just went briskly "oh yes certainly, I can manage a roast you know" as if she'd been cooking family meals all her life. But when we got there, Matthew hadn't remembered and she said she knew all along he would forget. Geoffrey had the gall to ask why she didn't remind him but she retorted that he should care enough about her to need no reminders. So we sat through a really awkward meal. Josh got grizzly and and Hannah, trust her, said she wished Aunty Evie was here which earned her a glare from Granny and an icy comment about children who had never been taught good manners.

I don't know how Geoffrey didn't strangle the old bat, but we had to keep in mind that she had just lost her husband. Actually, she was just as poisonous before Dad died as afterwards, so we couldn't really tell the difference.

She retires at the end of term and she has hatched an astounding plan to get her own back for all the nasty treatment she believes she's received at the hands of her colleagues. It's traditional at her school for anyone leaving to provide a lunch for all the staff and for everyone to join in with a celebration to say goodbye. So she's going to provide a lovely buffet which she's ordered from a local caterer, no expense spared. When everyone is duly assembled, she plans to say "I hope you all enjoy my lunch but I don't wish to share your company", then she's going to sit in the car while they eat it. I tried as best I could to suggest that her plan was entirely inappropriate and maybe she might enjoy it better if she stayed and joined in, but she is relishing the prospect of her moment of revenge. When I asked what they'd done that was so bad, she related a long story about them all going out for a meal but deliberately giving her incorrect directions so she got lost and went home instead. I began to remonstrate but Geoffrey was shaking his head behind her and I realised I was wasting my breath.

Pretty soon, we said our goodbyes and slunk away with abject relief. When I told Matthew, he laughed till I thought he would have a seizure. I wish I could dismiss her so easily.

MATTHEW

Dad escaped.

CHLOE

When Dad died and then Mummy retired, she started ringing me up at all hours which began to annoy Isla and Lucy. I seemed to be constantly having long conversations in the wee small hours that went round in circles and never got anywhere. Then I'd find myself nodding off to sleep and missing my cues when we were in practise sessions the next day, so I knew I'd got to pull myself together.

I'd got a little teensy bit behind with my share of the rent and Isla's wedding was coming up, so what with one thing and another, I wasn't surprised when the girls said maybe it was time to go our separate ways. It seemed the obvious thing to do to take leave of absence for a month and go home to help Mummy. Unfortunately, the month stretched into two and then the General Manager began to be rather urgent in his enquiries about my return, so for a while I decided I would have to commute which I'd done before but it's a ridiculous way to manage.

Well, I pretty soon came to the conclusion this was a mug's game and with Isla married and gone to Brussels, and Lucy and I no longer on speaking terms, the Concert Orchestra had become an uncomfortable place to be. So when I heard on the grapevine that there might be a position at the City of London Sinfonia, I went for it and was successful much to my relief.

I found myself a bedsit on Harrow Road in Westbourne Park, a nasty 1960's square block, but clean and tidy and affordable which is the main thing. Mummy was predictably distraught but I think I've been quite patient enough with her and it will probably do her good to be a bit more self-reliant. My new place is furnished so no need for a van this time, Geoffrey got all my stuff in the back of his Renault Espace and off we went with Olivia and Hannah to help. Olivia's help consisted of stringing up a set of fairy lights to make the room pretty and Hannah demonstrated her strength by carrying two lamps upstairs at once and only dropping one of them. She turned the cracked bit to the wall and we all agreed that no one would ever know.

When they'd gone, I sat down in the peace and quiet with my one working lamp and thought "poor Mummy." Then I contemplated the reality of sharing a bathroom and thought "poor me" but quickly I adjusted that thought to "poor fellow residents."

I do intend to pay every penny back to Lucy you know.

I've been a nurse with MacMillan for nearly ten years now, and although some people would find it depressing, I find it endlessly rewarding and uplifting. Yes, you're constantly saying goodbye to your patients, but it's rarely as unhappy as it sounds. At the end of life, most patients and families find peace and if I can ease a person into the next life with comfort and love, I know I've done my job.

People like Margaret are, thankfully, the exception to the rule. If they were all like her, MacMillan would have no nurses left. All she wanted to do was find someone to blame, just could not accept that sometimes life dishes out tough stuff and it's nobody's fault.

Her poor husband became so distressed at the prospect of her visits that we sometimes used to put her off, telling her he was asleep even when he wasn't. Poor man. He slipped silently away without any fuss. I suspect that was how he lived his life – in the background, uncomplaining and unnoticed. He was a true gentleman. I liked him very much.

7 *Bellevue Gardens*
Bedford

The Primrose Cancer Unit
Bedford Hospital
Kempston Road
Bedford

Dear Sirs

I can't begin to tell you just how your negligent actions have wrecked my life. I will never forgive you for the criminal neglect you offered my poor husband. I have instructed my solicitor to pursue all avenues to prevent you repeating the wicked evasion of your clear duty.

Time and again I suggested courses of treatment that have proven records in the medical sphere which it was your job to be familiar with. Every time, you refused to follow my advice and continued doggedly on a course which ultimately led to my husband's death. It is plain to me that if you are so unwilling to investigate up-to-date methods, you should not continue in your profession one moment longer. You are a danger to your patients and it seems to me that not one of you has any principles.

I hope you are proud of yourselves. You have left me a broken-hearted widow with an empty life ahead of me. How can you sleep at night?

You will be hearing from my solicitor very soon. I look forward to seeing you in court.

Yours sincerely

M. Johnson

Margaret Johnson (Mrs).

Twenty-Nine

MARGARET

I knew it would happen. Every last one of my children ended up abandoning me. I've finally found a buyer for my house, which wasn't easy thanks to the unbearable neighbours. Every viewer asked about gaga stuff like community spirit and the like, so I had to tell them that it was advisable to avoid our neighbours who organised a burglary on our home while my husband was dying.

The gentleman who has agreed to buy the place is going to let it out, so he wasn't interested in such matters and didn't even ask the question, just commented that it was a lovely area that was always popular with potential tenants. I didn't enlighten him, absentee landlords don't need to know all the gory details.

I've been ruthlessly clearing out all the abstruse paraphernalia that we've gathered over the years. Clive must have kept every offcut of wood and half length of wallpaper for our entire married lives. I hired a man with a van and he took two trips to the council tip with all the junk and expected me to give him extra money for the additional trip. I had to hand it over in the end because he threatened to empty the second vanload onto the pavement. Nothing short of blackmail if you ask me, but when I called Geoffrey, he said he was at work and couldn't come until the weekend, so there was no alternative but to give the grasping fellow his money and then phone Trading Standards to report him. I'll take a bet he's not declaring his income, probably owes a heap in back-tax.

I've taken all Clive's stuff, his clothes and books, his tools and his cameras down to the charity shop, which has given me a clutter free home. I've found a neat little bungalow, only two years old so everything is very modern and easy to run. The kitchen is a streamlined delight with integrated appliances and beautiful granite worktops. It looks a million dollars. There's a spacious lounge with an arch through to a dining area, one bedroom with an en-suite (mine, all mine) as well as a main bathroom and one spare bedroom.

Admittedly, the garden is tiny, but I can't manage anything bigger at my time of life. Geoffrey is coming down with a couple of his men to gravel the whole outside space, back and front, and Caroline is potting me up some nice mature flowering shrubs so it will all be simple for me to cope with.

The complicated business of buying and selling, "conveyancing" to give it its proper name, is a complete mystery to me and I'm sure it's quite unnecessary. I got Matthew to attend to it all in the end, I simply could not bear to talk one more time with the solicitor with all his needless clauses and sub-clauses and wheretofores and hereuntos. Good grief! Nearly drove me mad! But now the process is nearing completion, do you know, I'm rather looking forward to it.

CAROLINE

Phew! We finally got Mum moved in to her satisfaction but by God she's a demanding woman. Geoffrey has started calling her Mimi because he reckons those are the only two people she ever thinks of. Needless to say, she doesn't know that's why he calls her by that name, she preens and believes it to be an affectionate diminutive of Mum.

Bright and early on moving day, Geoffrey drove off with two of his labourers in the lorry and I followed in the car which I used for all her "delicates" because they couldn't be entrusted to the blokes. Thankfully, Sarah and George volunteered to have the children for the day because I don't think they would have survived Granny's wrath.

Her final act was to post a fat envelope through the letter box next door and she looked very satisfied as she walked down the front path but then instructed me to drive away fast so I don't want to think about what she'd written to the poor devils. They were always so inoffensive and friendly and the son was a talented disc jockey, in great demand and very well respected in the area. But I don't suppose it would have mattered if he was Noel Edmonds, somehow she never got on with any of them.

Her new bungalow is immensely suitable for her and we left her tucking into the casserole I'd brought along and looking very comfortable indeed. Let's hope she settles in quickly.

It was so nice to get home and find normal Sarah and ordinary George caring for the children, and a lovely meal prepared as well. They had been to the park and fed the ducks and George helped Nat fish for tiddlers in the stream so I'll have to bury them tomorrow then, the tiddlers that is, not George and Nat. Nat didn't understand he shouldn't take them out of the water to give them a stroke so now they're all floating on the top of the water. We've told him they're having a sleep. The cruel truth of life will come soon enough to smack him in the chops. In the meantime let him enjoy fishing with Granddad and earnestly giving guidance to Josh in every aspect of his life.

Josh is quite certain that he can run as fast, jump as high and hide as efficiently as his older brother. One day he will learn that calling "I bet you can't find me under the table" is not a good method to employ in hide and seek, and what a sad day that will be.

Childhood is far too fleeting; Olivia is hunkered in her bedroom most of the time studying hard for school exams and telling her brothers to pipe down, fat chance. Hannah takes things a good deal less seriously and would rather encourage her brothers to make more noise not less. I'm not confident about her exam prospects but as her only ambition is to follow Geoffrey into the building industry, maybe I shouldn't worry. And I freely admit that she's a dab hand with scaffolding though I fear that one day she will climb up faster than she's simultaneously building the scaffold tower and then come to a sticky end.

MATTHEW

The solicitor nearly had to act in his own defence on a manslaughter charge by the time Mother had finished with him.

CHLOE

Mummy is safely ensconced in her new bungalow and can hardly stop singing its praises. I daren't tell her that I think I'm going to have to move again, I'm finding it difficult to manage the rent and all the London living expenses. The fridge is empty most of the time, and I know I'm not paying proper attention to my diet.

I know full well that a hypoglycaemic attack is to be avoided at all costs, but I get distracted when I'm busy doing other things. It was lucky that when the attack happened, I was working and the first aider on duty came to my rescue. If it had happened while I was alone in the flat, I don't know where I would have ended up. It was very scary, I can tell you that much for nothing, and I'd prefer not to have another one. I'm just going to be more careful in future. But I need to find somewhere cheaper to live which probably means another flat-share.

I mentioned my little problems to Caroline and she sighed and went "I wish you'd just ask straight out when you want money off me" which I thought was a bit mean of her. Still, she sent me a cheque for £250, which will just pay off some of the interest charges, drop in the ocean if I'm honest, but it's the thought that counts I suppose. Mummy says they've got money coming out of their ears and grumbles that they could give her more help if only they were interested. Though I'm pretty sure they helped her with her move, so she saved the cost of a removals company at least. Maybe it could be a nice side line for them, Removals R Us or something.

Perhaps they could remove my tattoo that I got done on my butt and wish I hadn't now. But to be on the safe side, I won't tell them about it.

TIM CHATER
DISC JOCKEY SERVICES
"MR MUSIC"

That woman is mad. I don't mean mad as in angry, I mean mad as in mental. And now I am mad (as in angry) because she wrote a letter which made my Mum cry and my Mum is the kindest person anywhere. There are some new neighbours there now. They talk to us! They don't look the other way when they see us. They are like...normal! Wowza!

25 Meadow View
Bedford

Young, Meade and Young
12-16 Alms Terrace
Bedford

Dear Mr Young

It has become impossible to continue dealing with you in your professional capacity, or should I more accurately describe it as your unprofessional capacity? Time and again, I have tried to get some sense out of you, but your habit of talking in riddles has bamboozled me completely, as I'm sure was your intention.

Fortunately, my dear son was able to take over the task of wrapping up the legal requirements for the purchase of my new property. You should be aware that he is a very busy man, very important in the BBC, and can ill spare the time necessary to sort out the mess you have made of my affairs. I wouldn't be surprised if he doesn't commission an investigative piece into your practises as he must be just as exasperated as I am by the delays you have needlessly caused. So you can confidently expect to see yourself on Panorama or something of the sort, and you will have no one but yourself to blame.

I wonder how many of your clients have been treated in the same cavalier manner. I don't suppose you get much repeat business. How you sleep in your bed at night, I will never know. You can expect to hear from the Law Society very soon, which I trust will put a stop to the poor treatment your clients receive.

Yours sincerely

M. Johnson

Margaret Johnson (Mrs).

Thirty

MARGARET

What a lovely cosy home I have now. A few little tweaks were necessary of course. Like the granite worktops for example, that looked so sumptuous when I viewed the place, but actually are a right nuisance. Don't ever be persuaded to give them house room, they smear as soon as you look at them and unless you're willing to spend hours every day polishing them they won't repay you with that enticing showroom gleam.

Anyway, I've got better things to do with my time than polish, so I replaced them with good old formica. You can't beat the trusty old stand-bys. I've gone for white which has brightened up the kitchen noticeably and let's face it, you can't go wrong with white can you?

Chloe came to stay for a couple of days when I first moved in and we had a lovely Mummy and daughter session. She understands me so well and we get along like a house on fire. We enjoyed several treats, dinner at the local pub, a tasty Chinese takeaway, and I splashed out on a new coat for her, the one she'd got was so threadbare and disreputable. She surprised me with her unexpected cooking ability, though I was a bit taken aback when she presented her speciality: "posh stew" made with fillet steak. She reckons whenever she announces posh stew is on the menu, she has legions of guests turning up and I must confess, I believe her. I would turn up if I could.

When she went home again, I felt quite bereft all on my own. I thought long and hard and the solution suddenly came to me in a flash. So on Sunday I took myself off to church, which I haven't attended for many years. Oh, I can't tell you what a warm feeling of homecoming I experienced as I sat through that first service. I felt engulfed by peace and tranquillity and knew I was accepted just as I am. I felt at home amongst like-minded people, free from prejudice and vindictiveness. I hate the feeling of being judged and found wanting; it's a trait quite abominable to me. I loathe judgmental people with a passion and always do my best to put them in their place. It's one of my bugbears.

But to come into church and be surrounded by generous-minded folk was like sinking into a comfortable armchair. I can come here with no need to put my armour on beforehand, just listen to the teaching and be reminded of what is important in life. Balm for my sore heart! For the first time in as long as I can remember, I truly feel as though God's in his Heaven, all's well with the world.

CAROLINE

It's been a tough old time lately with one thing and another. Helping Mum with her house move was something we could have done without if I'm honest, but duty has been done. The business is under a lot of pressure and Geoffrey is the one bearing the brunt as usual. The building trade is always the first to feel the pinch when there's a downturn in the economy but Geoffrey is confident that it's just a blip. I'm sure he's right, it's always bounced back in the past.

He's employing his usual strategy in straitened times, and has invested in a couple of good sites that were being offloaded at such good prices that he couldn't resist taking the gamble. But they will stand vacant for now awaiting the right moment, so cashflow is difficult. And with less work coming in, we had to lay off staff. It's the hardest thing you can imagine, probably the hardest part of being an employer I would say. How do you choose? The longest serving? The Father of young children? The most reliable? You might as well draw lots if you're aiming for fairness.

Sometimes Geoffrey has looked quite drawn and I suddenly realised that his hair is completely grey. When did that happen? Even Sarah commented on his harassed demeanour, which made me feel properly guilty. Without thinking, I said a holiday would do him good, and she instantly said "George will take care of things!" like she'd got it all worked out beforehand, which she probably had. Jenny's parents have a holiday villa in the south of France which we've been regularly encouraged to use so without pausing long enough to allow any complications to scupper our plans, I booked the Channel Tunnel crossing.

We set to, filling our ancient Renault with all the junk necessary for a family holiday and heading off into the sunset with joy in our hearts and euros in our wallets. By Dover, we were all a bit fed up with listening to the same tape of Postman Pat on an endless loop, but Josh wasn't willing to relinquish his favourite in exchange for another of our wide-ranging cultural choice, ie Thomas the Tank Engine or James and the Giant Peach.

We were glad of the girls' hard earned linguistic skills when we approached our overnight stop at Beaune. Geoffrey practised over and over the phrase Hannah coached him in: "Voulez-vous coucher avec moi ce soir" until he had it word perfect. Fortunately, as he got out of the car muttering "voulez-vous…avec….ce soir", Olivia blurted out "No Dad! Don't say it!" and spoiled Hannah's marvellous joke but at least Geoffrey didn't get arrested for propositioning a poor unsuspecting pension owner with his unwitting offer of sexual favours.

The holiday was fantastic, day after day of blue skies and carefree hours, non-stop action in the pool or chilled relaxation to suit the needs of the individual. Hannah surprised us by sleeping for hours in the shade. I had been so preoccupied with Geoffrey that I hadn't even noticed how weary she had become. Maybe she needs to climb fewer trees when we get home and start being a bit more ladylike which would please Mum. The whole family had a blissful fortnight of going barefoot and unshackled and it did us all the world of good.

When our old knacker-heap of a car konked out at Calais, we were able to take it in our stride, in fact the entertainment value of being brought home by the Automobile Association contributed immeasurably to the whole holiday experience. Now we're home, and things are much the same but our load feels lighter and Geoffrey is enjoying himself looking at Range Rovers in the Auto Trader magazine. He's a laugh a minute. I confidently expect the replacement for our cranky people carrier will be a slightly less cranky people carrier but as long as it gets us from A to B, who cares?

MATTHEW

What the blazes did Chloe think she was doing?

CHLOE

I had the most amazing piece of luck when I was browsing in Notting Hill market shortly after I had given notice on my flat. I bumped into my old mucker Jimmy! Remember, from my first days in London when I ended up living in that shrine of grot before being rescued by Matthew and Dad?

Well, as I might have known, he had a mate who had a cousin who knew a guy with a spare room he wanted to let out, so to cut a long story short, I nipped over there and shook hands on the deal. I won't let Mummy see it, as she would not be impressed, but it's cheap. A little smidgeon of damp in the corner of the ceiling is apparent I will admit, and the mattress manages to be too soft and too hard all at once, but I will survive.

My credit card is sadly maxed out so I think I will do a bunk once again to avoid the rent arrears. I assure you, I learnt the lesson from my last experience and just as a precaution I didn't give my landlord entirely accurate personal details, so he won't be able to track me down unless he's the Hound of the Baskervilles or something. I know, naughty, naughty, naughty; but London is impossibly expensive when you're on your own.

I was going to ask Caroline to help me out a bit by increasing the 100 quid she's been sending me each month, but damn and blast it, she rang me to say she would have to discontinue payments until things picked up with the business. Just my bad luck! My good friend Sidney has put me on to the trick of balance transfers, so I've applied for a new credit card to switch my old card debt onto, which will give me a breathing space to pay some off with no interest charges racking up painfully. This is known by the technical term of "win-win" and almost seems too good to be true. I expect the financial institutions will end up caning us all in some new dastardly ruse yet to be devised, but in the meantime I will take every crumb they throw me.

Work is sometimes boring and sometimes thrilling, which I suppose is the same for every job in the world, however glamorous it might seem to the outsider. It would be useful if I learnt to drive, but how would I afford to run a car? I can barely afford to run to the bus-stop. The landlord at my local pub offered me a spot playing a bit of Irish traditional music on a Wednesday night, cash in hand, no questions asked. I'm considering it, that's how desperate I am, but I was seriously affronted when he referred to my Rodolfo Fredi violin as a fiddle. Philistine!

JIMMY

Surely you dint think I'd forgot her did yer?

5 Cambridge Close
Bishop's Rourke

The Automobile Association
Norfolk House
Priestley Road
Basingstoke

Dear Sirs

I am writing on behalf of myself and my family in order to say how impressed we were with your service earlier this week.

On Tuesday morning, we returned from a holiday in France, just managing to limp into Folkestone with a car full of panicking passengers and a dashboard full of flashing lights. After ringing the AA Emergency Breakdown Service at about 6.30am, by 9am, we were on the road, with our car (diagnosed with a blown head-gasket) on a low-loader, my husband plus two children in a hire car and myself with two sons being entertained by the inestimable Bob in his cab.

A changeover of drivers took place smoothly at the halfway point and we arrived back home in plenty of time for tea. The children all think the whole thing was terrific and look forward to being brought home by the AA every time we go on holiday. In addition, my husband has decided that he would like to be a Relay truck driver when he grows up.

Please accept the very grateful thanks of our enthralled family.

Yours faithfully
Caroline Fellowes

Thirty-One

MARGARET

Chloe is such a brave soldier. She's moved again without even telling me. She said she didn't want me to be worried about her, she just couldn't afford to keep paying the rent for a place of her own. I've thought long and hard and I've come to a difficult decision but now I've made it, I feel as though a weight has lifted from me.

I've been to see a solicitor and I've written a new will making Chloe my sole beneficiary. It's quite clear that as a musical artist she may give immense pleasure to many people, but she'll never be able to support herself. I've told her that after her death, I would like the estate to pass to the grandchildren, and she seems quite happy with that provision.

I wouldn't say the same about Matthew, who was unbelievably rude and cruel when I told him the news. "Do you seriously not understand the message you are conveying in this action?" he said to me, coldly, quietly, calmly, his measured voice dripping with icy disdain. "You clearly don't give a shit about anyone else but yourself and your precious Chloe and I hope it makes you very happy. But you'll have to excuse me when I tell you I want nothing more to do with you." And with a gentle click, burrrr, he was gone. Well, he's no loss to me.

He's never cared for me, and as for that wife of his, I wouldn't be surprised to hear that she leaves him now he's not going to get anything from me.

After that reaction, though, I was a bit nervous about ringing Caroline, but she's always been more tractable, and she just said "well, it's your money, Mum." Such a relief! I said "that was easier than I was expecting!" and told her all about the church bazaar I'd helped with on Saturday. She was a bit quiet, but she's had to take one of her kids to the doctor and they're doing some tests, which must be a worry to her. It doesn't matter how old your children are, they're always preying on your mind. You never stop trying to do your best for them, you'd give them everything you own if it would help them.

Luckily, my own children are well set up and need no assistance from anyone, but I'd be the first one they'd call on in times of trouble. That's what being a Mother is all about, isn't it?

CAROLINE

Hannah somehow hadn't seemed quite herself, nothing I could put my finger on, and yet....she was pale and listless and didn't shake it off. So I took her to the GP who thought it was just "one of those things", but to be on the safe side, he ordered tests at our local hospital.

What a thoroughly soul-destroying process! You wait for hours in a beige corridor before getting called through to a room where you have to confirm all over again the details you've already given three times that morning. By the time they'd eventually taken the blood samples the doctor had ordered, Hannah was exhausted and just wanted to get home.

I was peeling spuds, how prosaic, when the phone call came and life as we knew it ground to a halt. "Now, I don't want you to start worrying but just as a precaution, we'd like you to take your daughter to Addenbrooke's Hospital in Cambridge," said the nurse on the line. "They're expecting her on Ward C2 so they can do some further tests." As you can imagine, I floundered and stuttered as though English was no longer my first language. "When are they expecting her?" I managed to stammer out. "Well, now, actually," came the reply and I can't quite tell you what happened next but I don't think those potatoes ever got peeled.

Jenny came to collect Olivia to stay overnight with an obliviously exuberant Amelia, while Sarah and George hot-footed it over to sit with the boys "for as long as it takes, don't you fret lass", and Geoffrey and I were in the car with a wide-eyed Hannah in the back and her hastily packed bag flung in beside her. Tests, tests, horrible tests! Further bloods were taken and then a gut-wrenching bone marrow sample taken from her pelvic bone and finally, the heart-stopping verdict.

Acute myeloid leukemia, "not very common in patients of Hannah's age" explained the consultant as though that deserved a badge of merit and a celebration! It was recommended that chemotherapy should commence immediately; well it wasn't a recommendation really, simply the only possible course of action. The consultant talked about Stage 2 and Stage 3 and I didn't take in what he meant at all, but I understood enough to know that Hannah was in a bad way and that was why she was put on an intensive course of treatment.

She had a PICC line inserted into her chest which, little did we know, she would keep for six months, during which time she endured chemo doses once or twice a week. And when I say endured, that is exactly what I mean. She was sick every day for the entire six months, her hair went, she was whiter than the sheets she lay on and prey to every cough and cold that passed her way. We had to be very careful with monitoring visitors because an infection in her weakened state was a very serious matter indeed. Sometimes she just lay there and wept, tears rolling down her cheeks and plopping into her ears and what could I do?

There is nothing, nothing in the whole world that is worse than seeing your child so ill and there is not one thing you can do to make it all better. When we were feeling a little less grim, though, we might go to the playroom or the teenager's room and without fail, there would be someone else you would feel even more sorry for, so we tried to keep a perspective on things.

Hannah even reached the conclusion that she didn't have such a bad deal when one day it seemed that just about every child on the ward except for her had been administered the dreaded barium drink. Ward C2 has unanimously decided that a barium drink is not going to make it onto Macdonald's menu, not even with dunkin' doughnuts.

MATTHEW

The Bristol Royal has a fine childhood leukemia programme. But Caroline wanted Hannah close to her. I look at my healthy children and think how lucky I am.

CHLOE

My niece Hannah is very sick. I went and got her name tattooed on the back of my neck as a gesture of support but it backfired quite spectacularly when I got called into the General Manager's office and basically invited to leave the Sinfonia.

The thing is, we often have to wear formal evening gowns when we're performing, and visible tattoos or "excessive and inappropriate" piercings are strictly forbidden. I knew that perfectly well from the handbook I was given when I joined, but I went ahead and did it anyway. I suppose it was the last straw and I fully acknowledge I'm a twit because I knew I was already skating on thin ice, with questions being asked over my perceived lack of commitment. Perceived, my tattooed backside, anyone can tell I'm not the most committed member of the Sinfonia and I'm lucky they hadn't dispensed with my services before.

Surprise, surprise! There aren't a lot of openings for a tattooed violinist in the list of vacancies at the Job Centre. Thank goodness for my new credit card but my plan to reduce my debt is now up shit creek. One of my old colleagues at the BBC has an idea in the pipeline for a touring Chamber Orchestra, but it's not off the ground yet though I'm pretty sure I could get in if I say the word. In the meantime, I can't survive on sweet fresh air, so it's back to Mummy for a rest. Of course, I haven't told her the real reason behind my change of career direction. She thinks this new touring group is my big opportunity for fame and fortune and I'm not going to enlighten her.

Caroline's got a lot on her plate so I can't ask her for help, not until Hannah's better. According to Mummy, it's a long haul for her with a lot of horrible treatment. We're not able to go and visit her in case we give her an infection and Mummy says they're living in such a madhouse at the moment that it's best to stay out of the way. Still, once Hannah's treatment is over, doubtless Caroline will throw a big party for all the family to come and celebrate. Mummy will enjoy it, she loves to sit by Aunty Honor and point out the new things Geoffrey's done to the house. I might go too if I haven't started work yet, it's a long time since I saw everyone.

And I bet Hannah will like my tattoo even if the City of London Sinfonia does not.

JIMMY

I'm reeling her in. Softly softly catchee monkey.

25 Meadow View
Bedford

The General Manager
The City of London Sinfonia
4th Floor
9 Brighton Terrace
London

Dear Sir

I learn with shock that you, in your wisdom, have decided to take the incomprehensible step of dismissing my daughter Chloe Johnson. I would urge you to reconsider, as you have clearly taken leave of your senses. A more talented violinist you will never meet, and the loss to your orchestra must be incalculable.

I have tried to talk with Chloe about her dismissal, but she is too overwrought to make any sense. I warn you that she is a very vulnerable girl with such a sensitive nature that it is almost a handicap to her. Things that would pass over the heads of the average person affect her so deeply that she becomes physically unwell. If she suffers any long term ill-effects as a consequence of your abrupt decision, I will hold you personally responsible, and will take legal action against you as General Manager of the Sinfonia.

Furthermore, I am in daily contact with the ACAS advisory helpline. You may confidently expect to hear soon in respect of a case for unfair dismissal.

Lastly, I do assure you that this will prove to be your loss, not Chloe's. We never did think much of your tinpot little provincial musicians.

Yours sincerely

M. Johnson

Margaret Johnson (Mrs).

Thirty-Two

MARGARET

I know better than anyone what a worrywort Caroline is when it comes to her children and I hope she realises before it's too late that she mustn't forget she has other members of her family to think of. She's simply consumed by Hannah and I'm worried about the effect on her marriage. She lost one husband when she neglected him and Geoffrey is not even Hannah's real father, so she can't expect him to feel the same way she does.

Whenever she rings me, it's a hurried call in between dropping children off with one friend or another, or with Sarah or Karen about to turn up to take care of things while she dashes back to the hospital. It's no life for anyone, and I fear for the future. Once Hannah's treatment is over, they will all find it hard to get back to normal without resentment creeping in at the amount of attention Hannah has enjoyed while Caroline has effectively handed over her domestic duties to friends and family. I've heard of so many cases where marriages have been torn asunder in the aftermath of such traumatic periods. She doesn't listen to me of course, but she'll wish she had, you mark my words.

And Hannah isn't the first child to fall ill, you have to keep your sense of proportion. Many years ago, my Mother nearly lost me to Scarlet Fever. The episode became an unforgettable piece of family lore which was related to me so many times by my sister Sandra.

I was too young to remember it myself, but I've heard it so often that I can perfectly picture the scene. I grew sicker and sicker until the crisis came and my Mother, accompanied by a neighbour, sat up with me all night. The neighbour was famously doom-laden and kept announcing "she's going!" until my Mother reached the end of her tether. Unwilling to listen to one more mournful prediction, she threw the enraged neighbour out and maintained her vigil alone. She continued to doggedly sponge me down and in the early hours the fever broke. Legend has it that she saved my life, but I don't know whether I would go that far.

Anyway, she stripped the sweat-soaked sheets off the bed, replaced them with fresh bedlinen and went off to work leaving me to recover alone as best I could. I've often wondered why she couldn't show me the same devoted affection when I was well.

CAROLINE

We kind of knew that the treatment wasn't going to plan. As the course drew to a close, Hannah's blood counts were being monitored practically daily and the nurses and the consultants were looking very serious as they updated her records. I didn't want to ask, didn't want to make it real, but the Ostrich approach has never been renowned for its success.

One day, with Geoffrey present, the consultant invited us into his office to discuss the situation. Gravely, he gave us the information we definitely did not want to hear; that leukemia cells were still being detected which meant that the hoped-for consolidation phase was not an option. If she went through a repeat of the chemotherapy course, he put her chances of survival at only four in ten, which was a brutal statistic to try and assimilate. What all this boiled down to was that we had to face the prospect of stem cell treatment, better known probably as a bone marrow transplant.

While we caught our breath, he talked us through the procedure, explaining that the first step was to find a suitable bone marrow donor. Willing family members should be tested first as that offered the best chance of a good match, so our first job was to approach as many of our relations as possible to ask them to be tested. I said please could I be tested straight away and Geoffrey instantly said "Me too."

The consultant quizzically looked at him and gently said "You must be prepared that the likelihood of a match is not good given that you have no genetic link with Hannah." I honestly think that simple fact had not occurred to him until that moment, and the look that came over his poor face as the truth hit home is something I never want to see again. He absolutely broke down and cried like a baby, something he had never done before and never did again through the whole awful process.

Sadly, my own results were not brilliant and as expected, neither were Geoffrey's, but we were overwhelmed with offers from so many people who desperately wanted to undergo testing in the hope of being a match. Though Mum hastened to tell us that she was too old and vetoed Chloe on the grounds that her insulin dependent diabetes ruled her out. Which was all true, bugger it.

We managed to track down Phil, who as Hannah's natural Father stood a good chance of testing successfully, but before he underwent the procedure, we got the news that Karen's daughter Rosie had flagged up a near-perfect match. We celebrated that day, I can tell you! Hannah was very poorly and no time was wasted in preparing her and Rosie for the operation. Hannah required yet more chemo as well as a blast of radiation to boost her chances. As usual, the side effects were as vile as ever, but Rosie's match was so good that we were buoyed along by optimism.

On a warm summer's morning, the precious bone marrow was harvested from Rosie's hip bone and transferred to Hannah. And it took! I won't pretend she was instantly better, in fact the aftermath of the procedure is not at all pleasant, but we had been warned what to expect. So the gruesome ulceration of her mouth and throat was no surprise, and she bore the constant pain in her gut with the aid of her innate cheerfulness, or more likely her patient-controlled analgesia. She pressed that morphine button like it was her X-box controller and I know I'm biased, but her stoicism was the most admirable thing I've ever seen. All the nurses commented on it, not just her favourite nurse Jackie who always praised her whatever she did, but even the stern nurse Linda who was respected by all but held in awe and never crossed.

The important thing was that her blood counts began to improve with extraordinary rapidity, and the consultant's looks of concern were transformed daily before our eyes into smiles of quiet triumph. When he turned to us and said "I really think we've turned the corner here", they were the sweetest words we could have wished for, words indeed that for a long time we hadn't dared to hope we might hear. I think we were all a little overcome, and I had to leave Geoffrey with Hannah and take myself off for some private time.

I found the hospital chapel, and sat in the gentle peace and said thank you to every deity I could think of, well, the chapel is non-denominational after all. They all heard from me that day, God, Jehovah, Allah, Buddha, the whole bally lot of them. I guess they're all the same really. I could have broken into the Hallelujah chorus, but thought better of it. My singing might have caused a relapse. I would wish the whole loathsome experience on no one, but the sheer bliss of knowing she was in recovery made my heart overflow with gratitude.

MATTHEW

Addenbrooke's did OK.

CHLOE

Young Hannah came through. No party yet though.

I was offered a place in Nick Hallam's new Chamber Orchestra, which I accepted without even pretending to give it consideration amongst my many other options ha ha. Our first tour was off to Eastern Europe, which you might think unexpected, but know what? Even ex-communists and Bolsheviks like proper music. They're actually human just like you and me, there's a shock for you.

I think Mummy was worried I would be shot by the KGB or sent to a Gulag or something but actually the whole trip was quite charming. I'm not stupid, I am aware that most civilians do not live in luxurious home conditions but personally speaking, we stayed in some very nice hotels and spent five days as the guest Orchestra on a river cruise ship which was the best adventure ever. We got to stop off for the daytime trips and I've explored places I would never have dreamed of.

In the evenings we played old classics to elderly inebriated tourists who never noticed bum notes and were all happy as Larry. Quite a few of them really were called Larry as it happened. I'd grown my hair while I was staying at Mummy's, so the dreaded tattoo was out of sight. It might have given some of the old dears apoplexy or something.

Here's a piece of information high on the list of things you never wanted to know: they have a big chiller on cruise ships, and it's not for storing food. It's for the people who inevitably die en route because they're so ancient. That's cruising for you!

I make it a solemn rule never to get fond of my patients. They are all really sick by the time they come to us and we lose more than we would wish. If you invest your heart in every child, you wouldn't last the course. I am proud to say I am a highly professional nurse in this respect.

Hannah was very wonderful. I couldn't help myself. I loved her.

25 Meadow View
Bedford

Dear Matthew

This week's sermon was on the subject of forgiveness, and it made me think long and hard. I considered all the hurts you have inflicted upon me over the years, but taking heed of the vicar's blessed words, I am able to offer forgiveness to you.

I forgive you for the cruel way you shouted at me down the phone when I informed you of my new will. You nearly burst my ear drum, and Chloe was shocked when I told her about it.

I forgive you for apparently suggesting to Honor that I had ignored your Father's wishes in making Chloe my beneficiary. This was something that we discussed many times prior to his death, and I made my will with those discussions in mind.

I forgive you for excluding me from your family. I'm sorry that I have been unable to offer support during your divorce, but I can't help you if I am not informed of these developments in your life.

I forgive you for never taking my advice. You are getting your just desserts now.

I forgive you for engaging in secret meetings with Caroline to discuss my "mental health issues". I assure you I am the sanest person I know.

I could go on in the same vein, but it is very tiresome to do so, and I am above all the bitterness and recrimination that you seem to attribute to me. You have hurt me to the core, but I forgive you anyway, as a Mother and a Christian always will. However, will you offer the same clemency for all the wrongs I supposedly have done to you? Going on past experience, I doubt that very much.

So carry on your own sweet way. If you hate me so much, there is nothing more I can say. If you continue ignoring me and excluding me, it will ultimately be you and your children who will be the losers. I'm sure that you can work out what that means. I do not intend to have any further contact with you and would prefer you to make no further communication with me. And I would rather you didn't attend my funeral when I'm gone. It will be too late to make amends then.

Yours,
Mother

Thirty-Three

MARGARET

It was a relief to hear that Hannah was on the mend and we could all get back to some semblance of normality at last. Oddly, I haven't received many invitations to Sunday lunch and I'm strongly suspecting that Caroline is going the way of her brother. I wouldn't be surprised to learn that they've been discussing my supposed shortcomings and of course, she's always been so easily influenced.

She's never brought up the subject of my new will, but I'm so sensitive that I can feel the undercurrent when we speak on the phone. Everyone thinks she's so saintly but I know the real Caroline. She's been the most stubborn and intransigent of all my children; smiles on the outside and hatred on the inside. I can't bear her brand of hypocrisy.

Fortunately, I've got so many new friends at Church and I've made a point of nurturing some old friendships so that my days are packed with so many activities that I have no idea how I found time to go to work. I never miss Wednesday lunch with my sister Sandra, and I'm determined to make good on that old intention to travel; I'm off to Australia to visit my older brother who I haven't seen in, golly, ten years? Or probably more like fifteen? Anyway, I'm looking forward to it immensely.

I went to the Lake District on a Church trip and met a gentleman there who made it very clear that he found me attractive which was a major boost to my confidence. It's nice to know I haven't lost it yet! Of course, no one will ever replace my darling Clive, but a companion in my old age is a prospect that has obvious advantages. Anyway, Gerald and I have exchanged numbers and when I return from Australia, we're pledged to meet up again. Gerald says that as you get older, you learn the value of new friendships as well as old, and I couldn't agree more.

I told Caroline about him and she says we must both come over one day so everyone can get to know Gerald, but I could tell the invitation was made through gritted teeth and I said "you don't have to bother yourself if it's so very inconvenient." I feel quite out of sorts after I speak to her. The irritation that crackles down the line is extremely disconcerting.

She seems to have forgotten all the things I've done for her over the years. I told her the dates of my Australia trip so that she would know I wouldn't be available during that period, and she retorted "available for what?" quite curtly as though I'm not always on call in an emergency. I was quite cross I can tell you and I told her straight, I realise she won't make the effort for me, which is why I have made arrangements myself for my funeral. The little madam accused me of being mean-spirited which was absolutely uncalled for and I put the phone down. Now I suppose I've got to go and organise the damned thing or I'll look like a fool.

My whole family has always relied on me to carry it through every upset and I get thoroughly tired of it sometimes. At least it's confirmed in my mind that my new will was the right decision. Chloe is the only one who's ever cared for me. I'm off to the other side of the world on Thursday, and I can't wait to get away from them all.

CAROLINE

I've learnt a great many more medical terms than I ever expected to find a use for. The latest one to pop up is GvHD. That stands for Graft versus Host Disease. It also stands for disaster. It was the cruellest blow imaginable. Hannah was beginning to really perk up and we could see life returning to our Miss Mischief.

Then it began: odd little red spots on her hands and feet, then a rash and a fever, and back to hospital we went to have the rug whipped from under us all over again. More treatment, oh God, how could this happen to our brave girl? Immunosuppressants left her wide open to infection and the corticosteroids brought her back to the old days of needing a bowl always to hand as vomiting dragged her down to her lowest ebb. Nurse Linda, in her questionable idea of humour, said with mock severity that return visitors were not welcome on Ward C2, but instead of laughing along with her, Hannah burst into tears and was inconsolable. She refused to wear any of her funny hats and seemed to shut herself off from us.

Then she whispered to me "No more. Please Mummy. I don't want any more." And my heart stopped. I knew in that awful moment it was cruel of us to subject her to any more of this inhuman existence where the cure was worse than the disease. We'd been filling her tiny wasted body with poison for so long and she had had enough.

Our beautiful daughter left us on a grey rainswept day in February. It was like heaven was weeping along with us. Excuse me. I can't speak any more.

MATTHEW

Life is the most random web of insane tragedy.

CHLOE

I didn't know until about ten days after it happened. Mummy said in the confusion she just forgot. Anyway, they had the big party in the end, but sadly Hannah didn't get to enjoy it because it was her funeral instead of her celebration and I missed it because we were touring in the Philippines. Who would have thought? We go to the most amazing places, I think now what a waste of time it was being a member of those staid traditional orchestras when I could have been having fun and seeing the big wide world.

I don't think I would have been able to get back home anyway. I would have had to pay my own fare and as my financial situation remains as grim as ever, my credit cards would doubtless have been rejected. Anyway, what could I have done? Got the tattoo lasered? I'm not good in those situations, everybody would be crying and I would say something crass as usual and earn the displeasure of all present. Though I would like to catch up with some of the family. I rather fancy having a duet with my cousin Roger. I reckon I'm a whole lot better than him now. Perhaps the opportunity will arise in happier times.

Oh, I nearly forgot: the most unbelievable coincidence! I bumped into Jimmy at Manilla Airport. It turns out he has business interests out here. I'd never clocked him as a globe-trotting entrepreneur, but I obviously didn't know him that well. He gave me his card and told me to look him up when I get back home. I think I will, he was always a looker, but with a golden suntan he looked quite snoggable.

JIMMY

Told yer, dint I?

Dear Gerald

It was so lovely to meet you on our recent Church trip. I felt an instant meeting of minds and instinctively knew that you and I are kindred spirits. It was very pleasant to chat so easily with you. My keen sense of humour has often been commented on by my many friends, and your's seemed to dovetail so neatly with mine. I don't think I've laughed so much since the good old innocent days of Laurel and Hardy!

I realise you are eager to make firm arrangements to meet up again and have already taken a look in my packed diary to check when would be a suitable time. I lead a very busy life, so it was quite hard to find a gap! I am off to Australia shortly, travelling business class which is so comfortable. When I come home in six weeks time, I suggest we get our heads together to fix up a visit. I don't mind coming to you if that is most convenient, I have a lovely car, top of the range with leather seats which I find so pleasing to the eye. Alternatively, you would be welcome to come and stay in my luxury bungalow – don't worry, there is plenty of space, and you would have your own bathroom!

I have told my family all about you, and they can't wait to meet you. I look forward to hearing from you very soon.

With love and best wishes,
Margaret

Thirty-Four

MARGARET

Hannah's funeral was like a visit to the funfair, crowded with hordes of unsuitable people, hundreds of youngsters from her school and cycling club when anyone knows that a funeral is no place for children. Caroline was insistent that the day was to be treated as a celebration of her life not a mourning of her death, which was ridiculous of course. We all had to plaster smiles on our faces as if our hearts weren't breaking. It was quite impossible.

Family members with the most tenuous link were present, like Phil's entire family for instance. Completely inappropriate, they had no right to be there. Their Rosie basically killed her, let's not beat about the bush. I will never speak to her again. By all accounts, Hannah's suffering at the end was utterly unbearable, if she had been a dog they would have put her down.

After the church service, which was far too jolly for such a solemn event, we went back to the house to carry on the "celebration." As usual, it was a vulgar display of extravagant profligacy with drink flowing and food served in excessive quantities. But that's Caroline for you, always wanting to show off to as many people as possible in the hope of garnering their approval. She's plainly lost weight and I told her it suited her although actually, she never had much flesh to spare and she looks quite skinny and plain. But I was too polite to tell her the truth on such an occasion. It's the sort of advice that needs to be given in a private moment.

I asked my friend Gerald whether he would accompany me, but he sounded a little shocked and excused himself, saying he thought it wasn't the right time to meet my family. By a series of unfortunate clashes, we've been unable to meet up in person since I've been home, but I've rung him several times, and he's always the same, jolly and avuncular, the sort of man who is at ease in any company. I'm looking forward to getting our engagement diaries synchronised for a reunion. My goodness! I've just realised what I said there; I don't mean we're engaged, oh far from it, just a term to describe the social whirl of our lives!

I was seated between Honor and Sandra so I told them all about him which they found very interesting, though Ron glowered. I suppose he thinks I should be in purdah for the rest of my days, wailing in perpetuity for the loss of his wonderful brother. Well, I don't mean to say he wasn't wonderful, I seem to be tying myself in knots here, but while Clive is obviously irreplaceable the reality is that life goes on, doesn't it?

Matthew was there with his wife, glad-handing all and sundry, they always liked to be the centre of attention. We didn't speak. I was hard pushed to pick out their children amongst the throng. We have never been allowed to get to know each other. I think it's a wicked shame to deprive kiddies of the older generation's care and wisdom. But we grandparents have absolutely no lawful rights whatever in these heart rending cases. I've checked.

One thing only I asked my Mother to do, and that was to inform Chloe of our sad news, yet somehow Mum was so grief-stricken by the loss of a child she barely knew that she couldn't get round to that single task and Chloe never heard about it until it was too late.

I'm trying to keep my patience with her selfish ways, but it's really difficult when she is so demanding and ungrateful. I've tried to ignore the disinheritance thing but it's there in the background; the elephant in the room I suppose I should term it. The knowledge of her ultimate rejection of me is continually confirmed by her self-serving attitude. She never visited Hannah through her whole illness, not once, never offered to help out at home with the other children, and then played the grieving Grandmother at the funeral like she was a more talented actress than Meryl Streep. I really had no time for her performance and was most thankful that Aunty Honor and Aunty Sandra bore the brunt with far more tolerance than I could muster.

Geoffrey tries to buck me up when she gets to me, but my head is too full of my sweet Hannah to find space to accommodate Mother Duty as well. I told him at least we wouldn't be in charge of Mum's funeral as she's sorted it out herself and he said "oh good, when is it?" which was most disrespectful, tut tut.

Hannah's funeral buoyed us through the first sting of loss, I think that's the whole point of the exercise. The Church was packed and lots of people had to stand outside. Several of her schoolteachers attended along with a great crowd of her friends who cried with such sorrow it demanded the most supreme effort not to break down alongside them. The affection borne towards our Hannah was palpable and gave us strength over the coming days as we vacillated between having a huge weep and then going "oh did you see so-and-so in the Church porch?" or "I never expected thingummibob to turn up".

But it's been a very empty feeling for a long long time and try as I might, my mind keeps returning to the hamster wheel routine of what would Hannah be doing right now, or more likely, what trick would she be planning? I can't imagine a day when the soreness might recede. We've tried to give the kids "normal" times but it's uphill work. They still need treats even though there is a Hannah-shaped gap in all we do.

We took them to Alton Towers in the school holidays immediately following the funeral to try and give them some good memories of the period. We ended up standing in a queue behind the most gigantic woman you ever saw. If she joined Weightwatchers, she'd need to pay two membership fees. I don't know what's happened to me, I shouldn't be so judgmental. Maybe she has a glandular problem...or maybe she's just plain greedy.

Anyway, while we were standing in her immense shadow, her phone started trilling and Geoffrey muttered, sotto voce, "watch out, she's reversing." Silly fool. It reduced us both to hysterical laughter and next thing, tears were flooding down my face, while Geoffrey gripped my shoulder and quietly said "hold up girl". What kind of a fool did I feel? Laughing when Hannah is gone seems as though it should be deemed a criminal act. But I swallowed down the wash of silly emotion and we had the best day. It did us all good to have some fun.

MATTHEW

With a face as sour as a lemon, Mother attended the funeral. Shame it wasn't her's.

CHLOE

My life has settled into a good routine. We tour for two or three months at a time, and we've got a six-month world tour planned in the New Year which is mega-exciting. The music is not demanding, we could all play it in our sleep, but the audiences always appreciate us and we get rousing standing ovations for doing diddly squat, frankly.

In our rest periods, I go to Mummy's where I can live without dreaded expenses racking up. Juggling the credit cards is seriously boring and does my head in. At the weekends, I can nip off to London and stay at Jimmy's swanky Thames-side pad, smoke a little dope that no one needs to know about, go clubbing, have a drink or two, head back for Sunday lunch at the pub with Mummy and then a big sleep.

I wrote down my insulin instructions and pinned them on Jimmy's corkboard so that there are no mistakes, but Jimmy is surprisingly on the ball as far as all that's concerned. He's not what you'd call romantic, definitely the strong silent type but I think we suit one another in our own way. Neither of us is interested in settling down and starting a family, fuck, the very idea makes me nauseous. And fleeting liaisons with other willing participants don't give either of us jealous palpitations, big "so what" to all that if you ask me.

Sometimes I shock myself by paying off a bit more on my credit cards than I spend, but the following month normal service is resumed. I know what I need to do if I want to get debt-free: give up smoking, give up dabbling with my very small drug habit, give up drinking, give up London, give up FUN. Ain't gonna happen folks! I don't think about it any more, what's the point?

I've got my miraculous fall-back position which is my cushion of reassurance. Mummy's house will be mine one day, so I can sell it, pay off my debts and buy a smaller flat to live in mortgage free. What more could a girl want? Only nipple tassels and I've got several pairs.

SIMON

I was pretty surprised to hear from my sister Margaret, she's never been a regular correspondent and the last letter I got from her was some weird tripe about me nicking her lemonade or something. My wife Pat has never met her and she ripped up the letter and told me I had a seriously odd kind of family. Well, that's not true actually. I just have one seriously odd kind of sister. She was always one for a bit of drama. After I'd left England, I heard some tale she'd told about Pa getting up to dirty tricks with her. Poor Mum got upset, you can imagine, but Sandra and Ted and me just put it down to Margaret doing her thing. She gave Mum a lot of grief about it at the time, until my brother Ted stepped in. Being in the legal profession, he was able to nip it in the bud with the threat that she would find herself in court if she didn't stop harassing our Mother. It shut her up but she never spoke to Ted again. Not that he was too worried about that. Well, I'm obviously the brother in favour at the moment, because she's invited herself to stay for a "much needed" holiday. Pat is not looking forward to it. I've told her just live your life the same as every other day and don't let her tinkle your bell. It won't be forever and we'll be sure to have a laugh about it when she's gone home.

Ward C2
Addenbrooke's Hospital
Cambridge

Dear Caroline and Geoffrey

I couldn't let Hannah's funeral go by without being there myself and, as you saw, several of my colleagues felt the same way. It is rare that a child touches us in the way she did, in fact, we have to maintain a certain professional detachment or we would soon be unable to do our jobs. You will be familiar with my fellow nurse, Linda, who is renowned for her ability to retain a clear distance from her patients as a form of self protection. After Hannah's death, though, even she had to lock herself in the office for ten minutes, something unheard of in all my days on the ward.

But Hannah was not your average run-of-the-mill child, was she? She brought an enchantment to our sombre surroundings and as for her hats! They were famous throughout the hospital.

We at Addenbrooke's will always remember your Hannah with the greatest affection. It's been a lot quieter without her! I can't imagine how much you all miss her, but one thing I do know – she'll never be forgotten.

With every good wish for you and your family,
Nurse Jackie Mitchell

Thirty-Five

MARGARET

I had a very enjoyable time in Australia. My brother Simon and his current wife Pam treated me like a queen, chauffeuring me around and introducing me to all their friends. I renewed my acquaintance with Simon's two children who both have families of their own now, all very aquatic and sporty and dreadfully *enthusiastic* about everything. They began to make me feel tired just listening to them.

Oh, I remember now, it's Pat, not Pam.

I saw all the sights, went on a trip to the rainforest and got to cuddle a koala. Frightful animals actually, I wouldn't recommend cuddling them at all. Mine was quite vicious and gave me a nasty scratch down the side of my face before the attendant managed to prise him off me. Pam was quite concerned, but the rest of them made a great joke of it, saying I was obviously a tasty lady; no respect whatsoever.

The Australians as a race are astonishingly informal, even on occasions which call for smartness and proper behaviour. We went out for dinner one evening and I automatically put on my best dress and 15-denier nylons and my cultured pearls that Clive bought me. I asked Pam when she was going to get ready, and she said she already had, which was embarrassing.

She'd got flip-flops on! But she didn't seem in the least bit bothered, and when I realised that Simon was going in his shorts, it began to occur to me that standards are not the same over there. I don't know what my Mother would have thought of their general lacklustre appearance, but Pam just laughed and said it's too hot for dressing up.

I mean Pat, the woman's name is Pat, not Pam.

When I got home, Caroline invited me and Sandra over for Sunday lunch so she could hear all my holiday news, but unfortunately Sandra wasn't feeling well that morning so I went on my own. I showed them all my photographs and went through my holiday journal so I wouldn't leave anything out, but those boys are quite rude, fidgeting around like they had ants in their pants until Caroline told them they could leave the table and play in the garden. It's not surprising they have no manners when they're not taught to sit politely while their elders are speaking. It would have been a good education to them to listen to all my foreign experiences.

Caroline hasn't seen her Uncle Simon in years and has never met Pam, so she was very interested to see their pictures, and exclaimed over Simon's bald head. The last time she saw him, he had a healthy brush of black hair but it's all gone now. Gerald has a very manly head of hair, white as snow but plenty of it.

Caroline has yet to meet him, in fact I've only seen him once, we're both so busy it's ridiculous. Still, he is the perfect gentleman, treats me with old fashioned courtesy and makes me feel ten years younger. I'm looking forward to our next meeting very much indeed.

But a great shock befell me when I got home. Sandra had gone from feeling under the weather in the morning to being in intensive care by the evening. Claire rang me to let me know so I could arrange to visit her, but she couldn't tell me what was wrong as tests were still being conducted. But that night she fell into a coma and never woke up. I don't mind telling you, I cried and cried. Another connection lost.

Claire was kind but I had to ask her to leave and just crawled up to my bed where I hid myself away for three days until I could face the world again. I know it's the natural order of things, but nevertheless, when your own sister dies, it really hits home that your days are limited. The greatest lesson of life is to concentrate on the important things and let go of all those insignificant trivialities which waste so much precious time.

CAROLINE

It was a shock to lose lovely Aunty Sandra so unexpectedly, but as Claire said, it was better than a long drawn out illness and up to that point, she had enjoyed a long and happy life, well loved by her family and friends. What more could anyone ask? And it was nice to speak to Claire again. She's moved around such a lot that we rarely see one another these days, but as we said goodbye after the funeral, she said "don't be a stranger" and I plan to stick to that exhortation.

Mum is pretty upset. I think Sandra had become something of a lifeline for her, hauling Mum along on outings and activities which she enjoyed once she'd stopped grumbling about how exhausted she was.

Home life began to steady itself into a routine as we all got to grips with the gaping absence of Hannah. Boys being boys, Nat and Josh seemed relatively unscathed and carried on their daily hustle with as much vigour as ever. They are both extremely sporty lads, and immersed themselves in dashing around at top speed and falling into bed at the end of each day in a comatose state. Olivia though, was another matter altogether.

During Hannah's long hospital stays, she had practically lived at Jenny's, and Amelia was like another sister to her. So she missed her real sister and at the same time she missed her surrogate sister too. She ended up spending most weekends at Jenny's house and was almost like a stranger in her own home. I knew full well I hadn't paid her enough attention when all my energies were focussed on defeating Hannah's illness and I was paying a heavy price for it now. Jenny advised me to leave the situation to work itself out in the fullness of time. I knew she was right, but it sometimes felt like I'd lost both my daughters, which was a harsh reality to face.

Olivia was always academically inclined and her A-level results were extraordinarily good so she had pretty much the pick of her university choices. She ended up plumping for Durham where she was going to study English literature. It sounded like such an interesting course; I was quite envious and almost wished I could join her. Which would not have been welcome. We went shopping for all the odds and ends she would need when she was away, but it was an unpleasantly strained outing. We didn't seem to have anything to say to each other, we'd just lost the natural ebb and flow of general conversation and rubbing along together. I guess we're both grieving for the same reason, but we can't seem to help one another. I hate it. She's withdrawn herself from us and seems absolutely unreachable.

I hope Jenny is right when she says she'll come out the other end and be our own Olivia again. Patience is not something I have in abundance. Mum consumes all mine.

MATTHEW

Sometimes I felt guilty about leaving Caroline to deal with Mother. But the guilt was easily outweighed by my loathing for the mad cow.

Jimmy's got a bastard baby. That was a shock I can tell you. To him as much as anyone. He told the girl she had to get a DNA test before he would believe her, nearly ended up on Jeremy Kyle I think. Anyway, it turned out it was his kid in the end and now he gets all puffed up about his Jensen, that's the baby not a luxury motor vehicle.

He said he liked the name she'd chosen because he'll be the only Jensen in the playground but I'm not so sure. I reckon 50% of the kids won't be called Jensen and that's because they're called Chelsea. I think he's quite proud of his big achievement but then the bimbo hassles him because he's supposed to send money every month and he's not so keen on that part of fatherhood. Calls her a lot of names that can't be mentioned before the fucking watershed and wonders how a pushchair with a fancy logo can cost 700 fucking quid.

I think if you can't beat them, join them, except I don't want a baby so I got a dog instead. Stupid goddam idea, what do I do with the thing when I'm on tour? Not for the first time, I freely admit I didn't think it through. So I convinced Mummy that the best thing in the world for her was a pretty little doggy companion and let her think that I'd got him as a nice gift for her. The decider was that he's such a yappy creature, I convinced her he'd be better than any burglar alarm so she can sleep easy in her bed without worrying about an intruder breaking in to rape her.

More likely to break out actually once confronted with her hair in rollers and her face embalmed in night serum.

Child Support Agency 2
Freepost RTGJ-ZCRR-KKKZ
Post Handling Site B
Wolverhampton
WV99 1NE

Dear Miss Johnson

Information has been forwarded to this office which leads us to believe that Mr James Fullerton is residing or has resided at your address. We are currently conducting an investigation into non payment of Child Support in respect of a child/ children fathered by Mr Fullerton.

If you know Mr Fullerton is residing at your address, or if you know where he is residing at the current time, please inform us at your earliest convenience, using the freepost address recorded above.

Please note it is an offence to withhold information or to give false information which may affect the ongoing case against Mr Fullerton.

Yours sincerely

Flora Benton

Investigating Officer
Team 2/WR
Child Support Agency

LIFE GOES ON

If I should go before the rest of you,
Break not a flower nor inscribe a stone.
Nor when I'm gone speak in a Sunday voice,
But be the usual selves that I have known.
Weep if you must.
Parting is hell,
But life goes on,
So sing as well.

Joyce Grenfell

Thirty-Six

MARGARET

I had to give Gerald his marching orders. I thought long and hard, but he was messing me around and I won't stand for it.

We'd made arrangements to meet up in Warwick and when I got there, he was with a whole crowd from his allotment society. I was not impressed. Listening to old fellas boasting of their monster marrows and giant carrots made my eyes begin to glaze over. Were they serious? And did Gerald honestly expect me to regard all this information with fascination? He basically ignored me and tried to suggest that he hadn't been expecting me to turn up! So why did he tell me all about the details of the event then?

I always thought there was something shifty about him, nothing like my steadfast Clive. Really, I wasn't surprised to be let down by him, I was half expecting it, the way he kept putting me off and being vague about plans. His loss not mine I assure you. Come to think of it, didn't Matthew have some kind of lizard thingy that he called Gerald? Obviously the standard name for a cold blooded reptile.

Anyway, I've got rather a sweet little doggy now. Dear Chloe, thoughtful as ever, picked him out for me because she was so concerned for my security. Geoffrey may have fitted me up with a new burglar alarm but that won't deter a professional criminal will it?

My Monty has a bark that is devastatingly ear-splitting, in fact sometimes the neighbour shouts over the garden fence, stupid old woman. It makes no difference anyway, he just barks all the more so she's wasting her time.

I don't speak to her in any case. On bin day, she keeps taking my wheelie bin instead of hers even though I've clearly marked my address on the lid. She just shrugs and says "they're both the same aren't they?" That's not the point, I don't want her dregs in the bottom of my bin thank you very much.

I hear that my son has moved house though he hasn't had the courtesy to tell me himself and two-faced madam Caroline won't pass on his new address. Not that I want to see him, but if there was an emergency, I might need to get in touch urgently. I wonder whether he's had to move as a result of a marital split?

It wouldn't surprise me in the least, in fact I've been expecting it for years, but Caroline is tight lipped on the subject. I don't suppose there's any chance I'll get to see my grandchildren if that gruesome wife of his has them in her clutches. Doubtless she'll take Matthew to the cleaners. Let's hope he doesn't expect me to help him out. Damn nerve of him, when he hasn't spoken to me since yelling at me down the phone so frighteningly after I changed my will.

I wouldn't mind moving house myself to tell the truth. With all Chloe's stuff here, I could do with a bit more space and as for the woman next door, she's no better than she should be. I mentioned it to Caroline, thinking naturally that one of Geoffrey's builds would suit me nicely, but she just suggested that Chloe should apply for a mortgage to enable us to upgrade. What a preposterous idea! She can't afford to pay me rent, not that I'd ask her. How the heck does she think poor Chloe could take on a mortgage?

The trouble is, Caroline lives such a gilded life she has no concept of what it's like for us ordinary folk struggling along on the bottom rung of society. Instead, it would seem that she is taking some delight in passing on nasty rumours to her "compassionate" friends suggesting I've got a screw loose. Maybe instead she could look at her own failings and make some personal time in her schedule to offer me true care and compassion. She was always a spiteful madam.

CAROLINE

We had a fantastic time moving Evie and Matthew to their new place near the Cheddar Gorge. They've bought 16 acres of woodland and meadow and a real tumbledown old house that Geoffrey has advised them to knock down and start afresh. But they didn't buy it for the sake of the house, it was all about the land. They plan to establish an outward bound centre for youngsters to visit and to conduct training programmes to teach people how to preserve wildlife and natural habitats for sustainable living.

Mind you, there's no sustainable living going on just yet. You'd be astonished to find out how many unsustainable practises have to be put into operation before the sustainable bit starts to happen. And it's all eye-wateringly expensive, so Matthew will continue to work at the BBC, but the commute to Bristol is quite manageable. In the car that is, not by sustainable bicycle.

Their kids Reuben and Heidi already look like proper country children, all apple cheeks and wellington boots, and Nat and Josh joined in all their outdoor pursuits. They hauled trees and chopped logs and slashed at unruly undergrowth as if they were in the Amazon jungle, although of course, the only Amazon they're familiar with is the online version.

Olivia didn't join us although it was in holiday time. But she said she had a lot of reading to do for her English literature course and she stayed at home instead. If you ask me, she's got a serious case of the sulks and the situation is beginning to be rather tedious. There are times when I feel like giving her a hard shake and telling her to grow up.

So I have to take a walk round the garden when the red mist comes over me and I give the boys' rugby ball a severe kicking until the feeling passes. Geoffrey's favourite phrase goes through my mind then and "steady girl", I can face my daughter and wait it out. I only wish I knew how to talk to her. She never ever mentions Hannah.

The only common factor we seem to have currently is her university course work. How lucky I am that she chose a subject that has always been my first love, so reading the same stuff that she's studying was a pleasure rather than a chore. Every once in a while, almost against her will, we'll find ourselves discussing something she's working on and momentarily she gets quite animated. So I have hope that the old Olivia will come back to us. Mum had a bit of a surprise for us when she announced that she and Gerald have split up. The way she talked about him, I thought it had been a genuine case of love at first sight. But Geoffrey said maybe Gerald didn't have his glasses on at the time. He's so naughty.

MATTHEW

I've realised a dream. And my Mother has no idea where to find me.

CHLOE

That girl of Jimmy's has had another baby *and* it turns out he's got one from someone else as well. I don't know how I feel about it if I'm honest. He's not my boyfriend or anything, but it all feels odd. He doesn't seem to give a shit what happens to the babies and he's determined not to shell out proper maintenance for them. Then he takes it into his head to blow a shedload of cash on something like a crazy Lamborghini battery operated replica for little Jensen to ride around in. I'm not sure I like him that much any more.

But I wouldn't fancy telling him so. He's got a big knife in the freezer which I know about and a pistol in the toilet cistern which I don't know about. He's definitely not a man to cross. I've taken refuge at Caroline's on a couple of occasions when he's gone on a bender. I know he won't track me down there and I can wait in safety until I see him again once he's calmed down.

I'm really glad when I leave to go on tour, and the tours I like the best are the mega long ones, although Mummy sighs and whines when I'm getting ready to leave. Then Monty yaps and I think "Christ almighty, get me out of here." Amazingly, going to work has become the best part of my life, no hassle, just play the fucking Blue Danube or something and soak up the applause.

What I ought to be doing is sucking up to one of the old geezers who come to see us and maybe wear my low cut dress with a mighty cleavage on show. If a rich old guy married me to get his hands on my bazookas I could live out my life in luxury.

GERALD

The woman was a nutter. I've never had a stalker before, and I certainly didn't expect to acquire one when I was in my seventies. My mates have ribbed me nonstop since she turned up out of the blue on our allotment society outing, calling her my dolly bird, good grief. The only dolly she reminds me of is certainly not available in Toys R Us. I can't even recall mentioning our Warwick trip to her, but she does have a nasty habit of ringing up at odd times and catching me on the hop. You have to be polite after all but it's a relief to find we're no longer in a relationship. Not that I was aware we were in one in the first place. I'm thinking the safest place for me is a monastery.

Not Warwick monastery obviously. Too close to the danger zone.

Dear Jenny

It was with some astonishment that I learnt from my daughter Caroline that you, in your "compassion" are aghast at our family situation. What it has to do with you, I have no idea. She tells me that we have met, but I can't recall who you are and wouldn't know you if I passed you in the street, any more than you would know me.

I'm sure Caroline has told you all sorts of derogatory tales about my many supposed faults. She has hurt me in numerous ways over the years, ignoring all the support that I have unstintingly shown to her. Did she tell you that I gave her a roof over her head for a year or so when her first marriage failed? A failure which, I may add, she blamed on me, an accusation which came as quite a shock. The truth is, her marriage failed because her husband could not keep his trousers zipped, leaving me to care for his discarded wife and children.

I wonder whether she showed you the birthday card I spent days stitching to mark her 50th birthday? But no, that would show me in a good light, so I expect she shredded it without showing it to anyone. I certainly got no thanks for it.

I've thought long and hard about what advice I should give you in return for the sycophancy you have been guilty of. I suggest you read a Bible piece: Luke 6, verses 37, 38, 41 & 42. Then take the log from your own eye before looking for the speck in mine.

Yours sincerely

M. Johnson

Margaret Johnson (Mrs).

Thirty-Seven

MARGARET

I really don't have patience with that girl of mine. She thinks she can ignore me for months and then issue an invitation for Mother's Day lunch as though I've got nothing better to do than jump at her bidding.

I've thought long and hard and I've come to the conclusion that if she can't be bothered to have me on a regular basis, she can't have me at all. She needn't think I'm going there just to suit her whims and she knows full well that I never liked Mother's Day anyway. It's an insult to be asked. The whole commercialised hype of the day reminds me too much of my horrible Mother.

Come to that, Caroline reminds me of my Mother. The older she gets, the more she resembles her grandmother, which is no recommendation let me tell you. Of course, I'm fully aware of what's behind it all. She hasn't got the bottle to tell me to my face, but it's clear as daylight that she is holding a grudge against me over my new will. She won't come out and say the truth but instead she satisfies her resentment of me by inviting me over once in a blue moon as a palliative to acceptable behaviour. She never had any respect for me, and this is her ultimate revenge. And it's apparent that she's taught her boys to ignore me too.

That's the thanks you get for being a Mother. She's brazen enough to question my objections and openly doubts the facts that I've set out for her in black and white. Clearly, she just wants my money. I wrote and told her I never want to see her or speak to her again. Chloe was shocked when I told her how reprehensible she has been, but the dearest child sensibly told me to forget it and get on with my own life. It was such a comfort to hear her caring words. She's vowed to have nothing more to do with her greedy sister unless she mends her ways. Whatever would I do without her? She is such a blessing to me!

CAROLINE

Mother won't come to us any more. It's like a liberation. I don't invite her often enough so she won't come at all; a fine example of her weird and twisted logic. When I told Geoffrey, he got up and danced right around the room like Bruce Forsyth but without the grace and panache. Though his jokes are just as cheesy.

He's busy with a very special project at the moment; something I never thought would happen. Yes, at last, after years of building houses for other people, he's building one for us! Our house has been a lovely family home for us, but Olivia has decided she will stay in Durham with her boyfriend Luke once she graduates, and this place is definitely too big for us now. It's really exciting to plan everything from scratch and I'm so looking forward to moving in – if it ever gets finished. There are so many decisions to make that my mind is in a whirl. Like this: tiled floor? flagged floor? carpeted floor? wooden floor? what kind of wood? moulded skirting? painted skirting? wooden skirting? See what I mean? And we're only three inches off the ground so far, with another twenty five feet of decision making to go. I think I'll just leave it all to Geoffrey, then it'll be his fault if anything's wrong. It will come together in good time, no doubt.

Olivia won't be living with us full time again as she's heading out into her own independent life but we're all cool with that. The turning point for her came after she left to spend a year in Charles University in Prague as part of Durham's exchange programme. It was a massive challenge and after a shaky start she absolutely adored it and thrived in the completely different environment. Initially, we had a lot of reverse-charge phone calls where the only requirement was to give her reassurance and more reassurance and then tell her that if things were too bad, she should get herself on a plane and we'd meet her at the airport. I think that did the trick. Knowing that she could come home meant that she didn't need to and she began to thrive.

From a distance, we saw her blossom into an adult during that year of fending for herself. We all went out to visit at Easter and were blown away by the beauty of the old city. But there's no place like home and it was wonderful to have her back, in every meaning of the word. She must have felt the same, because when she came to choose her dissertation subject, she picked the Bronte sisters, or particularly the most fascinating of them all: Charlotte.

We spent a week in west Yorkshire, just the two of us immersing ourselves in all things Bronte and in due course, we worked together on her dissertation. One morning, as we batted ideas back and forth, she said "do you still miss Hannah?" My voice nearly got stuck in my throat as I was struck with an overwhelming rush of wildly heaving emotions. "Every day," I strangled out in reply. "Me too," she said and in the silence she tentatively reached out her hand to mine. Nothing much. Yet everything in the world.

MATTHEW

Evie and I live the life we always dreamed of. We must be the luckiest people in the world.

CHLOE

I'm in a sticky patch. I'm sure Caroline would help but I've promised Mummy I won't have anything more to do with her now she's turned nasty. Well, I'm not certain what she's actually done but Mummy has certainly been very upset. She's been writing to Caroline to try and sort things out but she says that the replies she receives are so vindictive that she tears them up and throws them in the bin.

Caroline stopped responding a long time ago and the big silence from her has left Mummy so distressed over it all that I'm worried she's going to make herself ill. She can't seem to stop mulling over and over the situation and then she rushes off to write another letter and gets upset all over again when there's no reply. So obviously I need to be supportive towards Mummy but I need to get a loan sorted out from somewhere or I'm in some crappy stink. I wondered whether it would be possible to raise a loan against the house, but it's in Mummy's name and I'm not allowed to borrow against a future inheritance. Fucking stupid! If I already had the inheritance I wouldn't need to borrow would I? The only option I've got left is to ask Jimmy but I foresee a future of doom if I take that route. On the other hand it's pretty much doom if I don't.

The problem is the crippling interest rates that make it impossible to live a normal life. Mummy and I both hate bankers but for opposite reasons. She hates them because they don't pay high enough interest rates and I hate them because they charge interest rates that are too high. There's a fucking conundrum for you. When Mummy starts to grumble about her investment income, we don't call them bankers, we use a similar word but with one significant difference. It's really weird hearing your mother use a swear word.

I hope she confesses to the vicar when she goes to Church or she might get a thunderbolt to the head. At least then I'd get my hands on the house. But I think the only thunderbolt I'm going to experience is heading my way from the bank or do I mean @ank?

JIMMY

My gal's heading for a fall.

25 *Meadow View*
Bedford

Dear Caroline

I have thought long and hard about your latest invitation to join you for Mother's Day. After due consideration, I have decided to turn down your request since it is plain to me that I am no longer welcome in your home. You didn't bother inviting me on your birthday, nor did you press me to accept an invitation at Christmas. At Easter I was ignored and when I came to you accompanied by my visiting brother Simon, you barely seemed to find time for me. My brother received all your attention, which was a painful reminder of times gone by when he was the light of my Mother's life.

You cannot fail to be aware by now of my dislike of Mother's Day, yet you have continued to invite me every single Mother's Day of your adult life. You never seem to realise what an insult it is to me to have Mother's Day rammed down my throat year after year when I always loathed having to buy flowers for a Mother who never cared for me. But you've never been able to get the message have you?

Of course, I know what the real problem is. You disapprove of my decision to make Chloe the beneficiary of my will but you are too deceitful to admit that is the reason behind your lack of goodwill towards me. Your children appear to have been encouraged to send the most cursory of thank-you letters in return for my Christmas cheques. I suppose they think I should send a greater sum, but unfortunately, I am a widowed pensioner. It wouldn't hurt you, or them, to learn to give consideration for that sad fact of life. One day, it might be you.

I will not write to you again, or bother you by expecting further invitations to your house. You have made your feelings towards me very clear by your selfish behaviour. I shouldn't be surprised. You have always been the most ungrateful, unappreciative and downright belligerent of all my children. I don't suppose you gave more than a passing glance at the card I spent weeks stitching for your 50th birthday. Enough. I do not choose to associate with you any longer.

Yours in sorrow,
Mum

Thirty-Eight

MARGARET

Claire rang to tell me that my dear brother Ted had died after a long illness bravely borne. I thought I'd better show the courtesy towards Caroline that she has failed to show to me, and I rang her number so I could let her know. What a palaver that mission turned out to be! The number was out of use, so obviously I thought I'd misdialled but no, there was no communication to be had via that route.

Eventually, I tracked down a number for Olivia and explained about Ted's death and told her I needed her Mother's number to I could inform her. She absolutely refused to give it to me! She's certainly a chip off the old block, just as resolutely contrary as her Mother. Evidently they've moved house without telling me but Olivia told me that Caroline doesn't want me to have either her phone number or her address. Did you ever hear anything like it? I'm her own Mother for goodness sake! Oh, was I riled!

Olivia said she would pass on the news about poor Ted, but there was no sign of Caroline or Matthew at the funeral. Cowards! So much for her pious pretence that the family comes first. If it's not she who is giving the party, she obviously isn't interested in paying the proper respect due. She needs to be the centre of attention to make it worth her while to make any effort for anyone else. She was always the same. And no thought for how this affects me, needless to say. Of my own family, I've lost my sister and my younger brother so now there's only Simon left and he's on the other side of the world! And with Clive's brother Ron being taken last year, our numbers are thinning out in an alarming way.

With all this stress to deal with, I dare say I'll be next and then it will be too late for tearful regrets from madam Caroline. She'll realise what she's lost only when I'm gone. One day she'll learn what it is to be alone.

Chloe is on tour again, and I had to have Monty put down. He kept cocking his leg up against the sofa. I had to think long and hard, but I can't be dealing with that kind of thing at my time of life. So my house is rather quiet now. I bet the wretched woman next door is thrilled.

CAROLINE

We didn't go to Ted's funeral in the end. I discussed it with Matthew and he agreed that Mum is so unpredictable that it would be wrong of us to take the risk of precipitating a scene. Instead, we met up with my cousin Claire and Ted's widow Hilde for a nice pub lunch and reminisced over family history.

Hilde brought some old photographs and it gave me a pang of regret to look at Mum as a child. She must have been innocent and unspoiled once. It seems a dreadful shame that the sweet smiling child has grown up to be a bitter harridan. Everyone should be able to take joy from life, and in fact, we came to the conclusion that good old Ted had done just that.

Oh, I must tell you, our new house has given us so much pleasure! I didn't realise how much time I wasted in keeping the old place spick and span. And it's nice to actually live in one of Geoffrey's creations instead of hearing his clients express their appreciation. Nat and Josh both have good big rooms which they have decorated to their own taste, well we won't dwell on that. Then there is a pleasant spare room for Olivia and Luke when they come to visit which is always good fun. We generally try to arrange a get-together with Jenny and Stu and Amelia and it's just like the old days except that all the children tower over us now. The lads are both avid rugby players and have legs like tree trunks and have started bringing *girls* home, oh my! I've warned them that girls have germs so they mustn't ever kiss them but they just chuck dirty laundry at me so I think they're hopeless cases.

We've earmarked a spot at the end of the garden and Geoffrey has already put in the footings for a little bungalow. We want to be prepared in case Sarah and George ever want to share our space, but for now they're happy where they are. They are noticeably old people now, slower and frailer but with very full days: sewing classes, computer classes, ballroom dancing but not the rumba I suspect. Well, maybe a rum baba with a nice cup of tea once they've slipped their dancing shoes off.

MATTHEW

I love to show off our reed bed which processes all our sewage waste. Most people aren't as interested in it as I am. Odd.

CHLOE

Jimmy is not a nice person.

I can see you all looking shocked and surprised haha. He helped me out "as a friend" but he doesn't act like a friend.

He keeps asking why I've never got any money. I wish I knew. One reason of course is that I have to keep giving my salary to him because apparently, that's the agreement we came to. I want to tell him that I don't remember making that agreement, but I don't think he'd have much sympathy with my protest. I've learnt it's bad for your health if you make a complaint to Jimmy. It's hard to hide from someone like him. He has people all over the place. It's like he's got tentacles or something. If only I had tentacles, maybe I could play several violins at once, and earn several salaries. Which Jimmy would severally spend I suppose. Short of getting a new secret identity, I'm seriously short of escape routes.

HEIDI

My Dad is in love with his reed bed. I am not. I like stilettos and false nails. I'm probably a disappointment, but my Mum laughs at the sight of my piles of cosmetics and sometimes she tries on my shoes. She makes a big deal about stumbling around as if they're crippling her but she looks good when I give her a makeover. We get some cute guys staying here for outward bound sessions and it's nice when they come on return visits. Dad thinks it's because they're keen on his reeds and his wildlife but I know sometimes they're keener on his daughter. But I am saving myself. Reuben has a friend who doesn't know yet that he is going to be my significant other. It will dawn on him soon enough. I've got a place at college in September to do a hair and beauty course. Dad thinks I'm joking. He doesn't realise children grow up, even his children. Lucky he's got Mum to cushion the blow. And at least he'll get cheap hair cuts. Now that's being self-sufficient.

25 Meadow View
Bedford

Dear Karen

*I am embarrassed to be forced to write to you in these terms.
I have only just found out that your dear Mother died some
months ago. I would not have dreamt of allowing the sad
event to pass unremarked but would naturally have sent a
wreath for her funeral and written a letter of condolence to
you out of respect for our happy relationship.*

*Unfortunately, Caroline petulantly decided not to
inform me of your Mother's death because she has taken
offence against me. What happened is this: in order to
protect my vulnerable daughter Chloe, I changed my will to
make her my sole beneficiary. Caroline and her brother had
apparently met in secret to discuss my will and had decided
that I should do what I did, but like the hypocrites they are,
they did not really mean what they said. Although neither
of them is in want, they plainly believe I should give what
I have to them, making Chloe homeless on my death while
adding my little pittance to their own great wealth. This
I will not countenance, but they have now taken the step
of excluding me from all family celebrations, hence I was
not able to be present at your dear Mother's funeral. I am
sincerely sorry to have brought up such selfish children who
have given me nothing but pain, and continue to ignore me
while playing happy families with people like yourselves who*

are not really family at all. I have no doubt that Caroline will have told you all about how badly I have supposedly treated her, wasting no opportunity to spitefully denigrate me to you and all her acquaintances. I don't suppose she showed you the birthday card I spent months stitching to celebrate her 50th birthday. But that would not fit the picture of a nasty Mother that she wants to portray, and is therefore not something she would wish you to be aware of.

I have thought long and hard about writing to you in this manner, but I am fed up of being represented as some monster figure by my malicious daughter. So now you know why I have not been present at any recent family events, as I expect you will have wondered why. I assure you it is not because I have died, or am no longer able to travel; I am quite simply unwelcome. I sincerely hope you never have to face the same treatment at the hands of your own child, who, with the aid of prayer, I have learnt to forgive for the role she played in poor Hannah's death. I was extremely close to my darling granddaughter, and miss her every day, as I am sure you must miss your dear Mother. I hope you are equally able to find forgiveness in your heart for my absence from your Mother's funeral.

I hope we may be able to meet again one day under happier circumstances.

Yours sincerely

Margaret

Margaret Johnson.

Thirty-Nine

MARGARET

I can't tell you how much I miss my brother Ted. He was a sweet little boy, used to adore me when we were growing up. He'd trot round like my little shadow, always wanting to do whatever I was doing. He'd happily play houses with me. He'd be the husband and I would ask him to do the washing up or he would be the patient while I bandaged him. All good fun until Mum wanted her tea towels back.

He turned out to be super brainy, none of us knew where he got it from. Once he got a place at the Grammar School, he wasn't my sweet little playmate any more, went all snooty and up his own back-side. Mum was so proud of him, he suddenly wasn't required to do his share of the household chores any more. His homework was much more important. She was right in so far as he went on to University, but she was wrong in the same old tale that his share fell on me. She was always one for favourites. Nice if you're lucky enough to be the favoured one, but that was never me in our family. Not with Mum anyway. Pa was another story.

University was a real big deal back then, I can tell you. The working class did not go. I think Ted was the first kid in the whole street to ever go and boy! did Mum bask in the glory! She could hardly form a sentence without a reference to Ted at University. He became a barrister eventually, moving in vastly elevated circles compared to the rest of us. We were left behind, although I think Sandra kept in touch. But you could tell he was embarrassed by his common family, especially Mum with her flat vowels and her dodgy grammar. And for all that he worshipped me when he was a child, he was quick to interfere in a minor tiff I had with Mum. Mr High-and-Mighty sent me a snotty legal letter threatening court action. He just couldn't wait to start throwing his weight around and showing off how important and official he had become on the back of his family's sacrifices.

That was the end for me as far as he was concerned. I can't bear that kind of self centred behaviour. But he was a sweet boy.

CAROLINE

We've had the pleasure of a visit from Evie and Heidi, doing the rounds of university reconnaissance trips. I don't know what her parents are going to do when they realise they are wasting their time.

Heidi is one determined young lady and she has made her mind up that she is going to college in Bristol to do a hair and beauty course. It doesn't quite fit the upbringing she has had, and I think Matthew and Evie are having a hard time relinquishing their dream of another naturalist in the family. She's asked me to act as diplomatic go-between.

It sounds like her parents have fallen into the age-old trap of still imagining their daughter is a little girl. Well, I assure you, she has well and truly grown up. She knows what she wants and she is going to follow her dream. She plans to have a chain of beauty salons by the time she's thirty, and I suspect she will succeed. Geoffrey says good for her. But he doesn't want to be the one to break the news to my brother.

Still, every cloud has a silver lining. Heidi gave me a fabulous haircut and colour. I feel super-glamorous now! It'll last until the first time I try to blow dry it myself I suppose.

MATTHEW

See what happens when you raise your children to think for themselves and to have an independent mind? At least she hasn't discovered boys yet.

CHLOE

Mummy will not let it rest. It's like it's the only subject on her mind. It was quite good fun to start with but now I want to tell her to put another record on. We had a good laugh searching on the internet to find Caroline's super-secret address and then we went on Google Earth and had a look at her house, very nice indeed. Smaller than the last one, but as Mummy says, they surely don't need all that space by now. Then she wanted to go to Zoopla to try and find out what it was worth, then the Land Registry to see whether Caroline's name was on the deeds. And we had to pay for that, fucking cheek, they're public records aren't they?

Anyway I didn't (couldn't!) pay, used Mummy's card instead, so now I know her PIN number which is a temptation I wish I didn't have. She wrote down all the facts and figures and got me to print off the picture from Google Earth then she wanted me to do the whole exercise all over again to find Matthew's place. Well, I'd had enough by then and actually said to her that I don't think it's good for her to obsess over it like this. So she didn't speak to me for the next 48 hours. It was a relief actually.

But just then I got an unexpected email from Caroline who'd used those same internet facilities to find me. She wondered how I was and what a shame that we'd lost touch and would I like to resume contact and so on. Talk about rock and a hard place! I knew that Mummy would blow a gasket if she found out I was communicating with my sister again. I didn't like to think of the consequences, so in the end I just casually showed it to Mummy. "You'll never believe who's contacted me!" I said breezily and wow! it was like giving her a shot of adrenalin.

She leapt on the computer and fired off a reply with her fingers stabbing down on the keys like she might break the keyboard. It made her happy again anyway, she kept going back into her "sent documents" file and reading the message over and over, laughing till the tears rolled down her cheeks. I tried to send a message of my own the next day, but Caroline must have shut the email address down because it kept pinging back at me. There was a cookie showing on the screen advertising a personal injury claims firm. I considered throwing myself accidentally down the stairs so I could make a claim but Mummy lives in a bungalow. Foiled again.

Dear Margaret

Thank you for your letter. I miss Mum but she had a long and happy life so I cannot feel too much sorrow. We didn't always have an easy relationship but I was glad that we had never given up on one another. Her death was gentle and loving and I believe her passing was eased by the close understanding we were able to achieve. It enabled her to have a peaceful death for which I will always be grateful.

I'm sorry to have upset you by not informing you of her death. However, passing on that information was no one's responsibility but my own, so please don't blame Caroline. Because it has been many years since you had any contact with Mum, it didn't occur to me that you would wish to honour her in her death. At any rate, we requested family flowers only so rest assured, the absence of a wreath from yourself went unnoticed.

I'm very sorry that you have become estranged from Caroline. I was aware of the fact but she has never discussed any details with me. I have always thought it regretful that communication has dwindled between you, but your letter has answered a lot of questions. The Caroline you describe is not someone I recognise. In short, she is the kindest person I know and has given immeasurable support to me in all sorts of ways over the years. Knowing her as I do, I am sure she would welcome you back into her family life if you were willing to make a gesture of reconciliation. Your situation must be horrible for you and, for your sake, I urge you to make that approach.

With my good wishes to you,
Karen

Forty

MARGARET

Chloe got obstinate and wouldn't help me search for Matthew's house on the internet and I couldn't quite get the hang of it. But when I typed in "Matthew Johnson Bristol" onto that Google bar in the middle of the screen, I found to my gratification that he is a member of the Clifton and District Ramblers Association. As I suspected, he is listed as single, but more interestingly, he has laughably claimed to be in his 40s! He must be desperate, we all know that's a wistful dream.

His photograph shows a very tanned and lithe figure, but I really can't say that he has aged well at all, in fact he's completely bald. I would have barely recognised him. Now, as anyone knows, I can't abide falseness in any guise, so my instant reaction was to make an entry onto the website debunking the lie he was promoting. While I was at it, I made sure to include the information that he has an ex-wife and two children, just to be on the safe side. Some unsuspecting girl might get taken in by his fantasies, and if he tells one lie, how many more will there be?

I knew it was my civic duty to protect members of the public from cheating bounders like him. I felt a great sense of satisfaction that I'd been able to expose his web of intrigue.

The world needs public-spirited people to keep it on track. The next day, I got the most fatuous reply from the Chairman of the Ramblers Association, insisting that I was mistaken in my claims and the reason the Chairman knew this to be so was because Matthew Johnson was his brother who he had known since his birth 46 years ago. What a lot of nonsense! He also informed me that their Mother was called Desiree, not Margaret, and went on to say that from the tone of my email, he was very glad that she, not I, was his Mother. How remarkably offensive, not to mention most unprofessional from someone in a position of responsibility. He invited me to rescind my website contribution and apologise to Matthew who he said was extremely upset.

I thought not on your Nelly my boy and sent back a reply confirming everything I had already revealed. He thoroughly deserves his come-uppance.

Sadly, there seems to be no integrity left in this world. I'm having an almighty ding-dong with the bank, which has sent me a credit card bill for a £5000 cash withdrawal. I've told them about a million times, the whole thing is preposterous. I have never in my life made a cash withdrawal using my credit card. I would never consider it, given the absurd interest charges those wan..I mean bankers foist upon the down-trodden consumer. And what's more, why would I take £5000 from my credit card facility when I could simply withdraw it from my deposit account?

But do they want to listen to common sense? Of course not. They are (ahem) *bankers* aren't they? So I have to face the fact that I have been the victim of identity theft, doubtless caused by the lax systems of the banks. I've told them in no uncertain terms that it is their responsibility to track down this disgraceful crook and lock him up for the rest of his life. How dare these lowlife people cause such distress to an innocent elderly widow in the twilight of her life?

Yes, it happened after all. George tripped on the stairs and dislocated his knee which was agonising. But from that moment, the pair of them decided they were ready to come and live in the bungalow, and we were thankful that they'd seen the light. George's little stumble could have been so much worse and we took it as a timely warning to get the building work completed quick smart and move them in. We had to be a bit ruthless with them in the end, because the bungalow is tiny and they didn't want to throw away anything from their old house.

The lamenting was heart-rending as old memories were consigned to boxes in our loft. But that was easy! Choosing which furniture to keep and which to consign to the charity shop took the negotiation skills of Kofi Anan. But once they'd moved in they were so comfortable and Sarah said that she felt like she was on holiday every day. That's probably because she was now living in a building the size of a park home, but it had everything they needed.

They trot up the garden each evening for their dinner like a pair of happy garden gnomes and the main thing is it's given us all peace of mind. There are days, I confess, when they are a pair of cantankerous old biddies and I wonder what have I let myself in for? Then Sarah will say in her voice that's grown old and quavery "I hope we're not a nuisance to you my dear. We're very grateful, you know." So that puts me in my place. They have always been so good to the whole family, they deserve their bit of security.

Josh is so sweet with them. He's in Sixth Form now, doing his A-levels this summer, so it's probably not cool for him to have his grandparents at the bottom of the garden but he's never uttered a word of complaint. He often takes himself down to their place and watches the football with Granddad.

He regards it as a success if he gets George so worked up that he lets slip a swear word. "Granddad said bugger" he will report with the utmost delight and Geoffrey is shocked and disbelieving. I don't think.

MATTHEW

I'm hearing some odd reports concerning my Mother. I thought I'd shaken her off by now.

CHLOE

Right, I was already up shit creek and now I'm somewhere worse, in fact I wish I was in shit creek because that was paradise compared to this. I did something really stupid with Mummy's credit card and the bank's been investigating and basically I'm about to get rumbled. I don't know whether I should go to Mummy and make a full confession before the truth comes out. If I throw myself on her mercy, she'll be sure to understand. But unfortunately that's not the half of it.

The interest charges on my credit cards were bad enough, but they pale into insignificance when compared with what Jimmy charges. I knew it would be a balls-up when I asked him to help me out, but I never imagined how bad it could get. So anyway, he came up with a scheme which he promised me would wipe clean my slate for good. All I had to do was take a package to Peru which was our first destination on our next tour.

Well, I'm not stupid, I knew perfectly well what the package would consist of, but I was beyond desperate by now. The plan was that we'd conceal the consignment in my violin case and it would be a doddle to smuggle it through customs. We were an orchestra after all! We go through airports all the time without any problem and as long as I delivered the goods to the guys who would meet me at our hotel, that was it! I would be in the clear, Jimmy would wipe out my debts and I would be back on my feet again, never *never* to repeat the stupid mistakes that have dogged my life. It was the only way out of the whole fucking mess so I agreed. Is anyone surprised? I never made a sensible decision from birth onwards. Who would expect me to change the habits of a lifetime?

But it was a cock-up. They were on to me, I realised when about thirty uniformed officers were all staring at me from the moment we got off the plane. When I clocked what was going on I was just shit-scared, I don't mind telling you. I faked a fit of illness, and actually it was hardly a fake, so I could dash off to the public conveniences. I got in the last stall and thank God! there was a high up window above the toilet. So I climbed on the rim of the loo and wriggled the latch open then threw my violin out the window. We went through customs without a hitch and I just told anyone who asked me where was my violin that Nick had taken it for me when I came over queasy. Brilliant! Although now it didn't seem as if there were any more customs officers than usual and they waved us through with general bonhomie and welcoming smiles. Then I had to try and sneak away round the back of the building to retrieve the violin and of course I couldn't find it.

By that point, I really did start to feel ill. I was looking disaster in the face. When I arrived empty handed at the hotel, there were a couple of heavies waiting and I won't ask you to believe they were happy. I tried to explain that the stuff they wanted was round the back of the airport somewhere, and if they found it, please could I have my violin back. I sincerely consider myself lucky to be alive. Or maybe not. And in case you haven't worked it out, a violinist without a violin is no use to Nick Hallam's touring orchestra, so bye-bye and close the door quietly on your way out please.

This is how bad things were: I had to call Caroline, and Geoffrey paid on his debit card for my flight home. They rescued me but they were unimpressed. They collected me from the airport and dropped me back at Mummy's without saying more than three words to me the whole time. And those three words weren't very pleasant.

NICK HALLAM
HALLAM'S TOURING ORCHESTRA

I tried to do the girl a favour when to be honest she's no more than a journeyman violinist, but she was down on her luck and I didn't like to refuse. Then she let me down big time. I'm on tour with a violinist down and dates to honour. Just the kind of thing to get a new orchestra a bad name before we get started. That's the last time I take a punt because someone knows someone who thinks I'm the pillock who'll agree to be taken for a ride. Anyone who asks me a favour in future is likely to get a broken nose.

25 Meadow View
Bedford

The Editor
The Bristol Post
Temple Way
Bristol

Dear Sir

I'm so worried, I hardly know where to turn. I've thought long and hard about the best step for me to take, and have finally decided to put the matter into your hands.

As a Mother who loves all her children immeasurably, I never imagined I would be faced with such a dilemma. Through an odd sequence of events, I have discovered something about my own son that needs to be publicly revealed. In short, my son has become a predatory pervert and it is imperative that the people of Bristol should be on the alert so they can protect themselves and their families from him.

You will undoubtedly tell me to go to the police, but I have already done so, and their systems are so slow and unwieldy that I fear someone will come to harm before my son is apprehended. So I am begging you to show an appropriate civic responsibility and use your newspaper to warn Bristol residents of the danger they are facing.

Yours sincerely

M. Johnson

Margaret Johnson (Mrs).

Forty-One

MARGARET

Chloe had some calamity with her violin and had to come home in the most distraught agony. I was the only person she wanted to see. She holed herself up in her bedroom and told me to tell no one she was there, take no phone calls for her and let in no visitors. She just wanted to hide away from the world. I knew exactly what that felt like, so I could empathise with her, well I always could. She's just like me. And the poor girl has been subject to so much bad luck all her life!

The bank, for example, is trying to have me believe that she is responsible for the identity fraud committed against me earlier in the year. They say they've tracked the transaction back to her bank account and I need to speak to her about the matter unless I want them to prosecute her on my behalf. My own daughter! That's likely! Instead of doing their job properly, they make an unfounded allegation and leave me to cope with it. Wankers!

I had to see my solicitor the other day and I told him the sorry tale in all its unexpiated glory. When I'd finished, he took off his glasses and, sighing, wiped his forehead; completely uninterested you see? Then he said "Mrs Johnson, if I were in your shoes, I would forget the financial loss and be supremely grateful that the bank is not going to pursue the case against your daughter." Another wanker! But I had to see him because of another problem that's raised its head, and this is the most ludicrous thing you'll ever hear. I've been trying to expose Matthew and his duplicitous carrying-on and now he's made a complaint to the police!

What happened was, I kept trying to make entries on the Ramblers Association website, but then they obviously blocked me so I couldn't send any more. Well, I was really worried about the kind of lies he might be peddling around the area. You hear such dreadful stories about predatory men leading a double life, respectable on the outside but prowling the streets for victims in the darkest hours of the night.

It was clear to me that the good people of Bristol needed to be warned against him, so I wrote to the local paper to publicise my son's misdeeds and they did a bit of an exposé piece without directly naming him. It was a kind of advisory tick list for young ladies out and about their legitimate business and in the meantime, the very eager journalist who contacted me began an undercover investigation. But he was taken in by Matthew's cover story. He got back to me to say it was a case of mistaken identity and his editor was furious with him and with me as well for all the time wasted on a spurious fairy tale. As you can imagine, I gave him a piece of my mind until I realised I was speaking to the dialling tone. In fact the world is full of wankers when you come to think about it.

Then the police contacted me. And we all know they're the worst wankers of the lot. They made a lot of threats about what would happen if I did not make a full public apology to the Johnson family and give an undertaking not to approach them in any way in the future. So now I'm getting prosecuted for trying to protect the public from people like my son. In other words, doing the job that the police should be doing themselves instead of harassing poor defenceless old widows. Hence my visit to the solicitor, who I have absolutely no confidence in. In fact, according to him, I am indeed defenceless as he says it is difficult to find an angle from which he can defend me.

So now, as a last ditch attempt to find a resolution, I'm expected to travel down to Bristol police station, at my own expense to add insult to injury. There, I am to attend a meeting with my son and draw the matter to a close without the need for a court case. I'm quite looking forward to it, actually. I'll see him eat humble pie!

CAROLINE

Mum has gone too far this time. She's my own Mother but even I can't find any excuse for what she's been up to. I went with Matthew to Bristol to attend the informal interview that the wonderful Bristol police force had arranged. They asked me to go too so that there could be as much confirmation as possible over the question of identity.

Matthew and I were introduced to the other Matthew Johnson and his charming Mother Desiree and they were so calm and understanding. They just wanted an end to Mum's lunatic letter-writing campaign, which by now had extended to the poor guy's workplace. He must have been at the end of his tether. But we felt confident that once Mum saw him, we would be able to draw the whole sorry scene to a rapid close. The fact that he looked nothing like our Matthew was difficult to overlook, and his mixed race parentage was pretty much a clincher.

Or so we thought. When they brought Mum in, for one moment I thought I saw some awareness flash across her face before she went blank and stern. She looked at her own son and said "I've never seen this man before in my life. What kind of trick is he trying to pull? I suppose he wants my money like everyone else." Matthew had told me he thinks she's psychotic and for the first time I began to think he was right. The senior office quietly suggested Mum might wish to participate in DNA testing in order to clarify matters. I thought she was going to punch him and he did too because he flinched away like a big baby.

"Are you calling me a liar?" she roared, with spittle flecking her chin. "Do you think I don't know my own son? How many times do I have to tell you? This is a conspiracy between my son and my daughter to get hold of my money. They'll see their sister out on the street so they can snuffle in the trough. They're evil, they should be locked up…."

And more of the same. She's off her trolley. It was quite unsettling actually. Seeing her mad vitriol right before my eyes made me feel….I don't know, almost fearful. It was a chilling scene to witness. It was like I'd stumbled into a particularly dramatic episode of East Enders. My immediate thought was for my kids, and I texted them all there and then, to tell them that under no circumstances were they to ever reveal their contact details to Granny. It didn't matter in the end. She was sectioned under the Mental Health Act. So we were safe from her for now.

MATTHEW

My Mother was bonkers. Officially.

CHLOE

I thought as long as I don't go out, don't see anyone, don't speak to anyone, just stay in bed, no one can get me. Nothing bad can happen to me here. I don't know if you've ever tried it but you get no peace.

Granny Gristle from next door kept rattling the letter box, calling "hello there! Are you alright in there?" so I pulled the duvet over my head until she went away again. Then there would be a nice pie or something on the doorstep so she had a kind heart really but I didn't want to see her. But even with her pies and casseroles and what have you, eventually the freezer was empty. I had to starve or do some shopping but of course my card was declined. I sat on the floor at the checkout and wept with fucking snot running into my mouth until the manager came out. I thought I was going to get chucked out but he packed up the food into two carrier bags and let me have it for nothing. I wished I'd put more in my shopping trolley then.

Obviously though, I can't keep trying that trick so I did what I always do; called Caroline. She went into mothering mode and came down to stay for a week. She cleaned the house, drew back the curtains, stocked the food cupboards and dragged me to the doctor. I was diagnosed with depression, well talk about the bleedin' obvious. So now, as well as insulin, I've got fucking 20g of Citalopram tablets every day on top. Caroline wouldn't stay so I went back to bed. Now she comes down every Wednesday and sorts me out and I know she's been talking about me to Granny Gristle. The old witch pops in every evening to check on me like she's my jailor or something and then I expect she trots off to phone Caroline with the latest bulletin. I might as well be a baby.

I wish I had my violin. I bet Jimmy's got it by now. It was quite valuable you know. My Daddy bought it for me. Not that Jimmy would give a shit.

Evening Standard

The body recovered on Wednesday from the water at Thames Ditton Marina has been identified as that of 49 year old James Fullerton. Police are working on the theory that this was the latest in a series of gangland revenge attacks. They are pursuing their enquiries and encourage anyone with information which may be of use to contact them at any police station or call Crimestoppers anonymously on 0800 555 111 using the reference TD/JF/ 2009

Category listing   musical instruments/ violin

Old violin, full size, 4/4,
two piece back, inlaid purling.

Condition: used
Time left: 1 day, 4 hours

£87.00 7 BIDS
_____ enter your maximum bid
Submit bid

Seller information:
Jensen Fullerton

Description
Seller assumes responsibility for this listing

Item specifics
Condition: used. Unwanted bequest. Traditional. Size 4/4
Style: violin believed to be made by Rudolf Fred

Forty-Two

MARGARET

Gaaaargh! Bastards! Wankers! Sodding God in sodding Heaven! I was a faithful servant all my life and the buggers have locked me away. Yaaaah! I'm being called home now. I do know that much. I'll see my wanker bastard Pa again. You watch out you wanking sod. No one would ever listen to me. Old wanker knows what he did though. Sandra just turned over and looked at the sodding wall. Just glad it wasn't her sodding turn any more I suppose. I had a trick – I could leave my body and float off to the ceiling. Look down on a little girl with eyes tight shut and a filthy man doing filthy things. It's happening again now. Off I float and look down on myself. Nothing much to sodding look at any more. Wasted life in a pristine hospital bed. Whoosh, I'm back. Not ready to meet my wanker Pa just yet. No one listened to me all my life. Bastard Pa. Wanker Ted with his wanking letters. Goddam Mother…"No one likes the little girl who cries Wolf". Christ! I hate them all! I hated them then, I hate them even more now! Wankers everywhere. Father! Why hast thou forsaken me?

I'd like to be able to say that Mum calmed down but nothing seemed to help apart from sedating her to a zombie state. That made her more tolerable, but it's not something that conforms with modern practice.

I tried to explain to her how her foolish mistake with the other Matthew Johnson had happened so she might gain some understanding of why she should rein in her reactions. I showed her on my laptop that if you typed Margaret Johnson, Bedford into Facebook, it came up with a buxom peroxided agent for Ann Summers lingerie. She peered closely at the screen and then wham! the laptop was sailing through the air. So then I needed a new laptop which was really inconvenient because it had the payroll history for all the staff. I had a right game re-entering all the information in time for the next payday.

Nat was kind enough to help me, but couldn't resist the opportunity to give me a lecture. "When will you learn to back up after each pay period?" he asked me, not for the first time I must admit. I patiently pointed out that I did back up, but he shook his head in exasperation. "No Mum, I mean on a memory stick not an A4 file where your columns lean further over to the left as you go down the page until they all run into each other at the bottom." "Well it's working isn't it?" I replied and he went "yes Mum" and gave me a hug. My lovely boy!

Anyway the staff got paid on time so that's the main thing. As for Mum, her disasters didn't end with being sectioned. Once she was in, she was given a full medical examination and here's the rub. While she'd been so engrossed in tracking down "Matthew" and saving the world from his evil designs, she'd taken no notice of her own problems. And still isn't interested, it has to be said. She's got breast cancer that has become so advanced as to be inoperable with secondaries well established all over the place. The doctor was gob-smacked to use modern parlance, and could not figure out how she had got so bad without the pain alerting her if nothing else.

I know how she did it: quite simply, she's fuelled by fury. Thanks to her own obstinate nature, there's nothing to be done now except keep her comfortable and await the end. She doesn't seem aware of any of it, her only avowal being to sort out that Matthew of hers before he murders someone. It's a dreadful thing to say about your own Mother, but she is a thankless taskmaster and I don't like her one bit.

MATTHEW

I pity the nursing staff who have to care for my Mother.

CHLOE

I'm just about keeping body and soul together living in Mummy's house. Matthew is in negotiation with the Office of the Public Guardian over management of Mummy's affairs and I'm able to use her income for now. With that and my incapacity benefit, I'm serving the interest on my debts but the banks are not letting up in their never ending fucking demands, threatening me with bankruptcy like that's going to help. Caroline still comes once a week with her charity parcel and her fucking Mr Sheen, like I care whether the place sparkles. She reckons I should go and visit Mummy as she's really sick but I can't face that just now. Can't she see that I'm sick myself? The whole world is against me, even Caroline told me it's time I bucked my ideas up and did something to sort out a future for myself. Mummy always said she was mean.

Office of the Public Guardian
PO Box 16185
Birmingham
B2 2WH

Dear Mr Johnson

It is with regret that I must inform you that your request to be granted Lasting Power of Attorney over your Mother's affairs cannot be fulfilled at this time. Unless she recovers her mental health to the satisfaction of this Office, she will be unable to lawfully authorise the LPA request.

It is my duty to inform you, therefore, that her affairs will instead come under the administration of the Office of the Public Guardian. This procedure will be activated as soon as practically possible. You will be kept informed at all stages of the process.

Yours sincerely

Hassan Hussein

Office of the Public Guardian.

19 Vaughan Street
Victoria
Melbourne
Australia

Dear Caroline

I'm real sorry to hear about my sister's illness. I sure wish I could make the trip to see her one last time but I've talked it over with Pat and she made me see sense. I'm just too old now. Pat says it will probably kill me if I sit in a plane that long. She doesn't beat about the bush, that wife of mine. She's probably right like she usually is. It's just that I've got this something on my heart. I can't make it right now, should have done something a long time ago, but we were all just kids. Will you just tell her from me, Simon says he's sorry. Just do that for me, Caroline. It's too late now for anything more. It'll haunt me to my grave. I hope my sis rests easy.

I don't suppose I'll see you again, but I wish you everything good. You're a good girl Caroline.

My love to all the family
Uncle Simon

Forty-Three

MARGARET

Those children of mine never let up. They're still trying to get my money. They're worse than my Pa. Wankers! Get out of here! Leave me alone or I'll call the police!

CAROLINE

Matthew is trying his best to sort something out to protect Chloe. As things stand, Mum's will leaves everything to Chloe but as far as we can make out, she'll lose the lot to pay back her astronomical debts. How they've spiralled away to this level I cannot understand. She simply kept applying for one loan after another and no one seems to have cross-referenced, just ticked the box and sent her another card or whatever. Matthew is livid and keeps saying something must be done to make the financial institutions more responsible and accountable.

But that doesn't help Chloe. The best plan we could come up with was to persuade Mum to change her will in our favour so that we could manage Chloe with a rod of iron and prevent any repeat offending. If Chloe is made bankrupt, which is looking more and more likely, she will at least be in the clear after the statutory period, seven years I think it is. Hardly ideal, but a small sunbeam on the distant horizon is a beacon of hope in the midst of a storm. Good grief, I've turned into a Hallmark card.

Of course, you can imagine Mum's reaction when we put our idea to her, but we made an appointment with her solicitor to ask whether he could visit her and persuade her that it was the best plan. But he put a spoke in the wheels immediately. "If you read any will," said he, "you will notice the emphasis on being of sound mind; and I'm sorry to point out that your Mother will not satisfy that criteria. Unless she recovers her mental capacity, I am unable to draw up a valid new will for her. I'm very sorry." So that was that.

We did our best. I think Matthew had lost heart by now, which I could understand after all the time he and Evie had devoted to getting Chloe out of trouble in her younger days. I find myself agreeing with him when he says we've got her out of enough scrapes and he's fed up with still doing so when she's hit her fifties. Will she ever learn? I've got my doubts to be truthful.

MATTHEW

I am sick to the back teeth with the pair of them.

CHLOE

I have been served with a High Court writ for the repayment of debts owed to Barclays Bank plc. What the fuck does that mean? I asked Matthew and he just went "Oh for God's sake Chloe." I spoke to Evie instead, she was always nice to me, but she said "Hey, stranger, you haven't bothered with me for years, please tell me what you expect me to do for you after all this time." Repudiation was the last thing I was expecting from Evie. She was like my second Mother! I can't understand it.

I cry most of the time. And eat the wrong things. I've had to increase my insulin doses and the doctor is seriously angry with me. He keeps giving me lectures on my stupidity and shows no sympathy at all. Whoever heard of a doctor with no patience ha ha. Oh God!

NURSE SALLY-ANNE LEWIS

Every patient at the end stage needs someone to hold their hand and ease their passage. Even someone like Margaret. She never stopped being angry, no matter what we tried for her. But although she made very little sense in her latter days, there was one recurring theme: her Pa. We often find at this point that our patients begin to look forward to meeting their loved ones in an afterlife, and I am firmly convinced that great comfort is given to them by that belief. So I explained to Margaret's family that although she seemed to be railing against life and death, I felt quite sure she was gladly anticipating a happy reunion with all those people who she loved but who have gone before her. In her own way, I think she was questing for her personal path towards the peaceful reconciliation we all desire in the end. She just had a different approach to most patients. Sometimes I think I could make a case for mercy killing.

Order for possession In the London High Court   Claim No. BB/25/12

Barclays Bank plc
                                                                 Claimant

Chloe Margaret Johnson
                                                                 Defendant(s)

On 3rd May   20ᵤ,

sitting at London High Court

heard   Barclays Bank plc

and the court orders that

1. The defendant give the claimant possession of 25 Meadow View, Bedford

   on or before 3rd June   20ᵤ.

2. The defendant pay the claimant £ N/A   for
   [and £   per day from   20   , until possession of the property is given to the
   claimant.]

3. The defendant pay the claimant's costs of £ N/A
   [The defendant pay the claimant's costs, within 14 days after they are assessed [and in the meantime pay
   the claimant £   on account of those costs].]
   [The claimant's costs will be added to the amount owing under the mortgage.]

4. The defendant pay the total amount of £ N/A   to the claimant [on or before
   20   ][by instalments of £   per   , the first instalment to be paid to the
   claimant on or before   20   ]

To the defendant

The court has **ordered you to leave** the property by the
date stated in paragraph 1 above.
If you do not do so, the claimant can ask the court,
without a further hearing, to authorise a bailiff or
Sheriff to evict you. (In that case, you can apply to the
court to stay the eviction; a judge will decide if there
are grounds for doing so.)

(If detailed assessment of costs is ordered)
The claimant will send you a copy of the bill of costs
with a notice telling you what to do if you object to the
amount. If you do object, the claimant will ask the court
to fix a hearing to assess the amount.

(If there is an order to pay money - paragraph 2,3 or 4)
Payments should be made to the claimant, not to the
court. If you need more information about making
payments, you should contact the claimant.

*(If there is an order to pay money, made in a
county court)*
If you do not pay the money owed when it
is due and the claimant has to take steps to
enforce payment, the order will be registered
in the Register of County Court Judgments.
This may make it difficult for you to get
credit. Further information about registration is
available in a leaflet which you can get from
any county court office.

Ref. ERT 22378/12

Forty-Four

MARGARET

Wankers took my teeth away because I bit the nurse. He shouldn't poke me with his needles should he? Does he think I don't know what going on? They're trying to euthanise me. He's probably hoping I'll leave him a legacy. Some woman keeps visiting me. Says she's my daughter. My real daughter is on tour with her orchestra. You should hear her play! Angelic seraphim: that's my Chloe. Give me my morphine. Quick!

CAROLINE

Visiting Mum was the most exhausting ordeal imaginable. Geoffrey said don't do it, it was too upsetting for me. But I'd talked it over with Karen whose attitude I'd always admired when she found herself in a similar situation. She said it was all worth it when her Mother finally said "I do love you Karen" just hours before she died. I had to agree with Karen when she told me I should never give up, maybe that moment would come for me. Karen's intuition was generally spot on and she observed that I would find it a hard struggle to come to terms with Mum's death unless I had made every effort to ease her passing with loving affection. Well, I don't know if I can manage the loving bit, I don't have Karen's fortitude, but I must do my best. She's the only Mother I've got and it's plain I won't have her for much longer.

If only she could go as peacefully as Sarah and George. I let myself into their bungalow one day when I hadn't seen them up and about, only to find them still in bed. They were having a lovely cuddle but then I realised that George was silently sobbing and Sarah was never going to wake up again. Poor George was gone within the week and we were glad actually, I'm sorry if that sounds wicked. But they were so devoted that it was impossible to imagine one without the other and in point of fact, it *was* impossible. I think that whichever one had gone first, the other would have followed swiftly after.

So we mourned because we missed them, but we didn't mourn too much because they had an enviable life. I hope Geoffrey and I go the same way. Once I heard a wise tale. "Who would you want to die first?" a new bride was asked. "Why, me of course," she replied. "I don't want to be left alone without my husband." "Then you don't love him enough yet" came the reply. Sarah and George could have been that bride and her husband, waiting for each other, unwilling to leave the other behind. We loved them dearly, largely to do with the fact that they loved us unstintingly. How sad that my Mother had never learnt that simple lesson.

MATTHEW

I don't know how Caroline put up with the old hag.

272

CHLOE

The vultures are circling. I don't know what Matthew's done but he's holding them at bay for now. I know it can't last. I don't bother to open the envelopes any more, just stick them straight in the recycling bin. I ought to leave it by the front door so the postman can put the letters in directly. Cut out the middle man.

Sometimes I play an imaginary violin, hold it in position and sweep my imaginary bow across the imaginary strings. It produces the sweetest imaginary sound. I've played the entire Four Seasons Concerto without a single mistake. Now that's an achievement to be proud of. I think Granny Gristle enjoyed it.

JOHN MILES
BAILIFF

I had instructions to make a call at Miss Chloe Johnson's abode for collection of debts owed under a County Court Judgement. I was unable to gain access as the defendant did not respond and all the doors and windows were found to be securely closed. Not everyone knows this, but bailiffs are not allowed to simply break in to gain admittance. We have to be invited in, and oddly, we are not always welcomed. Personally, I have no sympathy. People get themselves in messes thanks to their own greed and irresponsibility. If you owe, you have to pay. Simple as that. We'll be back. It's only a matter of time in these cases. The old woman next door told me the occupant was very ill. I've heard all that before. Apparently, the sister comes once a week but it sounds like the family has more or less abandoned her. That's families in this day and age I'm afraid. Oh, I've heard every story and every excuse. Interesting job this. Mega secure profession as well. As long as there are stupid people in the world, there will always be a call for a bailiff.

Dear Uncle Simon

I don't want you to waste another moment worrying about Mum and however you feel you may have wronged her. I've made the same mistake myself many times, and Geoffrey gets annoyed with me for thinking it's my fault when its just her way. Let's face it, Uncle Simon, she was always a belligerent old bird, and that didn't change even in her final illness.

I never knew what it was that made her so angry with everything and I guess I'll never know now. I could never get a handle on what made her tick, but she remained ferocious to the end. She died with a snarl on her face, and when the undertaker had to prepare the body for burial, she said it was like trying to make a tiger look like a pussy cat. She was so apologetic, but in the end we decided the best thing was to go with a closed coffin so it didn't matter, nobody got frightened! Tante Hilde let me have a copy of one of Uncle Ted's old photographs. It shows the four of you youngsters lined up in a row, all beaming at the camera without a care in the world. Oh, the innocence of childhood is so charming! I had the picture tinted and framed and we mounted it on the coffin, where it was widely admired. We all thought it a truly fitting epitaph now that Mum was reunited with her loved ones.

So please Uncle Simon, don't fret yourself over what's gone. We all have our life to lead and it's up to each of us to deal with the good and the bad. Let go of your worry and enjoy what you've got. We all send you our love,

Caroline

Forty-Five

MARGARET

"Do not go gentle into that good night,
Old age should burn and rave at close of day,
Rage, rage against the dying of the light."

Dylan Thomas

Welsh wanker.

CAROLINE

To the very end I could not engage Mum's affections. It didn't matter what I tried. She died a horrible excruciating death; just a bag of bones and dreadful pain that even the highest doses of morphine could not relieve in the end. But still her anger burned bright and strong as her flesh shrank away. She could not let it go.

I stroked her hair and tried to soothe her when the pain got bad but I had to stop. It seemed to irritate her more than it calmed her. I think she blamed me for everything that had gone wrong. She left this life without ever giving me her blessing. Too late now. I wonder what happened to her to make her the woman she became. And what could I have done differently? But no. Maybe she was just a wicked evil woman. Whatever: she's at peace now and nothing on this Earth matters to her any more.

But my long suffering husband is quite right. My Mother and my free-loading sister are parasites. They've leeched off me for years and enough is enough. Time for new things.

We have a gorgeous new grandchild, our very first! We were thrilled when Olivia and Luke told us they had a baby on the way. Olivia got a bit feeble and asked me whether she should call the baby Hannah, but I said don't saddle the poor baby with expectations that are impossible to live up to. This is a brand new child with a brand new life to live without someone else's shadow blighting it. There's no need to have a living commemoration to Hannah, we'll always remember her just as she was. Anyway, the baby came and they called him Jacob. He's beautiful.

Josh is helping his Father increasingly, and we're thinking we might start to wind down a bit. In a stroke of genius, Geoffrey signed me up for an online Creative Writing Course. I never thought he saw any significance in my juvenile dreams of authorship! Who knows where it might lead? The Booker? The Costa? The bargain bin at the book remainders?

My dear friend Jenny, madcap as ever, tells me I should write about the life of my own family. As if anyone would be interested in that! Anyway, I'm so looking forward to tackling my first writing task when it downloads on Wednesday. As long as I have one of the children on hand to assist with the momentous task of logging on to the class forum, the rest should be a doddle. And I can spend time getting to know baby Jacob, and at last, Geoffrey and I can chill a bit.

Life's too short to waste it dancing to everyone else's tune. I'm calling time on blood-sucking relatives. I am not a saint! It's my turn to make whoopy!

MATTHEW

My Mother is dead. The impact on my life is zero.

CHLOE

Oh what shall I do? What can I do? My life is a fucking shipwreck. I don't even have the energy to get out the goddam bed. It's all gone to buggery. What can I do? Keep breathing… in….out… in… out. Oh where can I go? What can I do? Someone help me please! I need someone to help me! In… out… in… out.

Caroline will know what to do.

I must go to her and she'll take care of me.

That's what I'll do.

Thank God for Caroline.

Always there.

Acknowledgements

"They fuck you up" by Philip Larkin, reproduced from "The Complete Poems" by Philip Larkin with the permission of Faber & Faber Ltd.

"My Violin" by Bruce Lansky, from "Miles of Smiles" by Bruce Lansky, © 2015. Reprinted by Permission of Running Press Kids, an imprint of Hachette Book Group Inc.

"If I Should Go" by Joyce Grenfell © The Joyce Grenfell Memorial Trust 1980. Reproduced by permission of Sheil Land Associates Ltd.

"Do not go gentle into that good night" by Dylan Thomas, reproduced by kind permission of The Dylan Thomas Trust.